ELVEN FURY

AGENTS OF THE CROWN BOOK IV

LINDSAY BUROKER

Elven Fury
Agents of the Crown, Book 4

by Lindsay Buroker

CHAPTER 1

ZENIA WHIPPED HER ARM UP to block, but she was a split second too slow, and Rhi's gloved fist glanced off her temple. Zenia winced and jumped back. Her heel came off the mat and onto the red clay floor tiles.

"You're out of bounds." Rhi lowered her fists and took a few steps back to the center of the sparring area. "My point."

"Wasn't it your point when you clubbed me on the side of the head?" Zenia, sweat making her loose exercise togs stick to her body, hesitated to follow her friend back onto the mat. She needed a break, and the tile felt deliciously cool under her bare feet.

"Nah, I barely touched you. No judge would count that. You *were* slow to block though. You should be sparring with me every morning before work."

"I'm usually in the office before dawn."

"Yes, and that's pathetic considering there aren't any trolls invading this week, and I haven't heard about any other dire emergencies." Rhi waved her gloved hand, an invitation for Zenia to return to the mat.

Zenia dragged her damp sleeve across her forehead and eyed the towels draped over the nearby bench. Elsewhere in the gymnasium, a couple of pairs of men wrestled or sparred, but the open area was mostly empty, with Kor's subjects busy at work this time of morning.

One of the sparring men noticed her looking his way, and he threw a wink, then looked her up and down. He turned his bare chest toward her, puffed up like a peacock, and flexed his muscles. His partner slipped past his distracted guard and landed an uppercut on his chin. The man staggered back but made a show of dismissing the blow, thumping a gloved fist against his bare chest and leaping back in to take revenge.

"Just because we thwarted that scouting party of trolls," Zenia said, not interested in the sparring men, "doesn't mean an invasion isn't still coming."

"Have your reports suggested it?" Rhi asked.

"Nothing has escalated this week."

"So, you're just in the office from before dawn to after dusk each day to avoid thinking about Jev's upcoming nuptials."

Zenia grimaced. "I'm attempting to do the job the king has entrusted to me, nothing else. It's a demanding position with a lot of responsibility." Zenia unwrapped her padded gloves. "I need a break."

"It's only been an hour."

"For some people, that's considered a long workout."

Rhi snorted. "Barely a warmup. Do you want to switch to a bo for a while?" She waved toward where her wooden staff leaned against a marble column.

"I don't carry a bo around town, so that wouldn't likely help me."

"You *could*. Don't Crown Agents get to wear what they want? And carry what weapons they wish?"

"A pistol is less unwieldy than a six-foot staff."

"But not nearly as versatile. There are times when you only want to thump people, not kill them. Come on." Rhi waved toward the center of the mat again. "Another half hour. This was your idea, remember? I thought we were going to visit informants, but you randomly dragged me in here for some reason. I usually work out in the castle gymnasium."

"I know. I'm expecting someone." Zenia glanced toward the large archway that led into the practice area, but it remained empty.

On the nearby mat, the two sparring men broke apart, one heading over to a bench. The one that had been posturing for Zenia dropped to the mat and did a series of pushups.

"Is it one of them?" Rhi waved toward the boys. They were well-built and handsome, and the one doing push-ups certainly knew it. He pushed his legs into the air, balancing carefully to do hand-stand push-ups. "Because if things don't work out with Jev, I'm sure that one would scratch any itches you have."

"I don't need itches scratched." Zenia looked away, hoping to convey that to the man. He kept glancing over, his head flushed red now, as he did his exercises. "Maybe *you* can get his address."

Rhi twitched a shoulder. "Maybe. I'm actually a bit tired of men."

"Going to switch to women?"

Rhi snorted. "No. I just mean that I went a little wild after tossing my monk's gi—and my oath of celibacy—aside, and it wasn't unenjoyable, but..." She shrugged again. "This will sound silly, but it was more fun when I was a monk."

"Sex was more fun when you were celibate?" Zenia arched her eyebrows, though she knew full well that Rhi had sneaked men into her room in the temple.

"When I was *supposed* to be. And there was the possibility of being caught. It made it riskier and more exciting. A couple of times, my gentlemen visitors had to hide under the bed or jump out the window if a fellow monk knocked on my door."

"I remember the morning you went out early to cut the thorny Bougainvillea away from your window."

"A bit belatedly," Rhi said. "I felt the need to apologize several times to Branik Chasinlar after he, in his haste to slip out before Archmage Sazshen entered, had numerous exposed parts perforated by thorns."

"Was everything exposed?"

"Yes. My point is, that I'm not finding sex quite as stimulating." Rhi looked over at the red-faced young man, who had completed his exercises and lay on the mat on his back, watching them. At her glance, he rolled to his knees and started a series of languid stretches to show off his musculature.

"Perhaps you should seek out a relationship, rather than a simple itch-scratching." Zenia looked toward the archway again, wondering if she should head into the rest of the gymnasium to look for her contact.

Rhi grunted dubiously. "I'm not looking to get married. Or have babies. Can you imagine me as a mother?" She waved down her stocky frame. The exercise togs didn't reveal her muscles, but Zenia knew they were there and that she could likely go toe-to-toe in a push-up competition with the young man.

"Not every relationship has to have that goal, I'm sure. You could seek out someone you enjoy spending time with, and maybe it would make you happy, no thorns or windows required."

"The way Jev and his engagement to another woman is making you happy?"

Zenia winced.

"Sorry." Rhi touched her shoulder. "I shouldn't have said that. I just meant... Oh, I don't know. Relationships seem like more of a complication than I want in my life."

"Understandable." Zenia hadn't thought she wanted that complication, either, not while she was busy settling into a new job, and yet... She'd fallen in love with Zyndar Jevlain Dharrow, the unattainable nobleman. At least unattainable for someone who wasn't noble herself. She sighed. "Let's go visit the baths. The person I need to see may be back there."

As Rhi went to pick up her bo, Zenia headed for the exit. The man who'd been trying to get their attention jumped to his feet and trotted over to intercept her.

"I believe the person you need to see is right here." He patted his pectorals and smiled at her, his gaze dipping to her chest.

Zenia couldn't imagine that she appeared sexy at the moment, with her hair pulled back in a ponytail and stray strands plastering the sides of her sweat-dampened neck. Admittedly, her damp exercise clothes clung to her body and outlined her figure. The man's long perusal up and down made Zenia uncomfortable.

"No," Zenia said. "I'm looking for a woman."

"That can't be. Women don't have the right parts." He let his hand trail down his chest to the waist of his trousers.

"Back off, pervert," Rhi said, coming over with her bo. "Nobody wants to see your parts."

"That's not true. Just last night, I entertained Zyndari Mekhari in her townhouse. She used the words stallion-like to describe me."

His buddy ambled over, and Zenia hoped it would be to tell him to quit being an idiot and get out of the way, but he planted himself behind his friend and in front of Rhi.

"Are you two headed for the baths? Why don't you join us?" He poked a thumb over his shoulder. "We can help you relax."

"No, thank you," Zenia said, missing the days when she'd worn an inquisitor's robe and nobody had dared step into her path, to flirt or do anything else.

"No, and I'm *not* going to thank you." Rhi jammed the end of her bo downward and would have hit one man's bare foot if he hadn't yanked it back in time. "Step aside. And keep your arms down. The aromatic stench of those pits is more likely to make your foes pass out than your wrestling skills ever will."

Unfortunately, her insult only made the man grin and look at his friend. "I like a challenge."

"Too bad you don't like soap," Rhi grumbled and moved to step around him.

He shifted, not grabbing her but blocking her path.

A hint of warmth came from the dragon tear Zenia wore on a leather thong around her neck, and it seemed to ask a silent question.

No, Zenia thought at it. *We don't need magical help.* She didn't want to use magic to hurt these men.

A sense of disappointment emanated from the gem, and though no words formed in Zenia's mind, it managed to convey an, "Are you sure?" notion.

"Move your ass out of my way," Rhi said, "or I'll move it for you."

"Go ahead and try." The man's eyes glinted. "I've been hoping you would ask me to wrestle since you first walked in."

Rhi lifted her bo as she lowered into a ready stance.

Zenia, less enthusiastic at the idea of fighting with these loons, especially since they seemed excited by the idea, said, "Rhi is one of the king's hand-selected Crown Agents. It's against kingdom law for you to impede her. Please step aside."

The man snorted. "Girls can't be king's agents."

The bare-chested man in front of Zenia seemed less certain. He took half a step back, lifting his bare hands. But his buddy scowled and lunged for Rhi, as if he meant to rip her bo from her grip.

She used it, striking twice in rapid succession, to block his lunging hands. The humor vanished from his face, and his fingers snapped into fists.

Zenia's dragon tear allowed her to sense people's feelings and sometimes thoughts, and she keenly felt when the man's thoughts shifted from wanting to show Rhi a good time to wanting to teach her her place, subservient to *him*. Zenia knew Rhi could take care of herself, but a true fight might bring the staff and end up with them kicked out of the gym.

Don't hurt anyone, please, Zenia thought to her dragon tear as she pulled it out from under her tunic. *But you can show them a little intimidating flair.*

The gem flared a blue so intense she had to squint. The men flung their arms up against its brilliance and stumbled back.

Rhi's would-be assailant recovered first and sneered at Zenia. "I've seen dragon tears before. You can't scare—"

The mat under his feet lifted and was yanked to the side, as if someone had gripped the end and pulled. Someone with the strength to knock a grown man off his feet. He tumbled sideways, crashing into his comrade.

More mats stirred, and Zenia and Rhi scurried to the safety of the tiles. At least a dozen mats lifted into the air, twisting and snapping at the two men like living creatures. They shouted in alarm, trying to get to their feet and run. But the mats blocked their efforts to escape, just as the men had blocked Zenia and Rhi from escaping.

The other people sparring in the gymnasium gaped, their eyes bulging at the sight.

Zenia rubbed her face. This flair was more conspicuous than she'd had in mind. She tried to impart the idea of finishing up and putting the mats back down to her dragon tear.

Some of them settled back to their spots on the tiles, but other mats swept in and wrapped around the two men. Soon, they were pinned and bundled like stuffed gort leaves, with only their bare feet and their faces free. Their very red faces. They struggled, attempting to wriggle their arms out and escape, but the mats only tightened.

"We should go," Zenia said.

"Are you sure?" Rhi chortled and waved at the pinned men. "I was hoping we could get a painter to come in and capture this on a canvas."

"I'm sure." Zenia hustled through the archway and turned toward the changing rooms, aware of the onlookers gaping after her. Her gem still glowed a bright blue, and she stuffed it back under her tunic.

"Normally, I would feel disgruntled that you jumped in without letting me thump anyone, but that was too delightful to complain about." Rhi peered back as they entered the shady hallway. "I didn't think you possessed such creativity when it came to mischief."

Zenia almost said that she didn't, that her dragon tear had been fully responsible, but she clamped down on her tongue. *Most* dragon tears didn't have personalities; they only did what the mages linked to them told them to do. Hers was special. Zenia still didn't know the full extent of its capabilities.

"Captain Cham?" a quiet voice asked from a closet full of stacked towels and robes.

Zenia halted, recognizing the young woman's voice. "Jia?"

"Yes, ma'am." A slender figure wearing the starched white uniform of the gymnasium staff stepped out with a stack of towels in her arms. She wore a blue and gold scarf on her head that seemed a fashion choice but that Zenia knew covered slightly pointed ears. "I understand you wish to speak with me?"

A door opened farther down the hall, and two women with towels wrapped around their bodies walked out blurred by a cloud of escaping steam. They chatted easily, heading for the changing rooms.

"Yes," Zenia said quietly. "Is there a good place?"

"Perhaps you require my assistance and I could accompany you to the women's baths." Jia lifted the stack of towels.

"I prefer to bathe myself," Rhi said. "Or have handsome men do it, those who are suitably respectful and appealing. Not like those toads back there."

"Ssh," Zenia whispered. "Go along with it." She nodded for the half-elf woman to lead the way.

They entered the ladies' bathing room, passed the main pool with a few women paddling back and forth, and chose one of the heated baths in the rear corner.

"Jia," Zenia said, stopping at a bench to disrobe, "this is my fellow agent, Rhi Lin. Rhi, this is an informant you didn't meet the last time we were making our rounds. I actually found her later on a special list that wasn't with the others."

Jia smiled faintly. "One that included dwarves and half-elves?"

"One that was made up of *only* dwarves and half-elves," Zenia said. "As well as a half-orc living outside of town that I introduced myself to earlier in the week. He said I looked tasty. I'm still not sure if it was a sexual comment or a literal one."

"That was Ox, right?" Jia asked. "It could have gone either way."

"How does a half-orc come into existence?" Rhi asked.

"You, being more worldly than I, shouldn't need me to explain that," Zenia said.

"Uh no, I being more worldly than you definitely need an explanation. Not on how equipment works, but on, er, *why* it would between those two species."

"Another time." Zenia waved away the conversation and nodded for Jia to share her information.

The week before, right after the dwarven ship had blown up and Jev had been injured, Zenia had received a note from the anonymous person who had now sent her three such messages. It had warned her to "Avoid the elf." The only elves Zenia knew were Jev's friend, Lornysh, and the former elven ambassador and his staff. The latter had all disappeared from their embassy before the troll incident started, so that only left Lornysh. Zenia didn't want to suspect Jev's friend, especially on the basis of an anonymous note, but the two previous notes had been accurate with their warnings. She hoped some other elf might be about, causing trouble, and that it referred to him. Or her.

"Your message said you wanted to know if there are any elves in the city, or if I've heard of half-elves involved in illegal activities, right, Captain?" Jia sat cross-legged, ostensibly holding towels for Rhi and Zenia as they slipped into the warm water.

"Yes, please." Zenia resisted the urge to wave for her to set the towels down and relax. She always felt uncomfortable having someone wait on her, but Jia was a secret informant, so they had to be subtle, lest someone think it odd that an agent of the crown and a gym employee were having a long chat.

"There are very few elves currently living in the city or anywhere in the kingdom. I only know of Zyndar Dharrow's comrade, Lornysh, here in Korvann." Jia raised her eyebrows. "Is it true they are friends? And treat each other as equals?"

"From what I've seen, yes."

"Amazing."

Zenia didn't know if Jia meant it was amazing a zyndar would consider an elf an equal or if it was amazing an elf would consider a human of any social status an equal. Maybe both?

"There used to be many half-elves in the city," Jia went on, "but most left when the war started and it became dangerous for them to live here. Some have created tiny enclaves of their own deep within the kingdom's forests, and some simply live nomadic lifestyles with few kin. As I'm sure you know, it's difficult to be a half-blood. Elves do not allow anyone with human blood into their cities, and humans... aren't as open-minded about the offspring of such unions as they once were.

Once, Korvann was a great trade city and all races were welcome here, but that was decades ago." Jia shook her head sadly as she gazed down at the fluffy towels.

"I think King Targyon hopes to make it such a place again," Zenia said, hoping she was right. From what she'd heard from Targyon so far, she believed she was. She just wasn't certain he would be effective at changing people's prejudices, prejudices that the war had done nothing to alleviate.

"Perhaps." Jia's sad smile did not suggest she was convinced. "For now, even those who were born in the kingdom and consider themselves loyal subjects must hide any evidence of their elven heritage." She waved toward the scarf covering her ears. "I do not believe any of them are looking to cause trouble, but there is something you may be interested in, something I didn't see myself but heard from others."

"Oh?" Zenia leaned against the tile edge of the pool and glanced at Rhi, who seemed content to let Zenia take the lead in the conversation.

"Apparently, a group of people was snooping in the elven embassy tower last night. Someone thought they saw at least one person with pointed ears among them."

"Snooping? Is it possible the ambassador and his entourage simply returned?"

"I don't believe so, ma'am. They didn't light any lanterns, and my acquaintance who observed the trespassing has a dragon tear. He sensed magic being used. He almost went to investigate, but he experienced a vision sent by the Fire Dragon, one of himself being engulfed in a magical ball of flame if he crossed paths with those inside."

Rhi snorted. "You mean he was afraid."

"Because of the vision," Jia said earnestly. "Yes, ma'am."

Zenia poked Rhi in the ribs, hoping she wouldn't dismiss Jia's belief in such things. After all the years they had worked in the Water Order Temple, Rhi ought to be used to people with genuine faith in the founders. Many monks and mages claimed to receive visions from them.

"Thank you for the information, Jia," Zenia said. "We'll look into it."

"Be careful if you do, Captain. A group of elves in one of the human cities is a very unusual thing these days. If they're here, you can be certain it's for a reason."

"Jia!" a woman in a white gymnasium uniform barked from the entrance to the baths. "We need the tiles scrubbed in the steam room."

"Yes, ma'am." Jia bowed her head, then set the stack of towels on the bench and headed off without another word to Zenia and Rhi.

As it should be. The value of the informants stationed around the city depended on others not realizing they were affiliated with the Crown Agents.

"Isn't Lornysh still staying in the tower?" Rhi asked when they were alone, save for the lap swimmers in the other pool.

"The last I heard, yes. I haven't spoken to Jev in several days, so I haven't received any updates about Lornysh's whereabouts. He could have moved on."

"Several days? I knew he hadn't been back to the office yet—that gift from his former lady is still on his desk—but I assumed you'd spoken to him since he's been released from the healers at the Air Temple."

"It's only been a day since they released him. His injuries were extensive, and even though the healers used the magic of their dragon tears, they kept him a bit longer to work him through various stretches and exercises to help him regain his mobility. I haven't visited him personally since that first day. Because..." Zenia had checked in with the Air Order healers several times to get updates on his progress, but she hadn't visited Jev personally since hearing about the engagement his father had arranged for him. She hadn't wanted to be seen lurking around him. And definitely not kissing him.

She closed her eyes, an ache in her chest. She and Jev had no more than confessed that they cared for each other—loved each other—when that news had come in, that Jev was to marry some zyndari woman. Soon.

"Ah," Rhi said with more understanding in her tone than usual. "Maybe you can have your dragon tear wrap up that other woman in a mat and toss her in the harbor."

Zenia smiled wistfully. "Don't give it ideas."

Rhi frowned at Zenia's stack of clothing, the dragon tear resting atop it. Zenia wished she hadn't implied the gem had a mind of its own, even if it seemed to have exactly that.

"Jev is supposed to be back at the office tomorrow," Zenia said. "We'll tell him about the elves and see what he thinks." She still needed to share the anonymous notes with him, too, and get his opinion on them.

"That we should show up at the tower and thump them, I hope," Rhi said.

"Thump them? I believe Targyon would prefer we foster peace and understanding among the races of the world."

Zenia was tempted to walk past the tower on the way back to the castle, and maybe she would, but she would be hesitant to wander inside without permission from the king. Even if the old ambassador and his staff were gone, it was still elven territory.

"Uh huh," Rhi said. "If they're trespassing and snooping, they get thumped. That's what I'm here to foster."

Zenia thought of Jia's warning that the elves had been using magic, and she had a feeling that going to face them with nothing but a staff wouldn't be a good idea.

CHAPTER 2

S WEAT DRIBBLED FROM JEV'S HAIRLINE, ran down his jaw, and dripped onto the anvil where he was painstakingly braiding thin gold and silver strands into a pattern that Cutter assured him was aesthetically pleasing. Or would be if he could stop screwing up. His grandmother weaved tapestries that were so beautiful, people paid handsomely to hang them in their castles—or they had before she had been exiled. Shouldn't crafting ability flow naturally through his veins?

"Dragon's udders," he swore, realizing he'd made a mistake three rows back.

So much for natural crafting ability.

Maybe he could blame his color-blindness, though he didn't truly have trouble telling which strands were silver and which gold. It was just that when he'd chosen a pattern for the chain, he hadn't realized it was so complicated and had so *many* strands.

"They don't have 'em," Cutter said from the anvil next to his.

The smithy, with sweltering heat rolling off the nearby forge, wasn't the ideal place for jewelry making, but Cutter had rejected Jev's suggestion that they ask Master Grindmor to use her shop. Probably because he was tinkering with something that was meant to be a gift for her, or so Jev assumed. Cutter had been vague about it, but he was frowning, muttering, and tapping his hook against his jaw a lot as he worked. It was definitely something that mattered to him.

"Dragons don't have udders?" Jev had meant it as a curse—his nanny had used it when he and his brother had been boys and she hadn't wanted to sully their impressionable young minds. "Are you sure? Have you seen a dragon recently?"

"Seen plenty of paintings of them. All udder-less."

"Yes, but in all the paintings, they're lying belly down on a mound of treasure." Jev worked his way backward on the chain so he could fix the error.

"Proof that they don't have udders. Udders would get unpleasantly cold pressed against all those gold and silver coins."

"Wouldn't body heat warm them up?"

Cutter gave Jev an exasperated look. "Is this the kind of nonsense you and Zenia talk about when you work together?"

Jev knew his friend meant it as a joke, but he couldn't keep from frowning at the mention of Zenia. She had no sooner professed her love for him than they'd learned he had been engaged to another woman. True, *he* hadn't had anything to do with that, but it must have stung Zenia. She hadn't been by to see him after that day in the Air Order Temple when his cousin had brought the news. Jev hoped Wyleria hadn't forbidden her to visit. He didn't think she would, but it was possible someone else in his family might have. It was also possible Zenia had simply found it too uncomfortable to come see him.

By the founders, that pained him. The healers had finally declared him fit enough to leave the temple and return to work, so he would see Zenia in the morning. And he would have a beautiful gift to give her.

He looked down at his dubious progress. If he had to stay up all night to finish it, he would have a beautiful gift to give her.

"We're usually too busy talking about work to discuss udders," Jev said, realizing Cutter was waiting for an answer. Either that, or he was taking a break from his own project, which looked like a combination between a tool rack and storage box.

"That must be a relief for the other agents in your office."

Jev stretched before bending back over his chain, wincing at a twinge that came from his ribs. His bones were supposedly all repaired, but his body kept sending him reminders that he had foolishly allowed himself to be caught in an explosion.

At least he had survived. That hadn't been a certainty by any means. That night when he'd thought he would die, his biggest regret had been that he hadn't told Zenia how he felt about her. Now he had, but it hadn't fixed anything.

"I'm thinking about going to go see Zenia's father," Jev said.

"What?" Cutter asked over the banging of a hammer on an anvil.

The two blacksmiths whose shop they were using weren't the quietest co-workers.

"Now that my ribs have healed enough to take a punch or two," Jev said, speaking more loudly, "I want to see Zenia's father."

He didn't truly think old Veran Morningfar would punch him, but when Jev made his request, it was possible the man would order some servants to punch him.

Cutter grunted. "Didn't know she had one."

"Zyndar Morningfar. He had an affair with her mother but didn't acknowledge her. That's why she's considered a commoner. But technically, she's only *half* common. Most people wouldn't consider that desirable, regardless—most zyndar, I mean—but it might help me sway my father into allowing me to marry her."

Allowing him. He grimaced, hating the way that sounded. Hating that he couldn't choose his own fate, not without his father's permission.

But that was what being the heir of a zyndar prime meant. He wouldn't be able to choose his own fate until his father passed away, and presently, the old man was as healthy as a race horse.

"Thought you were marrying some other woman now," Cutter said.

"I'm not. I'm going out to the castle to tell my father there's no way I'm agreeing to that betrothal. Tomorrow, after I check in at the office."

Jev had been tempted to ride home that morning, but his back was as sore as his ribs, and the notion of doing fifteen miles in a saddle had made him wince. He'd kept hoping the old man would come see him at the temple, as his aunt and several cousins had, but Father hadn't shown up. He'd sent his condolences and well-wishes for swift healing, according to Aunt Vivione, but that wasn't the same as coming to visit. It was possible something was keeping him busy, but Jev had a feeling his father didn't want to argue about the marriage, as he must surely know Jev would do.

"Humans overly complicate their lives." Cutter lifted his project, frowned at it, then thunked it down and grabbed a pair of pliers.

"Maybe only zyndar humans. I have this notion that being a commoner might be simpler. It's possible it's a naive notion. What are you making?"

"A portable folding rack and storage system for Master Grindmor's small jewelry tools. I thought she might find it useful when she travels for work, but…" He scowled at the project.

"What?"

"She's not only the best gem cutter in the kingdom; she's a talented metalsmith and crafter too. She could make this with one hand tied in her beard, so I'm not sure why… Well, she probably won't like it. It won't be good enough."

Jev pushed aside the urge to ask why a dwarf would tie a hand in his—or her—beard and said, "You're good too. She'll like whatever you make for her."

Cutter gave him a look that suggested he had the mind of a child. A simple child.

"Over there," one of the smiths said with an indifferent grunt.

Jev looked up in time to see a cloaked figure gliding toward him, the flames of the forge at his back and hiding his cowled face in shadow. An uneasy feeling swept through him, and he knew with certainty that this person was deadly. Menace rolled off him like a foul odor.

Jev tapped Cutter on the chest and pointed his chin toward the newcomer.

The two smiths said something to each other, set down their tools, and went outside. Had the cloaked figure said he wanted to speak with Jev and Cutter alone?

Cutter frowned and picked up a hammer. Jev didn't have anything nearby that could be used as a weapon. He folded his arms over his chest and lifted his chin, hoping to exude some of that natural determination and defiance that Zenia conveyed so well.

"You are the friend of Lornysh Grazharon?" the cloaked figure asked, not lowering his hood. Though his voice was cold, he had a lilting accent. A Taziir accent.

"Yes," Jev said, refusing to deny it, "but I guess not as much of a friend as you'd think since, in the years I've known him, he's never told me that was his surname." Grazharon *wasn't* Lornysh's last name—that was an elven word that translated to mean a pariah in exile—but Jev truly did not know the real one.

Cutter frowned, perhaps recognizing the word, too, but he didn't speak. He merely glared at the figure and tapped the hammer against his hook, making a soft *clink, clink, clink.*

"Where is he located?" the elf asked. "We know he is in this grimy human city."

We? There was more than one elf looking for Lornysh? That didn't sound like a good thing.

Jev shrugged, refusing to let any emotion show. "Then you know as much as I do. He comes and goes as he wishes and doesn't keep me apprised. You might check at the symphony. He's a fan of culture."

"*Human* culture." The elf spat on the floor, almost hitting Cutter's boot.

Cutter growled and surged in, raising the hammer. Jev lifted a hand, intending to intervene—whatever was going on, starting a fight wouldn't help anything—but the elf moved too quickly. *Incredibly* quickly. He caught Cutter's wrist and squeezed, twisting and forcing him to drop the hammer. Then he whirled Cutter around and thrust him toward one of the anvils.

Indignation and fear for his friend sprang into Jev's heart, and he lunged in, forgetting his desire not to fight.

He threw a punch, but something slammed into his gut before it landed. Pain from his still-recovering ribs blasted him, and he couldn't keep from gasping.

What had that been? The elf's boot? By the founders, he was fast. Jev hadn't even seen him lift his leg to kick.

Before he knew what was happening, he was spun about, his chest ramming against the anvil with Zenia's chain spread across it. A roar came from behind him—Cutter. His friend sprang for the elf, but energy crackled in the air, and a wave of power slammed into him. It wasn't directed at Jev, but he felt some of it, like a battering ram slamming into his back. His chest hammered the anvil again, hard enough that he worried his ribs would be broken once more.

Something cold wrapped around the back of his neck—fingers.

Jev thrust backward with his elbow and had the satisfaction of hearing the elf grunt as he connected. But then a strange icy power gripped him, and Jev couldn't move again. He couldn't even breathe.

"The time has come for him to pay for his crimes against our kind," the elf whispered in Jev's ear. "If you impede us, you will die." The fingers tightened, nails digging in painfully. "We know you were a soldier in your foolish war, that you killed our people. I would enjoy sinking my dagger into your spine right now."

Jev wanted to retort—hells, he wanted to *breathe*—but neither his lungs nor his tongue would move. He realized it wouldn't even take a dagger for this enemy to kill him. This lone elf had chilling power that made him wish Zenia were there with her dragon tear.

The elf's fingers left his neck, and Jev sensed him leaving—he didn't hear a thing, even though the smithy had grown deathly silent—but he still couldn't move. His lungs burned, crying out for air, but they were as frozen as the rest of his body.

A gasp came from the floor behind him. Abruptly, the power holding Jev disappeared.

He sucked in a deep breath and spun. The elf was gone. Cutter lay on the floor, curled in a ball, his eyes squinted shut.

Jev dropped to his knees beside him. "Are you all right?"

"Who in all the stone bowels of the earth was that?" Cutter demanded.

Despite the heat of the smithy, Jev couldn't keep from shivering. "Someone who I hope never finds Lornysh."

Jev stood shirtless in front of the mirror in his room in Alderoth Castle as he smeared the unctuous concoction that one of the Temple healers had given him all over his chest. He thought about knocking on Zenia's door to see if she was there and if she would rub some on his back, but he was reluctant to let her see him with fresh bruises across his flesh. The explosion had been a noble injury, but being beaten up by an elf was another matter. The skin of his throat was turning an unappealing blue-black. He smeared goo on it.

A faint tapping reached his ears, and he looked around the tidy room for the source. A mouse?

While he'd been away, a maid had washed the linens, made the bed, and picked up the junk he'd left on the floor, so there weren't many hiding places for rodents.

The tapping sounded again, and Jev realized it came from the large glass window that overlooked the dark courtyard. He grabbed his pistol from the holster that hung over his desk chair and edged toward the window.

It was too dark outside to see much. Night had fallen as Jev had walked up to the castle, leaving Cutter behind at the smithy to continue on his project—a surly elf wouldn't distract *him*, he'd declared.

Jev unfastened the latch, pushed the window open a couple of inches, and stepped back.

A cloaked and cowled figure pushed his way inside, and Jev leaped back. At first, he thought it was the elven magic user who'd attacked him in the smithy. But familiar silver hair tumbled out from under that cowl.

"Lornysh?"

"Who else were you expecting?" Lornysh spoke quietly and closed the window behind him.

His voice, Jev noticed, wasn't as accented as the other elf's had been. A sign that he'd been outside of Taziira for much longer?

"Coming through my window? In children's tales, it's usually the valiant lover of the princess. Oddly, it was never the valiant lover of the prince. It was always zyndar men who scaled the stone walls of castles and keeps and such. In hindsight, it's possible those tales were rather limited in scope." Jev thought of his cousin Wyleria, who apparently had a female lover, and decided those children's tales had failed to accommodate the full spectrum of audience tastes in a lot of ways.

"I apologize for not being your lover. Presumably, she can walk down the hall to reach you. The guards don't seem to have instructions to let me into the castle."

"Have you asked Targyon to give them those instructions?" Jev decided to focus on that statement rather than the one about Zenia. As much as he wished otherwise, she was not now, nor had she ever been, his lover. Though the handful of kisses they had shared had been achingly wonderful, and he vowed there would be more of them.

"No." Lornysh pushed his hood back. "I believe my stay in your kingdom is at its end."

Jev wrenched his attention back to the present, concerned for his friend and also distressed at the idea of him leaving in a rush. Or at all.

"Does that mean you saw the surly, abusive elf? Are you all right?" Jev glanced down but didn't see any droplets of blood on the floor around Lornysh.

"*Elf?* There's more than one. I've avoided them so far."

"I wish I could say the same."

Lornysh looked at Jev's bare chest and the gunk smeared on the bruises.

"I'm glad I only met *one*." Jev grabbed his shirt and, hiding a wince, tugged it over his head. He was as disinclined to let Lornysh see his injuries as he was Zenia. Especially since a single elf had so handcuffed him. Him *and* Cutter. Jev felt moderately better knowing Cutter hadn't had any more luck against their pointy-eared foe, but he would have preferred it if they had handled him and driven him out of their city with a boot in the ass. "Do you know how many there are?"

"I saw four at the tower last night."

"The elven embassy?"

"Yes. I believe they're looking for me. I sensed a whisper of Taziir magic last week, and I've been alert ever since. Fortunately, I spotted them entering the courtyard and slipped out before they came in. I'd had my bag packed in anticipation. I've been expecting this day, though I thought it might take them longer to send someone for me."

"They who? Who's after you?"

"I believe the four I saw are highly trained elf wardens. No doubt sent because I fought against my people in the war."

"Oh."

Jev didn't know what else to say. He'd often wondered at Lornysh's choice to do that, to kill his own kind and help the human army. Lornysh had never said why he'd chosen to do so, nor had he spoken about his past. Jev didn't even know which of the Taziir cities he came from or even for sure that he *was* from Taziira and not from one of the smaller elven communities around the world.

"So, this is some kind of death squad, sent to hunt you down and punish you for your choices?" Jev asked.

"Essentially." Lornysh lifted a hand, palm up. "I'm not strong enough to defeat them. Better if I go so you won't be endangered." He glanced at Jev's chest again, even though the shirt now hid evidence of injury. "I admit, I am not as prepared to depart Korvann as I expected to be. Even though I can't say anyone has been welcoming, save for you and Targyon, of course, I enjoyed the culture more than I expected, and the climate is acceptable. I find the heat oddly appealing after all those long, frozen winters up north."

"Lornysh, if you want to stay, and even if you don't, I'll help you. We'll help you. I know Cutter will, and I can't speak for Targyon, but I believe he would be willing to put some resources behind you too."

"Resources." Lornysh's mouth twisted. "Men. Men who would be killed. These are elf wardens, superior warriors and magic users. Your people couldn't stand up against them, and the Taziir have many reasons to loathe humans right now, so I have no doubt they would willingly leave bodies behind them. I cannot allow that, not on my behalf. I—" Lornysh broke off with a frown. "I believe the lover you're waiting for is coming."

"What?" Jev looked toward the door.

A knock sounded.

"Zenia?" Even though he was worried about Lornysh, Jev's heart sped up at the thought of her coming to visit him. He made himself walk casually toward the door rather than springing to answer it like a teenager in love. Had he truly, just a few weeks earlier, wondered if he would ever feel the kind of love he'd felt back in those days when he'd pined over Naysha?

When he opened the door, Zenia was indeed standing there, and she smiled warmly at him. He returned the smile and clasped her hands, tempted to kiss her, but not with Lornysh watching.

"Zenia, come in." Jev drew her inside, pleased when she came willingly and squeezed his hands back. "I'm glad to see you. I was just talking to Lornysh about…" Jev trailed off because when he gestured toward the room where Lornysh had been standing, he was gone. "Trouble," he finished, his thoughts turning grim again.

Zenia looked toward the empty room and then the open window, a warm sea breeze drifting up from the harbor.

"That's what I came to talk to you about too," she said.

"Oh? I was hoping you came to snuggle."

Her smile faltered, and he wished he hadn't made the joke. To him, all this arranged marriage stuff was an annoyance, but to her, it must seem like a rejection, if not by him, then by his social class and his family. And maybe in a way, she would see it as a rejection by him. After all, he was a part of his social class and his family.

"Sorry," he said, then closed the door. "Let's talk."

"About snuggling or about trouble?"

"I suppose we should be responsible and discuss the latter first."

"Yes."

Jev told himself he shouldn't be disappointed by her agreement and waved Zenia toward the bed and the desk, inviting her to take a seat wherever she was comfortable.

She chose the desk chair. "You say Lornysh was here?"

"Just a moment ago. I'm not sure why he took off. There's no reason he should find you a threat, though I suppose he could be on edge and worried about everything right now."

"Did you hear about the tower?" Zenia asked.

"That four elves that want to kill him were snooping around? Yes, how did you hear it?"

"An informant, but she didn't know—or didn't say—they were here for him."

"Lornysh believes they are, and I'm inclined to agree." Jev touched the back of his neck, remembering that cold grip and the chill of the elf whispering in his ear. Maybe it had been his magic, but he'd seemed to carry some of those cold northern forests with him. "I want to help him, but I'm not sure it's within my power."

He glanced toward Zenia's chest, thinking of her dragon tear. It lay nestled under the dress she wore, but he could see the leather thong around her neck. He fingered his pocket where a small pouch held the chain he'd made. After the elf had threatened him, Cutter had helped him finish it quickly, so he wouldn't have to spend the whole night in the smithy.

Zenia followed Jev's gaze and looked down at her chest.

He blushed. "Sorry, I was wondering if your dragon tear might help with the elves. That's all. I wasn't ogling your, uhm, lady curves."

She lifted her eyebrows.

"My aunts always told me not to ogle those, especially not with my hand in my pocket." He had intended that to sound amusing, but he remembered Zenia wasn't that experienced with men and sex, and worried it came across as crude instead. "I did make something for you. For your dragon tear. For both of you."

By the founders, why was he flustered? He knew she shared the same feelings for him that he had for her, so he ought to be past being awkward and bumbling around her, shouldn't he?

Maybe it was that he hadn't had opportunities to seek out women and sex in the last ten years. He'd been a normal enough teenager in that regard, but the opportunities had been fewer when he'd been away in Taziira, and he'd spent so much of that time lovelorn and mourning Naysha's choice to marry another that he'd rarely been in the mood for what opportunities there had been. And then after he'd been captured and used by that elven scout, he hadn't been inclined to have sex for some time.

"What is it?" Zenia asked, eyeing his pocket.

Realizing she might think he was being crude—again—he hurried to withdraw the pouch. "I made it. Cutter advised, and maybe he finished it off and stuck on the clasp, but I made most of it."

She came forward and took the pouch and loosened the strings tying it closed. He wanted to stroke her hair and her face, but he made himself clasp his hands behind his back. She poured the chain out into her palm, and he held his breath.

Would she like it? Or would she reject it because he'd used valuable materials? The gold and silver strands were pure and had cost him a little money, but he wouldn't consider it a lot. Still, she had rejected the suggestion of gifts from him before, not being willing to accept anything that she perceived as charity.

"It's for my dragon tear?" she asked, holding it up. Was that a smile touching the corners of her lips?

"Yes. I assumed the leather thong was temporary and that it—you—you and it—might like something a little more fashionable." He never quite knew how to refer to that gem of hers, especially since Cutter had mentioned it might be dangerous and possibly linked to a real dragon. "Not that I should claim an ability to make something fashionable. But I think it turned out all right. Cutter said it wasn't hideous. Those were his exact words, mind you."

Her smile widened. "I like it, Jev. Thank you."

She slid a finger along the chain. Her gaze shifted to him, their eyes met, and a zing went through him at the emotions that swam in hers. Pleasure, he was certain, and gratitude? Or maybe that was love. For him.

She stepped closer, the chain looped between her fingers, and rested her hands on his shoulders and kissed him. The zing turned into a much more intense feeling, and he wrapped his arms around her and kissed her back. He was so pleased she liked it. And that she'd come to his room. When she hadn't visited him again in the temple, he'd worried she was distancing herself, that she'd given up on them.

But she was here now, and she was kissing him like... damn, like she wanted him. Wanted *them*.

He had the urge to sweep her off her feet and carry her to his bed, but he knew nothing had changed for her, that she'd made that vow to herself not to sleep with a man out of wedlock, not to risk bearing a child that wouldn't have a loving father around to care for it. And her.

Maybe she was thinking of similar things, because she broke the kiss, dropping her face to his shoulder. She didn't step back, so he didn't feel obligated to let her go. Instead, he rested his palm on the back of her head, relishing the silky feel of her hair, and tried to keep her close. She was breathing more quickly than usual, and he allowed himself a moment of masculine pride, knowing she found kissing him engaging.

"Why," she whispered, "do you have to be so..."

"Amazingly appealing, alluring, and impossible to resist?" he teased and lowered his face to the side of her head, wanting to feel her hair against more than his fingers. It smelled good. *She* smelled good.

"Not an asshole zyndar."

He started to laugh, but he thought there was a note of distress in her voice. "Zenia," he murmured, stroking her hair. "I know you heard about my father's decision, but it's not going to stand. I love you, remember? I'll figure something out. *We'll* figure something out."

"I love you too," she whispered and slid her hand from his shoulder to the back of his neck.

For an instant, he remembered the elf's icy grip, but her fingers were warm and gentle, and when she pushed them up into his hair, he thought again of taking her to his bed. He made his feet root to the floor. As long as he and Zenia remained standing, he wouldn't be tempted to sway her to break her word to herself. Though couples *could* do interesting things while remaining upright.

No, he told himself firmly. He didn't push her hands away, but he kept himself from letting his roam. She felt far too nice, and it was far too tempting.

"I'm going up to see my father tomorrow, and I'll talk to him about us," Jev said. "And about canceling that marriage acceptance. He *will* listen to reason."

"Hm." She sounded skeptical.

Jev wanted her to be confident that he could and would handle things. He wished he hadn't told her before that he felt duty bound to do as his father desired and be a proper heir, a proper son. He *would* be those things, but he would also marry who he wished. Even if he had to break the zyndar class rules to do so.

"I think we should visit the elven tower first," she said. "I walked past it on the way back to the castle this evening, but the outer gate was locked, and I thought I should get Targyon's permission before scaling the walls and snooping in their territory."

"Snooping?"

"To see if the elves who were snooping there first left anything snoop-worthy to discover."

"I think they were looking for Lornysh," Jev said, "if we're talking about the same elves."

Zenia hesitated. "You believe a group of them came all this way just for him?"

"I think it's possible. He's dangerous. They might have believed they would need a group." He tilted his head. "Why? You have reason to believe something else is going on?"

"Possibly." She stepped back—he told himself it was only mildly disappointing, not catastrophic, when she unlinked her arms from around his neck—and slid a hand into a pocket of her dress. "I've been receiving infrequent notes of warning from an anonymous source. I should have told you sooner, but this is only the third one. I barely thought anything of the first one since it came after the event. And the second one—well, we were so busy that I didn't get around to telling you."

She held out a small folded envelope. Jev opened it and withdrew a single piece of stationery.

"Avoid the elf," he read, then turned it over. Nothing was on the back. "That's it?"

Zenia pointed to her name, Captain Zenia Cham, on the front of the envelope. "It's addressed to me and was mysteriously dropped off at the Air Order Temple while I was waiting for you to be healed. Someone knew I was there. The second one came to me here at the castle, delivered by an arrow that was shot over the wall."

"I find the fact that someone is keeping tabs on your whereabouts more concerning than the contents of the messages." Jev looked toward the window, wishing Lornysh hadn't taken off. He would have liked to ask if there was a magical way someone could be tracking Zenia. Was it possible the dragon tear gave off a powerful enough signature that some distant mage could feel it?

"I'm not tickled about it either. If the paperwork in the office and our cases thus far weren't keeping me so busy, I would put some effort into tracking down the person, but I haven't had much free time yet."

Jev winced, feeling lazy because he'd spent the last week healing and rehabilitating. He hadn't even been to the office since before they'd fought the trolls in the swamp. "I'm sorry. You're not doing my paperwork, too, are you?"

"I don't mind," she said.

"Oh, Zenia." Jev stepped close and hugged her again. "You don't have to do that."

"Actually, I do. Or someone does, at least. The foreign reports come in almost every day and are imperative to read right away. Some of them contain time-sensitive information."

"You shouldn't have to do that. I'll find someone else to help for when I'm sick or injured or have Dharrow duties that I can't escape. Maybe one of the other agents has good organizational skills."

She accepted his hug and rested her hands on his hips, but she was stiffer than she had been before. "Both your work and my work, receiving and going over all the reports, were handled by one person before. Zyndar Garlok. I refuse to believe he can do more than I can."

"*He* never left the office. All he did was sit at that desk all day. You're too smart to be wasted on that. I want you going out and doing research and solving cases when we have them. I'm sure Targyon does too. We'll find a secretary or promote—or maybe demote?—one of the agents to the job."

Jev thought of Rhi, but he hadn't seen her pick up a pen yet, and she didn't seem like someone who would be good at paperwork. There was Garlok, who was experienced, but Jev didn't want to admit to the man that he needed help. Nor did he entirely trust Garlok. Someone had been giving the town gossips a lot of fodder about him.

"We'll find someone," he reiterated.

Maybe he should have said that *he* would find someone. He didn't want Zenia to feel she had to take on the task. She'd taken on enough.

"I'll be back in the office tomorrow morning and will start the hunt."

"After we visit the elven tower," she said.

Jev smiled, amused by her persistence and determination. He didn't know if anything would come from it—he believed those elves had come for Lornysh and nothing more—but maybe he would find Lornysh still there packing. Jev had questions for his friend, and he also wanted to make another attempt at offering him assistance. Perhaps he would urge Lornysh to visit Targyon and see what he thought before leaving. It distressed Jev to think of never seeing Lornysh again.

"After we visit the tower," he agreed.

"And after you open your gift."

"My what?"

Zenia leaned back to look at his face while she arched her eyebrows. "The gift from Naysha that's been on your desk for over a week. What if you run into her and she asks you how you like it? You'd have to admit you never opened it."

"Oh." He'd forgotten all about it. And it made him uncomfortable to be reminded that Naysha had given it to Zenia, that the two women had interacted at all. He wasn't sure why, but it seemed like he should keep his ex-fiancé away from his new... girlfriend. He decided to think of Zenia as his girlfriend, even if it would be gauche to announce that to the world when his father had agreed he would wed Fremia Bludnor.

Something else he had to take care of tomorrow. It was going to be a busy day.

"Rhi keeps wanting to shake it to see if she can guess what it is," Zenia added.

"Has she?"

"Not while I've been watching."

"That doesn't answer my question."

Zenia smiled. "No, it doesn't." She let go and stepped back. It seemed like she was doing that a lot tonight. "Thank you for this." She held up the chain. "I better get to bed. We have lots to do tomorrow, and I haven't been sleeping that well."

"The dragon tear?"

She hesitated, avoiding his eyes. "I'm still having nightmares. I can't prove they're a result of the dragon tear, but..."

"They started after you began wearing it, right? Have you tried taking it off when you go to bed?" He waved toward its spot on her chest, assuming she kept it close, even at night. Most of those lucky enough to have dragon tears did.

"Yes. I tried hanging it on the doorknob and putting it in a jewelry box. It made no difference. I think we're linked now."

"You could try leaving it in here if you like." He waved to his desk, though after all that Cutter had said, he wouldn't be that eager to sleep with the gem in his room. Still, if there was a chance it would help Zenia rest more easily, he would do it.

Zenia touched her chest, a flash of alarm in her eyes, and a faint pulse of blue light seeped through the material of her dress. "Thank you, but that's not necessary. I like to keep it close. In case there's an emergency."

Jev shifted his weight. He hoped it wasn't exerting some influence over her to ensure she didn't let it go.

"Of course," he said, not wanting to object or give the dragon tear a reason to believe him an enemy or a danger to it—and when had he started to think of the thing as sentient? "You could also sleep here. Maybe being snuggled in my arms would keep nightmares away." Maybe she would be too busy dreaming about erotic things to do with him for anything else to drift into her mind.

Uh huh, wishful thinking, Jev, he told himself. More likely, *he* would be the one dreaming, especially if he slept with her in his arms. Maybe he had better rescind the offer, for both of their sanities.

"I…" Zenia paused.

Was she considering it? Or only trying to think of a tactful way to reject him?

"Just for sleep," Jev said, a clarification somehow coming out rather than a rescinding. "Nothing involving nudity," he added, though he believed she trusted him and his honor and that the clarification wasn't necessary.

She met his eyes, and he thought he read longing in hers, that she truly would *like* to sleep with him. Whether to keep nightmares at bay or just because she would enjoy it, he didn't know, but he had the urge to step forward and wrap his arms around her again, in case she truly was distressed by the dreams and longed for comfort.

"No," she said and visibly washed the emotion from her face, assuming her familiar determined expression with her chin up. "Thank you, but no. As long as you're engaged, it wouldn't be appropriate."

"I don't intend to be engaged for long, and nobody would have to know." He spread a hand, silently offering again.

"We're in a castle full of hundreds of people. Somebody would know." She smiled sadly. "Goodnight, Jev."

"Goodnight, Zenia," he murmured sadly as she slipped out.

CHAPTER 3

Z ENIA, PLAGUED BY ANOTHER NIGHTMARE, was
down in the office before dawn, the lanterns lit on all the desks
in an attempt to stave off the perpetual darkness of the basement.
And the darkness of that forlorn cave with that vile orc striding forward
and sinking its sword into her flesh. Her *scaled* flesh.

She shook her head, disturbed anew by the memories.

A part of her wished she had taken Jev up on his offer. She doubted
sharing his bed would have kept the nightmares away, but at least she
would have woken up in his arms, feeling safe and secure as her heart
tried to pound its way out of her chest. But, as she'd told him, one of
the maids would figure out if they were sharing a bed, or some other
member of the staff would witness her walking out of his room in the
morning. She didn't want to be a handle others could use on Jev to hurt
his reputation. Or to hurt him. Even if she hadn't cared about the gossip,
such behavior wouldn't be proper, not when he was engaged to another
woman.

It broke her heart a little to think that his engagement might turn
into a marriage. Even though she believed he wanted to be with her, she
didn't quite believe he would walk away from his family and his duties
as his father's heir. She was tempted to ride out to his castle one day and
speak with Heber just in case she could change his mind, but the man
surely remembered her as the inquisitor who'd stormed his castle, and
she feared she would only make matters worse. It wasn't as if she had
some great charm and could bat her eyes and convince him that she was
perfect for his son.

A faint query emanated from the dragon tear on her chest. She slid a finger along her beautiful new chain and touched the gem, not certain what the sensation meant. A vision came to her of standing before Heber Dharrow, the magic from the dragon tear trickling over to him, its powers of manipulation changing his mind.

She jerked her hand down to her desk, a chill washing over her.

She wouldn't contemplate manipulating someone into doing something to benefit her, and it disturbed her that the idea had come to mind, whether prompted by the gem or not. Besides, she'd never heard that one could use such magic for long-term manipulation. She would have to stand next to Heber day in and day out to keep him from changing his mind.

"Which makes it a moot point," she whispered to herself. "I have a job to do here."

Still, a weird feeling settled in her gut and didn't want to leave. Speculation. What could be... if she was willing to do it?

Zenia was relieved when the door opened, and she lifted her head, expecting the first of her agents was coming in to work. Having others in the office would make it feel less quiet. Less dangerous.

But it wasn't an agent. Two people walked in, a man and a woman, and she didn't recognize either of them. A guard was walking behind them.

"Captain Cham?" The guard peered around. "Is Zyndar Dharrow in?"

"Not yet," Zenia said.

"This is Zyndar Hydal." The guard pointed to the man, a slender fellow with spectacles. He appeared to be about thirty. "He's here to see Zyndar Dharrow. About... zyndar things."

Zenia snorted. That likely meant the guard had no idea.

"He said he'd be in this morning." Zenia glanced at the rectangular gift sitting on Jev's desk, along with a short stack of folders. Of well-organized folders. She was pleased she'd kept the reports from growing into mountains during his week of recovery. In her mind, helping him somewhat made up for the fact that she hadn't gone to visit him during his rehabilitation. It wasn't that she hadn't wanted to.

Zyndar Hydal adjusted his spectacles. "Perhaps we could check his room?"

"This is the king's private residence," the guard said, sounding grouchy. Judging by the bags under his eyes, he was due to come off the night shift soon. "I'm not taking you on a tour all over the castle."

"Zyndar," the woman said.

"What?" the guard asked.

"My cousin *is* of the nobility and deserves your respect, sir."

Hydal flicked his fingers in a dismissive gesture.

The guard grunted. "You can talk to Captain Cham or wait here for Zyndar Captain Dharrow. Maybe *he'll* give you a tour." The guard grumbled under his breath and turned and strode away.

As Zenia walked up the aisle between the rows of desks, the woman moved to a bookcase near the door. It was full of reference material, nothing of top-secret importance, so Zenia didn't say anything. The woman clasped her hands behind her back, perusing the books. She was younger than Hydal, in her early twenties perhaps, but she also wore spectacles and had a slender build and fine features.

"I know little about zyndar things," Zenia said, "but may I be of assistance? Oh, Zyndar Hydal. Aren't you the one that Jev put on the payroll as an informant?"

"On the payroll without pay, yes." Hydal smiled. "That's me."

"I believe Jev—Zyndar Dharrow—occupies a similar financial category on the books."

"*Jev* can afford not to get paid." The woman turned, holding her finger on the spine of a book. "The Dharrows have money flying out of their ears. It's no wonder half the women in the kingdom are scheming to get Jev to marry them."

Zenia's cheeks warmed, more at the topic than because she fell into that category.

Hydal made a patting motion in the air to his cousin.

"Don't shush me, Hux. Isn't his marriage what we came here to discuss?"

"Yes, I suppose." Hydal gave Zenia an apologetic look—had Jev told him that he and Zenia had feelings for each other?—and closed the door. "My pardon for being late on the introductions, Captain. I'm Huxley Hydal—Jev and I served in Gryphon Company together during the war. This is my cousin Severalina. She's a… friend of Wyleria Dharrow."

For some reason, Severalina rolled her eyes at the word friend. "You can call me Sevy. Zyndari Sevy." She looked back at Zenia, as if she expected some disrespect to her title at any moment. "Also, you have an alphabetical mismatch."

"Oh?" Zenia eyed the shelf. Agent Torson sat nearest to it and kept a log about books being checked in and out by other agents. "Ah, yes, I see."

Sevy arched her eyebrows. Asking for permission to fix it? Zenia nodded, and Sevy switched two books around, placing them in their proper order.

"Jev has indeed asked me to share any gossip I hear while attending zyndar social gatherings around town," Hydal said. "And also not to be seen here at the castle."

"Which is why we're here before the robins are even cheeping." Sevy grimaced.

"You didn't have to come," Hydal pointed out.

"I know, but I wanted to ask Jev about… things." She didn't look at either of them, merely pulled out a rarely used book and dusted off the top with her sleeve.

"I'm sure Wyleria is fine," Hydal murmured.

This resulted in an exasperated you-know-nothing look.

Zenia was tempted to run up to Jev's room and get him simply so she could deposit the unexpected visitors in his lap. But if Hydal was one of their informants…

"Do you have something to report?" Zenia asked. "I can write it down for Jev."

"Just that Fremia Bludnor may come out with an accusation against Zyndari Megloni Trocken or her family soon. She was nearly run over in the street yesterday—it's possible it wasn't as close as she's claiming it was—by a steam wagon owned by one of the Trocken family businesses. She believes Megloni was behind it, trying to kill her so Jev would be free to marry someone else. Namely, her. It seems that Zyndari Megloni also has her eyes on him but that her mother didn't get to Heber Dharrow's castle quickly enough to put in a marriage offer. The two mothers recently had a spat over it, during which Fremia was notably smug."

Hydal recited all this in a bored tone. Zenia wondered if women's gossip was the kind of information he'd imagined himself relaying when he'd volunteered for the job. Or had Jev dragooned him into it? Either way, it had to be far less scintillating than working in the intelligence-gathering Gryphon Company during the war had been.

"At this time," Hydal said, "I deem it unlikely that His Majesty's Crown Agents will be called in to investigate, but there was talk from Fremia of escalating it to the king, so it is possible you'll hear about it."

"I thank you for bringing it to my attention. Technically, domestic affairs are my domain, so I'm the correct person to report to for such matters."

"Mm, lucky you." Hydal smiled.

Just what she had been thinking. Even if Zenia hadn't felt romantic feelings toward Jev, she would have pitied him for having to deal with all these women who, from what she'd gathered, had more interest in him because of his family than because he was handsome, honorable, and a gentleman who brought thoughtful gifts to a woman. Her hand strayed up to touch the chain holding her dragon tear.

"I will let Jev know about it." Zenia, noticing Hydal tracking her hand, lowered it. She had no idea if more people than Targyon, Jev, and his close friends knew about her special dragon tear, but she didn't want to call attention to it. "Though he might prefer I didn't."

Hydal's eyes crinkled at the corners. "Likely not."

"Do you want to sit and wait for him? I'm expecting him any time. We don't have a waiting area with sofas and the like, but Agent Torson usually comes in late if you want to take his desk. And that's an empty one over there."

"Certainly." Hydal stepped forward, withdrew a handkerchief, and carefully wiped the wooden chair before offering it to his cousin.

Sevy crinkled her nose at the desk, ignoring the chair. "How can anyone work there? Look at that mess." She held up a paper with the remains of some beverage spill staining one corner, and loose paperclips tumbled onto the desk. "Can I straighten this?"

"We won't be here that long," Hydal murmured.

"Captain Cham?" Sevy held the paper up and shook it.

Zenia looked at the contents of the desk, debating if there was any sensitive material there that shouldn't be shown to outsiders, but she mostly saw pamphlets gathered from the universities in Korvann and nearby cities. Agent Torson kept an eye on student organizations and movements in case anything escalated into a potential problem for kingdom security or zyndar interests.

"Go ahead," Zenia said.

"It's not necessary to humor her," Hydal said.

"Trust me," Sevy said. "I am not humored."

She plucked up a wrapper and deposited it in the waste bin.

"You don't need a job, do you, Zyndari?" Zenia asked, half joking but also thinking of Jev's suggestion that they hire a secretary.

"Desperately," Hydal said.

Sevy looked at him. "*Hux!*" She drew the single syllable out into a couple of extra ones.

"She could use a distraction from relationship woes," Hydal told Zenia, ignoring the reprimand.

"Don't tell *her* that." Sevy looked like she would pitch over in mortification at some common woman learning about said woes.

"Why not?" Hydal asked. "She's Jev's friend."

"She is? You are?" Sevy's gaze fastened onto Zenia with new interest. "Do you know Wy?"

"Wyleria? Not well. We've spoken a couple of times, but that's it. I saw her last week when Jev was injured and she came to visit."

"You just saw her last week? Was she well? Or was she distraught and oppressed by the parochial tyranny of her family?"

"Ah." Zenia was starting to pick up on the relationship in question, though Jev had never spoken of it with her. "I was more concerned about Jev at the time. I didn't scrutinize Wyleria for a sense of being oppressed."

Hydal snorted.

Sevy sighed dramatically. She did, as she sighed, go back to straightening the desk. After a moment, she remembered Zenia's question. "What kind of job? Do you need another agent? Like a spy? I admit, I've always found novels and ballads about such persons quite intriguing."

"More of a secretary to the spy captains." Zenia smiled. She wasn't sure she and Jev could claim to be spies. They were the people who received reports *from* spies.

"So I'd be working for Jev?"

"Both of us, yes, but more him. His family duties require that he be out of the office often."

"Up at Dharrow Castle where he sees Wy, right? Does she ever come down here? Have you heard if anyone has shown interest in her mother's suggestions for marriage yet?"

"Zyndari Sevy, you see, has been forbidden to step foot on Dharrow land," Hydal said. "Not through any fault of her own, just as a precaution, I understand, so that she and her insidious ways will not unduly influence Zyndari Wyleria."

"I don't need you to tell her stuff, Hux," Sevy whispered, her cheeks growing pink. "But I accept the job. I just finished my university courses and hadn't decided yet what to do next. The Hydals aren't rich, so we can't be like Fremia and Megloni and lounge around, gossiping and scheming all day about how to get men. Who even wants a man?" She wrinkled her nose. "They smell."

"Really," Hydal murmured.

Zenia opened her mouth, then closed it. She hadn't realized the young woman would be interested or would accept the job offer on the spot. Zenia should have done a thorough investigation into her background first. She couldn't assume that she had the kingdom's best interests at heart just because she knew Jev's family. But she did have organizational tendencies, and it sounded like she didn't have any interest in making trouble for Jev, so...

"I'll need to do a background investigation on you before making things official," Zenia said, "but we will be happy to have you. I'll start making a list of your duties right away."

"A background investigation?" Sevy squinted suspiciously. "Would you need to do that if some *other* zyndari wanted the job?"

Confused by the question, Zenia said, "Certainly."

"My cousin feels that our family does not always get the respect it deserves," Hydal explained. "Or that zyndar in general are given."

"Oh. I don't know anything about your family."

"Therein lies the problem." Hydal smiled, appearing more reserved than disgruntled. "Few do."

"I just want someone good at organizing reports," Zenia said. "I don't care about zyndar reputations."

Surprisingly, Sevy appeared mollified by the statement. "I'm excellent at organizing. I was helping Wy with the Dharrow bookkeeping before, uhm, things."

Odd how often that word was being used in this discussion. But Zenia didn't care about zyndar relationships either. All she wanted was a good worker, and she nodded as she noticed that Torson's desk was already much tidier. This might work out.

"Are you sure you don't want me to thump her? Maybe this girl would decide you're not worth the trouble if there was a cranky Crown Agent with a big stick around every time she showed up."

Jev regarded Rhi—and her big stick—as they walked down the stairs toward the office. He'd run into her as he'd been leaving the kitchen and she'd been walking into the castle, and somehow, they had ended up discussing his engagement. If this could be called a discussion. Rhi had asked if he was still engaged, he'd said unfortunately, and it had quickly elevated to threats of beatings.

"Are you making this generous offer out of a desire to help me, a desire to see Zenia happy, or simply because you like pummeling zyndari women with your staff?" Jev asked.

"Can the answer be yes to all those things?"

"I suppose so. It does make you sound somewhat aggressive and belligerent."

"Perfect." She grinned and thwacked her bo against the stone wall.

They reached the office, and Jev held the door open for her, worried his shins might receive a similar treatment if he didn't. Rhi walked in first but stopped only a few steps inside.

A couple of agents were at their desks, Zyndar Hydal sat near the door, and Zenia was in the back, opening books and folders for a young woman Jev didn't recognize. By the founders, had she *already* found and hired a secretary? He rubbed his face, pleased to have an efficient colleague but distressed that she was so much more dedicated to their duty than he was.

The gesture brought a twinge of pain from his ribs, reminding him that he was still recovering from his injuries, but it seemed a poor excuse. He resolved to sleep less, work more, and figure out why Hydal was sitting at Agent Torson's desk.

Rhi looked curiously from Hydal to the new woman and back to him. Remembering that Jev had promised to introduce Hydal to Rhi, in the hope that a romantic connection might be made, he held up a hand when Rhi started toward her desk. Jev didn't think Hydal was the type of man to be intimidated by a woman with a big stick. He was less certain that Rhi was the type of woman to fall for a bookish man in spectacles.

"Rhi?" Jev said. "Allow me to introduce Zyndar Hux Hydal. He was my lieutenant in Gryphon Company and is very smart."

Hydal winced. Maybe that wasn't the best accolade to convince a woman of a man's sex appeal.

"He's also well-trained at hand-to-hand combat and has hidden ferocity that makes elves quake in their buckskins," Jev added in an attempt to improve the introduction.

Judging by the way Hydal dropped his face into his hand, it was possible Jev wasn't successful.

Instead of appearing intrigued, Rhi looked confused, perhaps wondering why the stranger sitting at the desk across from hers was getting a more thorough introduction than Jev had given anyone else in the office.

"He's a new informant," Jev said. "I thought you should know in case he approaches you with information at some point."

"You thought I should know about his hidden ferocity?" Rhi asked.

Hydal adjusted his spectacles. Un-ferociously.

"Yes, so it won't alarm you when it appears. Hydal, do you have information?" Since they had agreed Hydal wouldn't report to the castle often, Jev raised his eyebrows, fearing something important had brought him.

"Some that may catch you unaware later in the day if it's reported to the office, yes." Hydal summed up information he'd apparently already given to Zenia, and Jev did his best not to groan.

"Jev?" Zenia called. "Come meet our new secretary."

"*Zyndari* secretary." The young woman sniffed and adjusted her spectacles in a manner similar to Hydal's frequent gesture. "I'm told I'll be paid more than Hux."

"That wouldn't take much." As Jev headed to the back of the office, he guessed this was one of the three cousins Hydal had mentioned over the years. Jev hadn't known Hydal or his family well before meeting him during the war and didn't think he had met this young woman at any point. Even if he had, she would have only been ten or twelve at the time.

Jev glanced over his shoulder to see if Rhi had stayed to talk to Hydal, but she was heading to her own desk. Hastily. So much for his attempt to play matchmaker.

"I'm Sevy," the young woman announced when Jev joined them. "Wy's friend. How's she doing? Have you seen her recently?"

"She's well."

"Well?" Sevy's brows flew up, as if that was the last answer she'd expected.

"Is she not perhaps pining?" Zenia suggested.

"Pining?" It took a moment for his last conversation with Wyleria to come to mind, the one where she'd mentioned that her mother was seeking a suitable male marriage prospect for her after finding out that her interests lay with women. Was this the woman? Sevy seemed university-aged, but he supposed Wyleria was only twenty-five. She'd always been mature for her age, so he tended to think of her as older. "Yes, that's possible. Pining."

"I *knew* it," Sevy said.

"Sevy is going to help with your paperwork, Jev, but she's not sure where to file that." Zenia pointed to a rectangular gift in brown wrapping paper with a fancy ribbon holding it together.

"Ah, right." Jev picked it up but felt self-conscious about opening it in front of everyone in the office.

Zenia sat down and pointedly opened a folder. Rhi, Sevy, Hydal, and the other three agents in the office were not so discreet. They watched curiously.

The door opened, and one of the castle pages jogged in. Young Tamordon.

"Zyndar Captain Dharrow?" Tamordon asked. "His Majesty requests you join him for a meeting."

"Just me?" Jev glanced at Zenia.

Since they were equal rank, he felt they should both be brought in for meetings with Targyon. He could relay information, but he wouldn't want her to feel she was being left out because she wasn't zyndar or simply because she didn't have a past friendship with Targyon. Though it was possible this was about Jev and his family and had nothing to do with work matters. He grimaced at the thought, wishing the entire zyndar world would leave him alone.

"He only asked for you, Zyndar," the page said.

"All right. Thank you." Jev plucked up the gift, glad for an excuse to open it somewhere else without looking like he was embarrassed to do it in front of witnesses.

"Aren't you going to open that before you go?" Rhi asked as Jev walked toward her desk on the way to the door.

"No."

"He's probably afraid she sent him lacy underwear," Rhi said loudly, apparently believing the notion should be shared with the whole office.

"Men don't get lacy underwear," Jev stated firmly.

"What about that stuff the king wears that caresses his nether regions?" Rhi asked.

"Those are his pajamas. And they're not lacy."

"You've checked."

"I have to go." Jev picked up his pace, now relieved that Rhi and Hydal hadn't hit it off immediately. Hydal deserved a kind, supportive, and polite woman who didn't enjoy thumping people.

"Jev?" Zenia called as he reached for the doorknob.

"Yes?" He turned a little warily. He didn't think Zenia would bring up the king's nether regions in public—or at all—but he couldn't be positive.

"After your meeting, will you be ready to go to the tower?" Her expression was pensive. She must still think those elves were worth investigating.

"Unless Targyon has a new assignment for us, I'll be ready."

Zenia nodded and went back to instructing Sevy.

The page glanced at the gift a few times as he led Jev up multiple sets of stairs and to Targyon's office. Jev tucked it under his arm, determined that he wouldn't open it in front of anyone else. He was positive Naysha hadn't given him lacy underwear, but he *wasn't* positive it wouldn't be embarrassing. Just knowing she had brought a gift for him made him feel uncomfortable.

"Go right in," the king's secretary said as Jev entered the outer office, shedding the page at the door.

Targyon was alone inside, thankfully dressed in trousers and a tunic and not his pajamas. It was early enough that the latter would have been understandable, but after Rhi's comments, Jev didn't want to see them.

"Yes, Sire?"

"Have a seat, Jev. I want to talk to you about..." Targyon trailed off when he noticed the gift.

"Sorry, it's nothing." Jev resisted the urge to stuff it behind his back. He didn't think Targyon would believe Jev had brought him a gift, but it was an admittedly odd thing to carry into a meeting with one's monarch. The pale blue ribbon was crimped into little feminine bows at the ends. "Naysha brought it to my office a while ago, and I didn't want to open it in front of everyone," he added, somehow feeling it needed an explanation.

"That's your ex-fiancé?"

"Yes."

"One wonders what your *new* fiancé will give you."

"Fremia? Nothing, I hope. I intend to get the old man to rescind that marriage acceptance as soon as I can." Jev grimaced, worried this opening suggested the meeting would indeed revolve around him and his personal life rather than kingdom matters. Oh, how he would prefer to talk about a new case. Or even the trollish invasion. He made a mental note to ask Zenia if any of the reports that had come in that week had expounded on that.

"Will that be as difficult as I suspect?" Targyon asked.

"I see you've met my father."

"I've had two meetings with the zyndar primes since taking over the throne."

"Was he equally charming at both of them?"

"Obstinate and set in the old ways would be the way I'd put it."

"So, you didn't find him charming? He'll be crestfallen when I tell him."

"I doubt it."

Jev sighed. Targyon had definitely gotten a read on the old man. Sometimes, Jev felt him more like a grandfather than a father, though grandfathers were reputed to be jolly and spoil their grandchildren.

"I suppose that means you won't order him to cancel my engagement," Jev said. "He agreed to it without asking me. It's rather unseemly."

He'd meant it as a joke, but as soon as the words came out of his mouth, Jev wondered if Targyon could do something. He *was* the king. King Abdor would have left his zyndar to figure out their own affairs—and the affairs of their children—but Targyon was progressive. Surely, his poetic soul railed at the idea of arranged marriages.

"Quite frankly, I doubt your father would listen to me if I suggested it," Targyon said. "And if I ordered it... It's distressing coming up against the limits of my power and influence. I've already found the older generation of zyndar are less inclined to listen to me. Kingly status or not." His lips twisted with bitterness.

Jev wondered how those meetings with the primes had gone. Most of them were over seventy. He didn't envy Targyon his position. When he'd been Targyon's age, he hadn't even liked talking to people who were forty. Odd how that didn't seem so old anymore.

"If I see an opportunity to talk to him about it..." Targyon started, then ended with a grimace.

Jev could tell the last thing Targyon wanted to do was to talk to the old man about Jev's love life. He held up a hand. "Never mind. I'll deal with it. It's my family."

"Yes, very good." Poor Targyon. He looked so relieved. "What I called you up here about is the Taziir."

Jev straightened, thoughts of marriage dashed from his mind. "You heard about Lornysh? And his problems?"

Targyon blinked. "No."

"Oh. There are some elves in the city—wardens, Lornysh said— looking for him. Unfortunately, I met one. It was unpleasant. And so was he."

"What do they want?"

"To kill him, I gather. Revenge for the elves he assassinated during the war. I saw him briefly last night, and he's considering leaving the city. Better that than a confrontation he knows he can't win. I said we— at least Cutter and I—would stand with him, but he doesn't want us risking injury—or death—for his sake. Laudable, but I don't think I can simply stand aside while wardens try to kill him. I owe him my life several times over."

Targyon walked to the window and looked out onto the gardens below.

Jev cleared his throat. "I thought you might be willing to volunteer some resources to help him, or at least help drive hostile elves out of the city."

"I appreciate that Lornysh assisted our people during the war," Targyon said slowly—he sounded like he was trying to choose his words carefully. "And if he comes to me for help, I will feel obligated to give it, but my inclination is to stay out of elven business. Especially business that might pit us *against* the elves." He turned from the window to face Jev. "As I started to say, I sent a message to the Taziir king, requesting that he send another ambassador and as much staff as necessary to man the tower. I'm going to send a team to repair it. I know it's early to hope we can mend fences with our northern neighbors—perhaps they'll consider it early throughout my entire lifetime—but I wanted to at least make an overture. To let them know we don't mind them in our city."

"I mind those wardens in our city," Jev said.

Targyon spread his hand. "I do empathize, but Lornysh must have known there could be consequences when he made the choice to assist humanity. If he wishes to leave, that may be for the best. Until tempers cool."

"Until tempers cool? Those people live for centuries. They could hold a grudge for half of eternity."

"They are Lornysh's people. He must have known he would one day have to deal with them again."

"He couldn't have known he would have to stand alone," Jev said, his face hot. He had expected Targyon to be more sympathetic, more willing to stand up for their friend.

"As I said, Jev, if he asks me for help, I will provide what I can. I'm definitely not unappreciative that he helped my uncle during the war—that he helped us. I just don't know the whole story, so it's hard to know which is truly the right one to side with, and I can't afford to make mistakes by choosing the wrong side." Targyon cocked his head. "Do you know?"

"Know what?"

"The whole story."

Jev hesitated, wanting to say that he did and that he was positive his friend was the wronged party. But he couldn't.

"He's never told me much of his past," Jev admitted.

"Ah." Targyon picked up a piece of paper on his desk. "This is why I called you up. I sent my invitation to the Taziir king right after Ambassador Shoyalusa left. The response arrived on a merchant ship that came in last night. Your Elvish is better than mine. Will you check my translation?"

"Yes." Jev stepped forward and looked over a pale green sheet of paper covered in a flowing, elegant script. An Elvish script. Interesting that the Taziir had chosen to respond in their own language. Jev knew there were plenty of elven scribes who knew the human tongues. He supposed it was a message in and of itself. If Targyon couldn't be bothered to translate it, they couldn't be bothered to have relations with him. "There's a poem," Jev said as he read. "About how the sea is harsh and many ships never make it to shore."

"Yes. There's a message in the symbolism, I assume."

"Actually, the whole letter is in verse."

"And vague. I noticed. Does the pod of orcas guiding the ship to harbor after it's recovered from a siren attack mean they're sending someone?"

Jev read the poem a couple of times, trying to see beyond the literal translation. An academic who studied their culture would be a more appropriate resource right now than a soldier who only knew the Taziir through battle. And through his friendship with Lornysh. Jev did know that even elven nonfiction tended toward poetry and symbolism. He'd once read an instruction pamphlet on how to season frying pans that had involved a dragon cave allegory.

"It does seem to have an optimistic bent underlying the numerous warnings," Jev said. "And I agree that the ship guided by orcas suggests the elves will be sending someone to guide us through treacherous waters with their infinite wisdom."

"That's not exactly what I asked for."

"From what you've told me so far, being king is more about wearing silky pajamas in a big bedroom in the castle than getting what you want."

Targyon's forehead wrinkled. Jev made a mental note to chastise Rhi later for putting the king's nightwear in his mind. Not that chastising would do anything to her. She would probably consider it flirting. Maybe *Hydal* should chastise her.

"There wasn't a date mentioned anywhere, right?" Targyon asked.

"No. The orcas could show up tomorrow or in ten years."

Targyon snorted. "On the chance that it's tomorrow, go to the elven tower, will you? Take Zenia. She has a lady's eye. See what needs to be done to make it livable, and requisition people from the castle to help."

Jev was about to object to what sounded like being named head maid, but Targyon kept speaking.

"Also, look around and see if the old elven ambassador left any documents or letters behind that would be useful to know about. They seemed to have advanced warning of the troll problem. What else did the ambassador know? And what was he reporting back to his king? Don't remove anything, but if a translation would be useful…" Targyon spread his hand.

"You're suggesting we should snoop in the elves' drawers?"

"I would like to be able to consider the Taziir allies again—that's why I've invited them to send another ambassador, in the hope that they'll see it as a peace gesture—but I'm under no delusion as to why the ambassador was here in the first place. To keep an eye on Korvann and report back to his people."

"It's why *we* used to have an ambassador in Taziira," Jev said.

The last he'd heard, the human ambassador had mysteriously committed suicide.

"Yes. Since we were the instigators in the war, I can't blame the elves for being suspicious of us, but what we need to know is if anyone is having thoughts of revenge."

"Against more people than Lornysh?" Jev touched the back of his neck, remembering again the elf warden's threat to kill him.

"Yes. Let me know if you find anything to suggest that my overtures of peace are naive. Things are going moderately well with the dwarves— I've moved those craftsmen out of the castle and into their new quarters and shops in the city—but we need more allies and quickly. And the elves, since they were our allies in the past and have no love for trolls, may be our best bet, along with the dwarves."

"I'll take a look, Sire."

"Good. And do take time to see your father. I wouldn't want my most trusted advisor to be grumpy and out of sorts because he's forced to marry a woman he doesn't love." Targyon smiled.

"I'm your most trusted advisor? Sire, you need to raise your standards."

"Undoubtedly." The smile faded, and Targyon added, "Also, and I hate to say this, but… since you're under some public—zyndar— scrutiny right now, it would be better if you weren't seen with one woman while you're engaged to another."

Jev grimaced. He didn't want this lecture from the kid he'd commanded only a couple of short months ago. "I understand, but I haven't even *met* the woman I'm engaged to, not since she was a little kid, and I honestly can't remember her from a bunch of other kids that were that age together. And I have to work with Zenia. We *are* colleagues."

Targyon's expression grew pensive, and Jev feared he might decide it wisest if he changed that fact. By firing him? By firing *her*? He couldn't do that. Zenia was good at her job. She was made to do this kind of thing. Jev hated to admit it, but he was the disposable one.

"I'll be circumspect, Sire. But I *do* intend to get my father to agree to me marrying Zenia. In the meantime, if you could make her a zyndari, that would be useful." It probably still wouldn't be enough to satisfy the old man, since she would be new zyndar instead of from an old and established family, but Jev smiled wistfully at the thought of Zenia being considered a noblewoman without need of any intervention from her father.

"Historically speaking, it required a great deed that the entire kingdom was aware of before a king elevated a commoner into the nobility."

"She *did* halt a troll invasion."

"I wouldn't assume it's been halted. Delayed, perhaps. Besides, weren't you and Lornysh the ones to kill all those scouts?"

"She was the one who led us to them."

"Also, historically speaking, commoners elevated to the zyndar class were male, with their wives and children granted the status through the man."

"I know that, but these are modern times. Can't we have some modern rules?"

"There isn't any land left to grant unless you want to give up some of yours. That's the main reason nobody has been added to the class in almost two hundred years."

Jev would happily give up some of his family's land, but he didn't own it. His father did.

"Go check on the tower, please, Jev." Targyon flicked his fingers in dismissal, or maybe to indicate that he'd grown weary of the conversation.

Jev walked out without a word. It wasn't Targyon's fault that he was growing into his role of king and absolute ruler, but at that moment, Jev had liked it better when he'd been Targyon's superior officer, and his young protege had been eager to please.

Jev, finding a moment alone, finally opened the gift he'd been carrying around for an hour. Fortunately, it wasn't underwear. It was a biography on the legendary zyndar general, Govrato Gorndor. Naysha had written a quotation from the general on the first page and added a note of her own.

"To lead great men, one must first become great oneself." You're on your way, Jev. I have faith in you. Be well.

~Naysha

Jev closed the book and took a bracing breath. He was skeptical that he was destined to be a great leader, but by the founders, he resolved to deal with his family problems like a man.

CHAPTER 4

ENIA RODE OUT THE MAIN gate at Jev's side, wondering if they were making a mistake by not bringing along a platoon of soldiers or a squadron of guards from the castle. Jev didn't seem to believe there would be trouble at the elven embassy. Either that, or he was busy thinking about something else.

He had barely said two sentences to her since returning from his meeting with the king. When he'd left for that meeting, Zenia had been disappointed that she hadn't been invited—she'd assumed it had to do with work—but she'd used the time to give their new employee instructions and watch her start on some tasks.

"Do you think we should pick up some men from the watch headquarters on the way to the tower?" she asked over the clip-clop of their horses' hooves on the cobblestone road leading down the hill and into the city.

"No," Jev said.

"It's been a couple of nights since the elves were seen poking around, but should we assume we won't run into them? I know it's broad daylight, but they must be staying somewhere in the city while they look for Lornysh."

Jev frowned, and Zenia wished she hadn't reminded him that his friend was a target.

"I'm guessing they're not staying anywhere so easy to find. Also—" Jev twisted in his saddle to make sure nobody was riding or walking within earshot, "—Targyon wants us to poke through the old ambassador's desk drawers to see if he left any interesting documents behind. Before a new ambassador shows up, making it difficult to snoop."

"Is a new ambassador coming?"

"Either that, or we can expect a pod of orca whales in the harbor soon."

Zenia stared at him, trying to decide if that was a joke she didn't understand or something that was actually likely. Jev appeared more grumpy than jocular today.

He noticed her scrutiny and smiled—it appeared forced. He leaned over and patted her shoulder. "It's likely the elves are sending someone, yes. Targyon wants us to make sure the tower is livable and also to investigate while we have the chance. I'd rather not investigate with the watch looking on. Zyndar are noble and honorable and do not rummage through other people's drawers. At least not with an audience looking on."

"All right, but if an elf warden jumps out of one of those drawers, I'm going to remind you I suggested bringing reinforcements."

"If an elf warden jumps out of a drawer, I'm not sure all the watchmen in the city would be of any help."

Zenia stirred in her saddle, surprised by the statement. "They're not *that* powerful, are they?"

"They're powerful." Jev rubbed the back of his neck, and Zenia noticed faint bruises on his skin. "I may have been exaggerating, but not by much. I saw one battle an entire platoon of the king's men and win. Or at least get away. And he left twenty men—twenty skilled veterans— dead in his wake. They have magical swords that are more than equal to our firearms, and they're trained with magic as well. Strong magic. Lornysh is a warden, and he once admitted to me that he was considered a weak one, since his skills are more heavily combat-oriented and magic isn't his strength."

"I've seen him use magic."

"Yes, he has some. He's just not a natural at it. He…" Jev trailed off, squinting toward the city gate.

A single side-saddle rider was heading up the road on a handsome chestnut stallion.

"That's Wyleria." Jev hesitated before lifting a hand.

Zenia could guess the reason for the hesitation. She believed he liked his cousin, but Wyleria had been the bearer of bad news lately.

"I hope she's not here to tell me I'm marrying someone else," Jev grumbled.

"That's not legal."

"There could be a backup woman lined up. In the event Fremia comes to her senses."

"That may be legal."

He gave her a bleak look and slowed his horse as Wyleria trotted up to them.

"Good morning, cousin." Jev forced another smile. He seemed to be doing that a lot lately.

Zenia wanted to hug him, but that certainly wouldn't help matters, not with his cousin watching.

Wyleria, after smiling at Jev, frowned slightly at Zenia. Because they were riding into the city together? Zenia lifted her chin. She and Jev were colleagues, damn it. They were supposed to work together. And ride places together.

"Good morning, Jev," Wyleria said, focusing on him. "Your father has decided that I should be the one to keep telling you news you may find unpleasant. My mother apparently told him I'm your favorite cousin, thus making me the natural choice. But if they keep sending me with unpalatable news, I'm sure that won't be the case for long." Wyleria smiled, but her eyes held concern. She probably truly worried Jev would stop talking to her.

"Four founders, there isn't really a backup woman now, is there?" Jev blurted.

Wyleria's eyebrows drew together. "Backup woman?"

"It's a joke," Zenia said. "I think."

Jev shook his head.

"No, I'm here about Fremia," Wyleria said. "Aunt Vivione decided the two of you need to meet. She invited Fremia up to the house for lunch tomorrow, and you're expected to be there to entertain her."

"Entertain?" Jev looked at Zenia, and she had the distinct impression he wished that she weren't here to hear about this. And also that he could make this Fremia woman—and their engagement—disappear.

"Yes, entertain," Wyleria said. "Be charming and compliment her beauty. I suppose you could be odious and say her hair looks limp and greasy, in the hope that she'll back out of the marriage, but that probably won't work. Her mother has been around Dharrow Castle a lot, talking to your father, and I get the feeling she's behind the engagement as much as Fremia is. Maybe more."

"Why lunch?" Jev asked. "I have work to do. I can't spend the whole day up at the castle."

"Don't you need to talk to your father, anyway?" Zenia asked. "Perhaps if you went early, there would be time for a long discussion in the morning."

"Nobody has long discussions with the old man."

Wyleria wore an expression of agreement.

Zenia merely gazed at Jev, hoping he was only joking and realized this would be a good time to go up there. If Jev didn't change his father's mind, Zenia definitely wouldn't be sleeping in his bed anytime soon. Or ever.

Jev must have read her expectations—her hopes—in her gaze, because he straightened in his saddle. "You're right. I'd planned to go to the castle anyway to talk with him. Firmly."

"I'll grant you my best wishes for that endeavor," Wyleria murmured.

She tugged at the reins, as if to turn her stallion, but Jev lifted a hand.

"You may want to go up to Alderoth Castle for a visit." Jev shifted his hand, pointing over his shoulder. "Your friend is up there."

"Friend?"

"Zenia hired a Sevy Hydal this morning to help keep us organized. I gather you know each other."

Wyleria's eyebrows flew up. "Hired?" she mouthed, looking at Zenia.

Zenia shrugged. "She came in and organized a bookcase and an agent's desk without being asked. She seemed a likely candidate."

Wyleria's expression shifted from surprise to genuine pleasure. "She is. She's very smart. She's not always the most mature young woman, but she's been helping me with bookkeeping, and is even part of the reason a couple of the family businesses turned a handsome profit last year. That's where I met—" Wyleria glanced at Zenia, and her cheeks grew pink. "That's how we know each other and became friends."

Zenia, having already gathered it was more than a friendship, only nodded.

"If she's there, and the guards will let me in, I believe I will go check on her," Wyleria said. "Unfortunately, she's not welcome at Dharrow Castle right now because of... reasons."

"They'll let you in." Jev guided his horse to the side of the road to make room for her to pass. "Just watch out for Zyndar Garlok. I'm not convinced he's not the person feeding gossip about me and Zenia to others."

"Yes." Wyleria sighed. "That's something I must avoid, lest word get back to my mother. I fear I'm not in any better position than you, Jev." Her expression was apologetic and commiserative when she waved goodbye, and she included both Zenia and Jev in the gesture.

"Maybe I should tell my father I want to marry a man," Jev said as he and Zenia continued down the hill toward the city gate. "Then if I later suggested you, he might be relieved that you're the correct sex to produce heirs with me."

"There is that tavern keeper across the street from the elven tower who wanted to see you with your shirt off," Zenia said.

Jev shuddered.

"You'd have to get rid of that reflex if you wanted to convince your father you were in earnest," she observed.

"Probably. I think he'd just have me disowned though."

The guards nodded respectfully toward Jev as he and Zenia passed through the gate. Zenia wondered what she would have to do to earn that kind of respect. Be zyndari? Be a man? Save the city from a flock of dragons? The latter, probably. Even when she'd been a renowned inquisitor in her vivid blue robe, the guards had been more likely to eye her warily than nod respectfully.

A blind man with a cane, a tin, and a turtle sat cross-legged in front of a bench in a small park a couple of blocks from the elven embassy. He wore a ragged white robe, such as the Air Order mages donned, but Zenia didn't sense any magic about him. If he'd once worked for the Air Order Temple and had wielded a dragon tear, that had been long ago, and he'd likely had to turn the gem back in.

"Your fortune and the blessings of the founders for a coin," he called to them in a wispy voice, though Zenia didn't know how he'd seen them.

She watched with bemusement as Jev veered over, dismounted, dropped to one knee in front of the man, and placed a couple of coins in his tin. This wasn't the first time she'd seen him stop for one of these self-purported seers to get his fortune. From what she'd seen of him thus far, he wasn't overly religious or superstitious, so she didn't know if these were serious entreaties, or if he was simply showing kindness by giving them some money.

"How's your fortune looking?" she asked when he returned, his expression wry.

"My summer is going to be fraught."

"I could have told you that, and you wouldn't have had to pay me."

"But would you have also blessed me?"

"I don't think I get to do that anymore, now that I'm not working for the Water Order. The Blue Dragon might return to our realm to smite me down for blasphemy."

"That's why I paid an expert."

She snorted at the idea of the blind man being anything more than a beggar or a charlatan, but she didn't say anything more.

They reached the elven compound without any more interruptions and tied their horses near the tavern. Jev did not go in to flirt with the barkeeper.

The gate to the embassy was closed with a padlock securing the wrought-iron bars. Zenia had noticed it when she'd walked by the day before. Another reason she hadn't ventured in on her own. She assumed the ambassador had placed it there as he left, but it was also possible watchmen had come by and done it, not wanting vandals or homeless people to take up residence in the vacant tower. Or mostly vacant. Lornysh had been sleeping in one of the rooms. Was that still the case? If he was smart, he would have moved on.

Jev tugged at the padlock. It was solidly attached and free of rust. "I guess we climb."

Zenia eyed the high wall, then touched her dragon tear. A hint of eagerness emanated from it, like a dog longing to go off on adventures.

"I think I can get us in more easily." She stepped forward and envisioned the padlock opening, as if a key had turned in the mechanism. She didn't want the lock broken if possible, not the way it had been at Master Grindmor's place the last time she'd used her dragon tear this way.

"Oh?" Jev asked.

A soft click sounded, and the lock fell open.

"Huh," he said. "It slays trolls, burns crocodiles to ashes, *and* opens locks. Versatile."

This time, the gem emanated pleasure.

"Yes," was all Zenia said.

They pushed open the gate and walked into the compound. It had rained a few times since the fire had burned down what had once been a lush treed garden, and new growth fuzzed the ground between the paths. Most of the trees were skeletal and charred, too damaged to ever sprout leaves again. Here and there, a few bushes had escaped the flames, but Zenia had no doubt that a new ambassador would want to start a new garden. A shame it was necessary. The old one had been mature and beautiful.

Also guarded by magical creatures, she remembered, peering between the skeletal trees. Would they still be about? Or would the old ambassador have taken them with him? Or dismissed them to whatever magical place from whence they had been conjured?

"I think they're gone," Jev said, noticing her gaze. "But maybe your dragon tear can sense whether there's any magic around."

"It probably can," she agreed, clasping the gem. The last time she'd been here, she hadn't been as aware of the variety of its powers as she was now.

The gem warmed in her grip, and her vision seemed to change, a strange blue tint coming to it. That hadn't happened before, and she almost let go. But then she saw bright spots in the blue, and it reminded her of the time in the marsh when she'd asked the gem to show her the locations of life all around them. This time, she realized, it was showing her magic. A few dark blue dots appeared on the ground or in the trunks of trees, but they were dwarfed by a whitish-blue glow around the entire cylindrical shape of the tower.

"Zenia?" Jev touched her arm.

The indicators of magic faded, her vision returned to normal, and she lowered her hand. "Yes?"

"You got glassy-eyed there. I wanted to make sure you're all right." He glanced at her chest, where her dragon tear glowed with blue inner light. "I assumed you weren't thinking of me naked."

"No." She looked at him. "Do women often get glassy-eyed when they do that?"

Jev released her arm. "They *do* look distracted. And drool a little."

"Would you be offended if I said I was perplexed about why so many women want to marry you?"

He grinned. "Nah. I'm positive you're the only one that would be interested if I wasn't Heber Dharrow's heir."

Zenia wasn't so sure about that. Even though she'd teased him, he *was* handsome. And considerate. And a good kisser. It was only his humor that some might find questionable.

"Is it wrong of me to wish you weren't?" she asked.

"I don't think so. I've wished it from time to time myself. Life would be simpler."

"The guards wouldn't nod at you when you pass through the gate if you weren't zyndar."

He snorted. "How distressing that would be."

Zenia wondered what it said about her that she longed for what he barely noticed. Maybe if he'd been born common, he would see the world differently. No, that wasn't a maybe. He definitely would. But having been born into the nobility, he was like a fish born in the sea. He had no idea the water around him even existed.

Jev started walking again toward the door.

"The tower is either full of magic," Zenia said, matching his steps, "or it's magic itself."

"I'm not surprised. I don't think we have to worry about magical booby traps. I sneaked in through a window once before and wasn't incinerated by incendiary caltrops."

She hadn't been imagining that would be a problem, but now she did. "I'll see if I can get my dragon tear to pinpoint magical items once we're inside. Maybe the elves left some interesting artifacts behind."

"Ah. Good idea." Jev reached for the latch but hesitated. The door was already ajar.

"Do you want me to go first?" Zenia knew her dragon tear could create a barrier around her to protect her.

"It's unmanly to hide behind a woman. The Zyndar Code of Honor forbids cowardice."

"That didn't answer my question." She tapped the gem to let him know *why* she was offering.

Her reasoning might have been logical, but he still stepped inside first. Zenia stuck close to him as they entered the shadowy foyer, the only light bleeding in through shuttered windows. A set of stairs spiraled upward along the wall, and two doors stood open on the far side of the foyer.

The hairs on the backs of Zenia's arms rose, and she shivered. It was at least twenty degrees cooler inside than under the early summer sun outside, but that wasn't the reason for her chill.

Thanks to her link with the dragon tear, she sensed magic all around them. It emanated from the walls of the tower and seemed to float in the air itself. It did not feel like friendly magic. Maybe it was her imagination, but the tower seemed to know they were non-elven intruders and had decided they weren't welcome.

"Do you know where the ambassador's office is?" Zenia asked as her eyes adjusted to the dim lighting. She wanted to finish this task as quickly as possible and get out.

"I didn't get the full tour last time." Jev headed for the stairs. "I was busy chasing that elven scientist." He paused at the base of the stairs and peered through the closest door. "That looks like an office, but I want to check and see if Lornysh is here before snooping. He's probably moved out, but if not, he might know where the juicy stuff is. You can start poking around in that desk in there if you want. I'll be right back."

Zenia shook her head, still very aware of the magic all around them. "I'll stay with you."

"Because you'll feel safe standing next to my fierce virile manliness? Or because you think I might get myself in trouble without you and your dragon tear to keep an eye on me?"

"Whichever one your ego wants to believe."

"Definitely the first thing, then." Jev flashed a grin over his shoulder as he climbed.

They ascended several levels, the stairs going round and round along the tower wall. There were only a couple of doors on each landing, all of them closed. Fortunately, Zenia's unease and certainty that unfriendly magic had surrounded them in the foyer faded as they climbed higher. Whatever it was, it seemed to be centered down below.

Zenia lost track of the levels. Jev stopped on a landing and veered toward an open door, but he paused before going inside and looked at the jamb. In the poor light, Zenia almost missed the splintered wood. Someone had forced the door open.

"That's Lornysh's room?" Zenia asked.

"Yes."

Jev, his expression grim, stepped inside. He gazed toward a shuttered window, then toward the bed. It was unmade, with the blanket fallen to the floor, and Zenia could make out something thrusting out of the pillow.

As Jev walked further into the room, ceramic shards crunched under his boot. The air smelled of flowers, and Zenia spotted a vase that had been knocked over. Dried petals mingled with the shards on the floor. A desk chair was overturned, one of the legs broken off.

She couldn't tell how long ago this had happened. The night the elves had been seen here? Or had they returned last night and caught Lornysh here? She didn't see a body, but that didn't mean they hadn't bested him. They could have kidnapped him. Or carried his body away after they killed him.

Zenia did not share the thoughts with Jev. He'd moved closer to the bed and was looking down at it. The hilt of a dagger stuck out of the pillow, the blade embedded deep.

CHAPTER 5

J EV POKED THROUGH THE DRAWERS in the old
ambassador's office desk and tried not to think about the signs of a fight
that he'd seen in Lornysh's room. Especially the dagger stuck in his pillow.

He wished he knew where his friend had gone after leaving the
embassy. Had that fight happened before or after Lornysh had visited
the castle the night before? Jev had no idea.

"There's a lot of magic in here," Zenia said quietly. She was
examining a bookcase on the wall opposite the desk. "Most of it is
built into the tower, but there are a few artifacts around. My dragon tear
doesn't know what they do."

She held up an elephant carved from jade as an example.

Jev had lit a couple of lanterns so they could snoop more effectively,
so he could see that the carving had been made by a highly skilled
craftsman. He would have to trust her that it held some magic since
he had no way to verify that. Very occasionally, he could sense strong
magic, usually when it was about to be used against him, but without a
dragon tear, he was just a mundane human. All he had were hunches and
intuition. They were unreliable, at best.

"Leave the artifacts," Jev said. "We're just here for information."

He was a little surprised that thieves hadn't risked elven ire—and
magical booby traps—to loot the place.

Zenia set the figurine back down. "I can't read any of these book
spines, I'm afraid. They're all in Elvish."

"Actually, some are in Preskabroton Dwarf, Jynnish Troll, and
Orcish, the ones dealing with magic mostly." Jev had quickly perused

the bookshelf when he first lit the lanterns. "But you're right that most are written in Elvish. They're atlases, cultural compendiums, city guides, and other things a world traveler—or traveling ambassador—might find useful."

Zenia looked at him, and he hoped he hadn't sounded overly pedantic. Languages were the one thing that had always come easily for him, and he even knew a smattering of many of the ones he hadn't studied in earnest for the army.

But she smiled, looking pleased with him. "What do orcs write about?"

"The last Orcish text I read was a recipe book that expounded on the differences between cooking wild game meat and cooking the sentient races such as humans and elves. Apparently, elves are stringy and need to be tenderized with an acid. Lemon juice was recommended. Also actual acid."

Her pleased expression faded. Maybe he should have lied.

"I'm never positive when you're joking and when you're being serious, Jev."

"Maybe it's for the best that you don't know in this instance." He pushed another drawer shut. So far, he'd found numerous papers and journals that had been left but nothing Targyon would consider useful information. Or information the Crown Agents office didn't already have in its filing cabinets.

Zenia came over to the desk and started lifting books and bins and looking under them. The elven ambassador hadn't been much more organized than Jev was, and the desk was a mess. He noticed a few envelopes in a bin and pulled them out. One was addressed to an Ormaleshon, and Jev froze. He recognized the name, having intercepted a few military correspondences to the elf.

"That's King Yvelon's secretary. The elven equivalent to a secretary, rather. The position involves being a spiritual and magical advisor as well as handling communications from representatives from other elven communities. And from elven diplomats stationed around the world, it seems." Jev grabbed a letter opener and slipped it under the fold.

"Wait." Zenia leaned across the desk and gripped his wrist. "That has magic in it."

"Which?" Jev held up the envelope and the letter opener.

She gave him a don't-be-silly look and pointed at the envelope.

"That's surprising, actually." Jev turned it over in his hands. "I don't think it's easy to embed magic in paper."

There was a green wax seal closing the flap, and Zenia pointed at it. "That's the source."

Jev recognized the stamp on the seal. He assumed it was the ambassador's personal or family mark, but he'd seen it before. It took him a moment to realize where.

"Ambassador Shoyalusa's dragon tear."

"What?" Zenia asked.

"Remember his dragon tear? We saw it at Targyon's reception. It was a tree. This is exactly the same. It almost looks like he used the gem to stamp this." Jev risked touching the edge of the oval embedded in the hardened wax.

"Maybe he did and it conveyed some of his magic."

"Do you think yours could do that?"

Zenia's nose wrinkled, and Jev couldn't tell what the expression meant.

"No?" he asked.

She touched her dragon tear. "I got a sense of… indignation."

"Ah, being a stamp is beneath it, eh?"

"I think so. I'm going to see if it can render that magic harmless, in case the seal is designed to keep other people from opening the envelope. It's hard to tell."

Jev imagined her occasionally overzealous dragon tear incinerating the envelope, but he held it up obligingly. The wax melted and dripped into a gooey mess on the papers on the desk. And his hand.

Zenia nodded. "Go ahead. The magical bond was destroyed."

Jev wiped the wax off the back of his hand. "If you say so."

He opened the envelope, drew out a single piece of paper, and unfolded it.

"It's not my anonymous advisor," Zenia said, eyeing the script.

"Did you think the elven ambassador was likely to be that person?"

"No, but I'm looking at every desk and handwriting sample I come across with extra scrutiny right now."

"Understandable," Jev mumbled, his eyes locked on the page as he translated it. "This is addressed to the king as well as his secretary, and it's surprisingly blunt for an elven letter." There was nothing about orcas. Jev wished there had been.

"What does it say?"

"Lornysh is here."

Zenia looked at his face. "It mentions him by name?"

"It does. And that's *all* it mentions."

"I didn't think he was that important. I mean, not to diminish him, but I didn't realize he was newsworthy to his people. To his king."

"To be honest, I didn't either." Jev lowered the page, wondering why the ambassador hadn't sent the letter. Maybe it hadn't been necessary. After all, the elven princess, Yesleva, had seen Lornysh at Dharrow Castle when she'd come for that artifact. The elves had known for a while that Lornysh was here. Was it possible King Yvelon had sent these wardens to avenge those who Lornysh had assassinated over the years?

Jev shivered, feeling the chill of the dim tower. He'd never approved when King Abdor had asked Lornysh to assassinate elves on the army's behalf, always feeling the tactic dishonorable, even if the elves themselves preferred guerrilla warfare to meeting in the open on a battlefield. But Lornysh had accepted the assignments. If he was now a target of the Taziir, he could only blame himself.

Still, it distressed Jev. He couldn't help but want to protect his friend.

"What's that?" Zenia whispered, her gaze toward the floor between the desk and the door.

A grayish blue mist was seeping into the room from under the closed door.

"I don't know. Is it magic?" Jev stepped around the desk to stand beside her and drew his pistol, though it would do nothing against mist.

Zenia hesitated before responding. Maybe her question had been directed at her dragon tear instead of him.

"Yes," she finally replied.

"Dangerous?" Jev asked.

"Yes."

"Let's get out of here, then." He stepped toward the door, but hesitated. His pistol would be useless against magic. On a whim, he ran to the bookcase and grabbed the jade elephant. He had no idea what it did, but if nothing else, he could throw it at something.

He expected Zenia to make a joke, but her face was pale, her eyes concerned. Her dragon tear glowed on her chest.

"There's something in the foyer," she whispered.

Jev stopped two paces from the door. "Not *someone*?"

"Two elves, I think, and…" Her eyes grew distant as she gazed at the door. Or through it. "I'm not sure what you would call it. A magical presence."

"That would be better avoided?"

"Likely."

Jev ran to one of the shuttered windows, having no compunctions against fleeing trouble, especially since this was Lornysh's trouble. Unless the elves had seen Jev and Zenia enter the tower and objected to them sniffing around.

The shutters would not open. He didn't see a latch or lock, but they refused to budge. It was as if several heavy metal bars stretched across them on the outside even though Jev didn't remember seeing anything like that when he'd visited the tower before.

"More magic?" he asked, trying the second window. Again, the shutters did not budge.

"Yes," Zenia said. "I—"

The only door flew open so hard it banged against the wall. Jev ran and jumped, skidding on a rug as he hurried to put himself between Zenia and whatever force had done that.

He glimpsed shadows moving in the foyer above more of that mist, but he couldn't see anything solid. Nothing sprang through the doorway at them.

Jev pointed his pistol and advanced slowly. He still gripped the jade elephant in his other hand, and he almost cast it aside. But something moved out there, another dark shadow, and his knuckles tightened around it.

An icy draft whispered across his cheek, almost a caress. His heartbeat thundered in his ears. He didn't need a dragon tear to tell him magic was all over the place. Malevolent magic.

Gritting his teeth, he continued walking forward. Maybe if he kept whatever it was busy, Zenia and her dragon tear could do something.

Through the shadows in the foyer, the door that led outside was visible. It was shut. And locked?

As Jev stepped across the threshold and into the foyer, a shadowy tendril wrapped around his wrist.

He cursed and tried to yank his arm back. The tendril squeezed, and a blast of pain shot through his body. Something incorporeal tore his pistol out of his grip.

"Shadow golem," he blurted for Zenia's sake. He'd seen something like this once during the war, seen his men hurled against trees by the dark magic entity.

More tendrils snaked around him, as intangible as shadows themselves. He kicked and punched, trying to knock them away, but he encountered only air. And yet, the magic wrapped around him like some macabre lover. Then it picked him up and hurled him across the foyer.

Jev tore his dagger out as he flew through the air, and he twisted, trying to land on his feet. His shoulder slammed into the far wall. He snarled as more pain blasted him, but he managed to get his boots under him and landed in a crouch.

He was only four paces from the door leading outside. He lunged toward it, hoping to open it so Zenia could sprint through the foyer and escape.

But someone sprang into his path. A tangible person this time, not the shadow golem. A person with a green glowing longsword that highlighted the fine features of his elven face.

Strange slender snakes writhed up and down the blade of that glowing sword. One flicked toward Jev. It didn't have eyes or a mouth, and he realized it was a vine rather than a snake.

Not that it mattered. When the elf swung his sword toward Jev's face, the edge appeared as deadly as expected.

Jev whipped his dagger up to parry. His smaller blade was inadequate, and he knew it, but he didn't expect the magical sword to cleave right through it. But it did.

Startled as his broken dagger clattered on the floor, Jev almost tripped over his own feet in his haste to get back. The elf lunged after him, his pale green eyes deadly cold. He raised his sword again, and Jev had no weapons left with which to defend himself.

Unless the figurine counted. He hurled it at the elf's feet, hoping it would explode with fiery magic.

It bounced up and hit the elf in the shin. His eyebrows twitched, and he kicked it away without looking.

An unearthly keening echoed through the foyer, the noise reverberating off the stone walls. That made the elf hesitate. He turned his head, his gaze latching onto Zenia.

She had stepped out of the office, her hands raised, and a blue glow emanated from her fingers. It pulsed, pushing outward, and the light grew stronger in the room, the shadows fading slightly. Was the dragon tear battling the golem? Could it win?

Jev had no idea, but he took advantage of his foe's distraction. He kicked, trying to catch the elf in the hand to knock his sword away. He connected and had the satisfaction of hearing a startled gasp as the elf's sword clanked against the stone wall. Unfortunately, he didn't let go of it.

Before his foe could bring it back to bear, Jev lunged in. He knew he couldn't best a trained elf in a sword fight, especially when he didn't have a sword, but the elf's superior speed and agility might be less effective in a wrestling match.

His adversary almost evaded him, but Jev caught him around the middle and bore him to the hard stone floor. The elf bucked like a spooked horse trying to fling its rider.

Jev's ribs ached from his old injuries, and his shoulder stung from the new one, but he didn't let go. He managed to grasp the elf's wrist and keep the sword from reaching him as he used his weight to his advantage, getting on top of his opponent and pinning him.

Another wailing keen echoed through the foyer. Zenia gasped—in pain?—but turned it into a determined snarl.

Maybe if Jev could keep the elf busy a little longer…

Green light flashed in Jev's eyes, and some magical energy flung him away. He went flying and smashed against the wall again, the blow knocking the air from his lungs and stunning him. For a moment, he couldn't move; he could only crumple to his back.

Something snaked around his leg. Another untouchable shadow from the golem?

Jev cursed, fear giving his body what it needed to move again. He tried to yank his leg away before the tendril could fully grip him, but it was too late. The thing pulled him across the floor, his shirt rucking up and rough stone scouring his back.

The elf stood over him, his glowing sword in hand, and a sneer on his aristocratic face. The tendril wrapped around Jev's leg was green and came from the sword, not the golem. The magical extension was one of several sprouting from the blade. A second one wrapped around Jev's arm and hefted him into the air.

"I saw you in Taziira," his enemy snarled. "You invaded my homeland and killed my people. For that, you will die."

Weaponless and dangling off the floor, Jev didn't know how he could object—or keep the threat from coming to pass.

"The war is over," he blurted. "Your presence here is an act of—"

Blue light flared, filling the tower with brightness that burned Jev's eyes like the sun. The tendrils released him, and he tumbled to the floor again.

He rolled away and scrambled to his feet, wishing he had a weapon. Founders' teeth, where had his pistol gone? He couldn't shoot an incorporeal golem, but he could shoot a damn elf.

He patted around, hoping to find it, but all he brushed against was the stupid elephant figurine.

"She's more powerful than it is," someone yelled in Elvish.

It wasn't the elf Jev had been facing. He cursed again, realizing the second one Zenia had mentioned was in there too. Fighting her?

A blur of white came from across the foyer. The second elf. He also wielded a glowing sword, this one with the appearance of a frosty icicle, and he hefted it as he raced toward Zenia.

She still stood with her arms raised, blue light flowing from her fingers and creating tendrils that wrapped around the shadowy entity in the center of the foyer. She'd caged it, but the elf...

He roared and lunged toward her with his glowing white sword. Jev hurled the figurine at him.

It struck the elf in the temple, almost startling him into dropping his blade.

Before Jev could feel any satisfaction, the elf with the green tendril sword jumped at him from the side. Fear for Zenia gave Jev strength and speed. He ducked the blade slashing toward his head, tendrils writhing, and lunged in, leading with his elbow. He slammed it into the elf's solar plexus.

A rush of air knocked Jev's hair into his eyes, and a thunderous crack sounded. He had no idea what was going on, but his opponent seemed even more startled than he was, so Jev hammered his chest again and again. Finally, the elf kicked him, knocking him back, and sprinted out the door.

Jev looked toward Zenia, but a cloud of dust filled the room. Light shone in from one of the walls. It was daylight, not some magical glow. Someone had knocked a huge hole in the side of the tower.

More snaps and cracks sounded, this time from above. Jev envisioned the entire structure collapsing.

"Zenia!" he shouted, rushing through the foyer, batting at the dusty air and hoping he wouldn't rush right into the shadow golem's grip.

But it seemed to be gone. He made it across the foyer without encountering opposition and finally spotted Zenia, slumped against the wall by the office door. It looked like her legs would buckle at any second and she would end up on the floor.

He snatched her up in his arms, lifting her so he could carry her outside. Her dragon tear dangled from its chain, no longer glowing. Zenia's eyes were glassy, her limbs limp.

"Zenia, are you with me?" Jev ran toward the hole in the wall, watching for the second elf. Where had he gone?

Pieces of mortar and stone clunked to the floor. Jev almost tripped over a fallen bookcase as he drew close to the tower's new exit. He ran around it and out into the afternoon light.

"I'm all right," Zenia whispered. She gripped his shoulders, then let go. "I can walk. I just—that took a lot out of me, even though my dragon tear did all the work."

"I will happily carry you all the way back to the castle if you wish." His ribs groaned and his shoulder throbbed, but he meant what he said.

"I think it'll be faster if we both walk. Or better yet, find our horses."

Reluctantly, Jev set her on her feet, but he kept a hand on the small of her back in case she needed support.

Rubble clacked to the floor of the tower behind them. Jev thought he saw a figure dart through the charred trees near the back wall of the courtyard.

"We better go," he said over the ominous snaps. He hoped the tower didn't collapse. It was bad enough he was the reason the gardens had burned. "Especially if that golem—I can't believe you just called it a *presence*—is still around. Do you know if it is?"

"I'm not sure." Zenia jogged wobbly toward the front gate, her dress flapping around her legs.

"I was hoping you would say you nobly vanquished it and it would never set foot in our world again." Jev stuck close, glancing all about as they hurried away. He no longer sensed the magical creature, but he knew those two elves were still around, and he feared they were not that injured.

Would they follow him and Zenia through the city? Or stay here, near their people's compound?

The wrought-iron gate was open, as they had left it. Jev and Zenia darted through, and he swung it shut behind them with a booming clang and peered warily between the bars.

But there was nothing chasing them. The mist had been replaced by a more natural stone dust wafting out of the hole in the tower. The structure itself had not collapsed—yet. Darkness lay beyond the gaping hole in the side, but Jev no longer saw shadows stirring in it.

"The dragon tear defeated it." Zenia stopped and leaned her hand against the courtyard wall. "I'm not sure if it's incapable of returning, but I no longer sense it nearby."

"Good," Jev said, then grimaced. He was still in front of the gate, and he spotted a cloaked figure climbing over the rear courtyard wall with a sword on his back. A faint white glow seeped out of the scabbard.

If Jev had possessed a weapon, he might have given chase, but he didn't even have an elephant to throw. He decided he would leave his pistol and get another one from the castle armory. He'd spent enough time in that tower today.

As the sounds of stones tumbling down faded, Jev grew aware of voices. He turned, expecting to find dozens of tavern goers outside, peering at the elven compound.

There *were* a lot of people outside, but they were up on the roof rather than in the street. And they were looking down the hill toward the harbor instead of at the tower.

"Something else going on?" Jev wondered what else could have commanded their attention, especially with what had seemed to him monstrous noise and destruction going on inside the tower.

"Maybe we should take advantage of our luck and go back to the castle." Zenia touched her temple, and her finger came away bloody.

"Or to a hospital." Jev frowned, tempted to reach up to stroke her face. Now that he had time to examine her in the daylight, he spotted other cuts. He feared they would both be covered with bruises before long. "Are you badly hurt?"

"No." Zenia lowered her hand. "I'll be fine. Are *you* all right? You were the one..."

"Heroically distracting the golem so you could use your magic on it?"

"Is that what you were doing when it flung you into the wall?"

"Wasn't it obvious?"

"Hm."

An appreciative whistle came from the rooftop, followed by numerous low murmurs.

"I'm going up to take a quick look," Jev said after glancing toward the tower again to make sure the elves had truly departed. Not wanting to leave Zenia behind, just in case, he added, "Will you humor me and come along?"

"You just want the barkeeper to see you with a woman so he doesn't whistle at you," Zenia grumbled.

"Precisely."

Jev led the way into the dimly lit tavern and headed for the back stairs that he knew from past experience led to the roof. The barkeeper wasn't around. Maybe he'd gone upstairs with everyone else.

Jev wondered if another great dwarven steamship had arrived. The one that had sunk in the harbor had been massive and absolutely magnificent. He wished he'd had the opportunity to truly explore it— and that it was still upright and steaming across the seas. What a loss that must have been to the dwarven people.

A crowd filled the rooftop deck, with people standing on chairs and tables to see better. Jev still couldn't tell what anyone was looking at. Something in the harbor? Or down the slope on the way to the waterfront?

Behind him, Zenia made an irritated sound when someone bumped her with an elbow. Jev used his own elbows, trying to protect her and make some room. Then, inexplicably, the crowd parted around them. A bubble of space appeared, and they were able to walk to the edge of the rooftop where they had a view of the harbor.

Jev noticed Zenia's dragon tear glowing and an expression on her face somewhere between bemusement and concern. Had the gem chosen to help of its own accord?

Zenia's expression changed to one of awe as she gazed toward the harbor. "That's a beautiful ship."

Jev pulled his gaze from her dragon tear, then halted abruptly. "That's a *Taziir* ship."

He supposed that was a statement of the obvious. The craft that was sailing into the harbor looked more like the limbs and foliage of a great deciduous tree than a ship. Branches and vines were twined together, forming the frame and somehow making a waterproof vessel. Leaves sprouted from the branches as if they were attached to a tree growing in the earth instead of a ship sailing across the sea.

All the greenery obscured the deck, such as it was, and Jev couldn't see any elves moving around on it, but a raised platform rose from the bow, reminiscent of the platforms in the treetops where the Taziir had their villages. He could see people out on it.

Wishing for a spyglass, Jev raised his hand to shield his eyes from the sun and squinted. There was a woman in a rich green dress almost the same shade as the foliage. She had blonde hair, and he immediately thought of the elven princess who'd come for the artifact. Yesleva. He didn't think she had ever shared her name with them, but he knew it from the intelligence reports.

The elf woman was too far away for him to make out her face and be certain of her identity. It was unlikely this was the princess. Why would she travel in the open when she'd come in secret before?

Two male elves in the greens and browns of wardens stood behind her, and Jev shivered, having all too recently seen similar clothing. And were those swords sheathed at their sides? Swords like the magical one that had almost lopped off his head?

"I've never seen an elven ship before," Zenia said. "Except for pictures in books. They're far more impressive in person."

"Yes." Jev had seen their vessels before, though not often. For the most part, the war had been fought on the soil of Taziira, the elves allowing—or luring—the humans into their forests before striking.

"Do you think that's the new ambassador?"

"Uh." Jev hadn't been thinking that, but Targyon had sent a request for one, so it was possible. If it was...

He grimaced and looked toward the tower. With the people in the way, he couldn't see much of the destruction, but he had no trouble remembering that huge hole in the wall. And he remembered that Targyon had wanted, among other things, for him to spearhead a cleaning operation. Jev had definitely not done that.

"We better get back to the castle and report everything to Targyon," he said.

And hope we're not in trouble for knocking a hole in the wall of the elven tower, he added silently.

Zenia had to jog to keep up with Jev after they left their horses with the stablehands and headed into Alderoth Castle. The grounds were busy with other people riding into and out of the stable at top speed, and she suspected Targyon had already heard about the arrival of the elven ship.

As they ran in through their usual back entrance, the one that led to the Crown Agents' basement office and also to the kitchen, laundry, and working area of the castle, they heard shouts and the clattering of pots and pans. Servants rushed to the kitchen, trays tucked under their arms as they adjusted their uniforms.

"Looks like an impromptu feast is being prepared," Zenia said, as Jev charged not toward their office but toward the stairs that led up to Targyon's office and suite.

"Elves arriving is a big deal," Jev said over his shoulder.

They passed more servants on the stairs, butlers heading to duty stations. Here and there, maids stuck freshly cut flowers in vases and removed any that were old and withered.

"Did the dwarves get a feast and this much attention?" Zenia wondered.

"I'm not sure. I was busy being blown across the harbor at the time."

She patted him on the back when they reached the landing, but she only had time for a few pats before he was off again, heading toward Targyon's office.

"His Majesty is in his suite," the secretary said as soon as they entered the outer office. "But he said he's not to be disturbed. He's bathing and dressing for our guest."

"Does he know who our guest *is*?" Jev asked.

Zenia hadn't been able to guess from their distant perch on top of the tavern, but she assumed the ship carried a contingent of important people. Or was it just *one* important person?

She thought of the warning she'd received to *avoid the elf*. Not elves. Elf. Which one? She couldn't help but wonder again if it was Lornysh.

Maybe he wasn't a danger to her or Jev specifically, but what if this was another group of his kind who wanted him dead? Or what if this group had sent the other group? Simply standing next to Lornysh might be enough to get her or Jev killed by friendly—or indifferent—crossfire.

"An elven emissary," the secretary said.

"How unspecific," Zenia murmured.

"I bet it's our new ambassador." Jev grimaced. "I need to talk to Tar—the king—and warn him about the embassy's state of disrepair. It will only take a minute."

The secretary opened his mouth in protest, but Jev, hurrying back into the hallway, did not see it. He strode toward the door to Targyon's suite—and toward the two bodyguards blocking it.

"You're going to interrupt him in the bath?" Zenia whispered, trailing after him. "Surely, it can wait twenty minutes."

"I want to report what we found and let him know, in case he intends to send the elves to their new embassy. You know what the tower looks like right now." He faced the guards as he spoke, the words as much for them as for her.

Zenia didn't usually ask her dragon tear to allow her to see his thoughts, but she sensed his urgency was only partially about the tower. He also wanted to report that letter they'd found about Lornysh. He believed things had gotten worse for his friend.

"Zyndar Dharrow," one of the guards said respectfully but also warily. He doubtless hoped Jev wasn't going to demand to be let in.

"I need to report to the king," Jev said. "He sent me on a mission, and I have the results. He'll want them before he goes to see the elves."

The guards looked at each other, neither moving from in front of the door.

"He said he wasn't to be disturbed, that he was in a hurry," the more talkative one said. "If you wish to wait—" he gestured to a table and a couple of chairs in an alcove a short ways down the hall, "—I'm certain you can speak to him when he comes out."

Jev frowned and looked at Zenia. Would he ask her to manipulate the guards into letting him in? She had used her dragon tear to do that once before and hadn't felt comfortable about it then or now. Since this dragon tear was so powerful, it was a little too tempting to use it to wave away problems. An image of Heber Dharrow popped into her mind, reminding her of one of the problems she wanted to wave away—or manipulate into getting out of the way.

"Fine," Jev said, stepping toward the chairs. "We'll wait—"

The door opened, and Targyon came out in socks and trousers with his shirt half-buttoned. He waved a silk cravat in one hand and a jacket in the other. They were of slightly different shades of green.

"Marea," he called down the hallway, not seeming to notice Zenia and Jev. "Marea, I need more color options. Do you know where the cravats are?" He noticed Jev, and his cheeks colored for some reason. "There has to be more contrast. Or no contrast. These are too similar. But not similar enough." He stared down at the items, then rushed inside.

One of the guards scratched his head. He'd stepped aside when Targyon burst out, leaving the doorway somewhat accessible.

Jev headed for it. The guard lifted his hand.

"He invited me in," Jev said.

"What? He called for the maid."

"In what was a clear cry for fashion help." Jev pushed the hand away. "This is a job for a zyndar."

The guard wasn't determined enough, and Jev pushed past. Zenia slipped through after him.

"Aren't you colorblind?" she whispered.

"Yes, so?"

"How are you going to help him pick a cravat?"

"I'm not. I'm going to tell him to relax and put on something regal."

Targyon, who had disappeared into his bedroom, rushed back out again, heading toward the parlor, as if he'd left something in there, or was simply looking all over in a mad dash.

Jev stepped forward to intercept him, gripping him by the shoulders. "Sire."

"Jev!" Targyon said. Zenia expected to hear exasperation in his voice or maybe even a threat, but Targyon gripped him back. "She's here. She came back!"

"Uh, who did?" Jev asked.

"Yesleva. The elven princess."

"The one who came for the…" Jev glanced at the door and lowered his voice. "The Eye of Truth?"

"Yes. I don't know what she wants yet, but what if *she's* the new diplomat? I suppose that's unlikely given her societal rank and importance to her people, but what if she *is*? Did you know she's an artist? I asked to see her work someday. Maybe she brought some pieces along. She's a scholar, too, you know. She can read all four of the First Races' ancient languages."

"You can, too, can't you?" Jev released Targyon, looking like he might also want to scratch his head.

Zenia found herself less puzzled.

"Yes, but she's a *woman*," Targyon said.

A plump gray-haired maid rushed in with no fewer than eight cravats, all in shades of green.

"Marea," Targyon blurted, abandoning Jev. "That's perfect. Will you help me choose one?"

"Of course, Sire."

"I'm confused," Jev murmured to Zenia.

"His Majesty has a crush on the elven princess," she responded equally quietly.

"Oh." Jev brought his fingers to his mouth. "Oh dear."

Zenia only nodded. It seemed to be the month of marriages—or desires for marriages—that society, or parents, would never allow to happen.

"Is the tower all right, Jev?" Targyon selected an attractive pale-green cravat. "Did you get any information you needed out? I ordered a cleaning team to be sent down right away."

"Ah." Jev lowered his hand. "I'm afraid you'll need to send a construction crew."

"What happened?"

"It was already in some disarray..." Jev looked to Zenia, as if for confirmation.

"Broken vases on the floor and a dagger in a pillow qualify as disarray, yes," she said.

"And then there were two elven wardens there, who conjured up a shadow golem to try to kill us. While taking swings at us with glowing magical swords." Jev rubbed his shoulder. "We did find out that the ambassador wrote a letter to tell his king that Lornysh was here in the city. He didn't send it, but... it does seem that his people are aiming for Lornysh. And these elven wardens could be trouble for more than just him. They threatened us simply because we showed up at the tower."

Targyon, busy buttoning his shirt, didn't look up. "I can ask her if she knows anything about it. She's on her way up. I wish I'd had more notice. Do you think she'll like a feast of human food? I'm having the chef cook gort three ways. Elves like greens, right? And berries. We're doing a berry compote for dessert. Am I forgetting anything?"

Targyon looked earnestly at Jev, frowned, then turned his earnest expression on Zenia. Craving a woman's opinion? Marea had, perhaps wisely, fled after delivering the clothing accessories.

Zenia stood taller and tried to appear worldly about such matters. "I know little of elven culinary preferences, I'm afraid, but perhaps a gift would impress her with your thoughtfulness?"

"A gift." Targyon whirled and peered around his suite. "Of course. I should have thought of that. What would she like? I have… a castle. Do you think there's anything good enough in it for an elven princess?"

"Maybe some flowers from the garden?" Zenia had been touched when Jev picked flowers for her.

"Elves consider it gauche to cut plants if it's not for medicine or sustenance," Targyon said.

"Didn't you write some poems when we were in the field?" Jev asked.

Targyon frowned. "The stuff I wrote during the war was moribund and overly flowery and verbose."

"Perfect."

Zenia couldn't tell if he was teasing Targyon. She hoped not.

"Have a scribe copy one for her," Jev said, sounding sincere in his suggestion. "In pretty letters and on nice paper."

"A scribe? I'll do it myself. You two—" Targyon waved at Zenia and Jev, "—had a big battle, you said? Take the rest of the day off. I'll let you know if she needs anything from my agents. Thanks for the help!" Targyon sprinted out of the room.

Zenia wondered if she should have pointed out that he was only wearing socks on his feet.

Jev stared at the empty doorway. "I didn't mean for him to leave. Or dismiss us. You'd think he would want one of his spy captains with him at a dinner with a foreign dignitary."

"Perhaps not if he plans to read poetry to a lady."

A lady who was probably a couple of hundred years older than Targyon. Zenia feared nothing would come of their king's infatuation.

"I had intended to make a more thorough report," Jev said.

"Maybe it would be within the realm of our duties to arrange a construction crew so Targyon doesn't have to worry about it?" Zenia suggested.

"And send him the bill afterward?"

"There may be skilled laborers here who are already on the payroll and can do the job." Zenia had seen workmen on scaffolding around the castle a couple of times since she'd started her job.

"I'll check into it," Jev said. "You should obey our monarch and take the rest of the day off."

"What would I do? It's not even dark yet."

"Relax. Read a book. A book of poems, perhaps. Though I can't recommend elven poetry. Or you could come with me to look for Lornysh if you're bored. We could get dinner somewhere in town on the way. But..." Jev shifted his focus from the doorway to her. "I suppose someone might misconstrue that as a date if they saw us. I hate that I have to care about what people think. I *will* talk to my father tomorrow. And put an end to his meddling."

Zenia didn't think that would be as easy as Jev thought, but she tried to give him an encouraging smile. She would have loved to go with him to find his friend—and enjoy a dinner. It was the time of year when people ate on the patios outdoors, enjoying the sea breeze and the view of the harbor. And holding hands as they walked along the boardwalk afterward, the sun burnishing the waves as it set.

But not Zenia and Jev. Not tonight.

"Go find Lornysh," she said. "I'll figure out how to send a construction crew to the tower."

Jev hesitated. "I don't want you stuck with all the grunt work while I wander around the city."

"If it makes you feel better, you can grunt while you wander."

"Would you find that sexy?"

"Grunting?"

"Yes, in a manly and somewhat savage manner. It would be very un-zyndar-like."

"Then it would have to be sexy, yes. I hope you'll show me after you find Lornysh." She waved for him to go.

"Zenia, I'll—"

"Go." She rested a hand on his chest. "Your friend needs you."

He hesitated a little longer, then clasped her hand and kissed her on the cheek. "Thank you."

As he jogged out of the suite, Zenia tried not to think about the tingle she'd felt at the brush of his lips and how nice it would be if they *could* have that dinner out together. With or without grunting.

CHAPTER 6

C LANGS EMANATED FROM ARKURA GRINDMOR'S
jewelry shop, along with a grinding noise, the sounds promising
the master crafter had not gone home for the night. Jev hoped
Cutter hadn't either.

Jev hadn't seen Lornysh since the night before, and after seeing the
aftermath of the fight in the tower, he was worried. He didn't know where
to look to check up on him. Despite all his mentions of symphonies,
museums, and theaters, Lornysh never spoke of *going* to them, only
of having been. If he was smart, he was lying low, or he'd left the city
altogether. The idea made Jev sad. He at least wanted a chance to say
goodbye to his friend.

Hoping Cutter would know where Lornysh had gone, Jev headed
into the shop.

Heat blasted his face when he opened the front door, reminding him
of that smithy and being attacked by that elf. A different elf from the two
who'd ambushed Jev and Zenia in the tower. How many wardens were
in the city? Lornysh had said at least four.

"Jev?" The grinding stopped, and Cutter looked up from a machine
in the corner of the front room. A loupe and several blue gems lay in
front of him.

"Are you allowed to talk?"

Jev peered around for Master Grindmor. Every time he'd spoken
with the bearded dwarf female, she had been brusque. He had no trouble
envisioning her cracking a whip to keep her new apprentice at work.

"I'm a grown dwarf, Jev. I can talk whenever I want."

"Why don't I hear the sounds of sapphires being cut?" a bellow came through the door behind the display counter.

"And as a grown dwarf, I like to work while I talk." Cutter turned the machine back on and held a gem attached to the end of a stick to the grinding tool.

Jev grimaced, approaching warily as blue dust flew. "Have you seen Lornysh lately? Since yesterday?"

"No, but I heard there are elf wardens all over the city like ants on a honeyed rock tart."

"Have you ever noticed that all of your baked goods have the word rock in them?"

"Because they're hefty. Like all good pastries are." Cutter cut off the machine again, his face grave as he met Jev's eyes. "They're after Lornysh, aren't they?"

"Yes. And they're happy to kill any war veterans they happen to chance across on the way." Jev touched his bruised shoulder. "One would have killed me today if Zenia and her dragon tear hadn't been nearby to help."

Cutter frowned. "Wanton killing isn't very elf-like. Didn't your people sign a treaty with the Taziir before leaving?"

"Of a sort. It was more of a promise that we were done infiltrating their continent and wouldn't bother them again unless provoked."

"Coming to your city and killing people isn't provoking?"

"I don't think they've killed anyone yet. Just issued threats. Painfully." Jev thought that warden *would* have killed him, if he'd been able. "Zenia and I were in the elven embassy, so we were technically trespassing."

"Hm."

"Lornysh came to see me last night and said he might have to leave."

Cutter's bushy eyebrows rose. "You didn't offer to help him with these elves?"

"I did. He said he doesn't want us to risk our lives on his behalf."

"What? There aren't many elves in the world that I like. If you can't take such risks on behalf of one who you do, what's the point in befriending someone with pointy ears?"

"That's what I told him. More or less."

"Friends fight to protect friends. That's how it works, Jev."

"I agree. I have an errand I need to run tonight—" an errand that, if successful, might make his chat with his father easier, "—but after that, I'm going to check some of the cultural events going on in the city to see if I can find Lornysh."

"Cultural events?" Cutter curled a lip.

"Do friends not go to cultural events to protect friends?"

"That's asking a lot."

"I can check by myself. I just came by to see… I was hoping he'd come to say goodbye to you. If he means to leave."

Master Grindmor stomped out of the back, slapping her palms together and sending puffs of fine powder into the air.

"You." She pointed a finger at Jev. "Should've known it was some chatty zyndar distracting my apprentice. He's far too old to start training, so it's mostly charity that I'm teaching him anything at all. He doesn't need interruptions."

"I was telling him about the hostile elven wardens in the city," Jev said, not commenting on her charity—or the fact that silver dust coated her beard. "Cutter and I both fought in the war against their kind, so we'll need to be careful."

"More elves? They come on that sissy tree that floated into the harbor, masquerading as a ship?"

"No, they came on their own earlier in the week." Jev wondered how long the wardens had been here looking for Lornysh and what kind of ship they'd arrived on. "I could use your apprentice's help to make sure our friend is all right."

"You want to be the one responsible for delaying his training?"

"It *is* three hours past the end of the work day," Jev pointed out.

"The *human* work day. It's shocking your kind get anything done, what with all the sleeping and playing you do. Cutter, how much does this friend mean to you?"

"A great deal, Master."

"Fine, go help him. But I expect payment in the morning." She rubbed her dusty fingers together and stalked toward the back room again. "And take that hammer along. You need more than a pointy hook against wardens, not that I'm suggesting you cross elves with that kind of training, mind you."

"I will. Thank you, Master." Cutter lifted his hook in a cheerful wave.

"You have to pay her if you take time off?"

"In pastries, yes. Now that a dwarven baker has set up in the quarry square, it's easy to bring her quality ones." Cutter headed for his faded tool pouch. He'd carried it all through the war, so Jev recognized it easily.

"Quality ones with rock in the name?" he asked as Cutter opened the pouch.

"A pastry isn't worth eating if you can't throw it and knock someone unconscious, Jev."

"Maybe we should get a dozen to use on the elves."

"You couldn't carry a dozen, but I can pick you up some in the morning."

"Thoughtful. Thank you."

Cutter withdrew a smithy hammer that was blunt on both ends and had the heft of the aforementioned pastries. Jev had seen it dozens of times before, and he wondered why Grindmor thought Cutter needed it against elves. As far as Jev knew, it was just a tool. Cutter had used it to repair all manner of armor and weapons the soldiers had brought to him during the war.

"Vastly improved." Cutter smiled and brought it over, holding it reverently in his hands. "See?"

Jev was about to say he didn't see anything, but he noticed the hammer appeared newer than he remembered, completely free of scratches and dents. And was that a faint silvery-blue sheen to it?

"She imbued it with magic," Cutter added.

"Oh? What does it do?"

"It's impossible to break now, and it's attuned with the earth. Like me."

"Does that mean it doesn't bathe often and smells like rocks?"

"It means it'll thwack an elf in the nose with extra oomph. Isn't it wonderful? She did it as a reward for my adequacy."

"Adequacy? Is that the flattering word she used?"

"It is." Cutter beamed and held the hammer to his chest as if he planned to snuggle with it in bed. Maybe he already had.

"A minute ago, she said you were old and barely worth training."

"She's harsh because she wants me to work hard and live up to my potential. That's how I knew I was doing good. When she said I was adequate."

"You're an odd dwarf, Cutter."

"No, I'm an adequate one." Cutter stuffed the hammer through his belt. "I'm going to make a special holster for it later. I can still use it as a tool, but I intend to carry it with me when I go into battle now."

"For thwacking elven noses?"

"Precisely. Once I learn how, I'll imbue one of your weapons with magic, so it's better at thwacking too."

Jev touched the pistol he'd grabbed from his room earlier, refusing to go unarmed now that he'd been attacked multiple times. "Any chance you can do it tonight?"

"Probably not. I'm still learning about enchanting weapons. All of my original training was on carving gems and drawing out and enhancing the power of dragon tears. You could ask Master Grindmor, but even for her, it would take some time. And she has a long list of tasks. She's in high demand, you know."

"And I haven't proven my adequacy to her."

"Don't feel bad. It's a difficult task." Cutter waved toward the door.

"Do you think that could block an attack from a warden's magical sword?" Jev asked as they headed out.

"I have no doubt it could. Shall we go hunt them down and verify that?"

"Let's find Lornysh first. Er, after I run my errand." Jev hoped Cutter wouldn't want to try his shiny new hammer on Zenia's father. Maybe he should have gone on his errand by himself before coming to get him. "I can handle it on my own if you want to meet me at the Lovariath Art Museum. There's a gallery opening tonight, and they're serving elven wine, so I thought Lornysh might be tempted. I won't be long. My stop is nearby."

"Jev." Cutter pointed his hammer at his chest. "Do I *look* like the kind of person who wants to arrive early to drink elf wine and look at paintings?"

"The wine is free."

Cutter wrinkled his nose. "But elvish. And not ale. Where are you going that you don't want to take me?"

"You're welcome to come. I'm going to see Zenia's father."

"Why? Is he sick?"

"He might be after I punch him in the face."

"You're going to do battle and wanted to foist me off at a museum? What's wrong with your noggin, boy?"

"You're right. I don't know what I was thinking."

"Clearly."

They walked out of the industrial area and toward a high-end neighborhood where many zyndar families kept townhouses. Along the way, Jev peered down all the alleys and into all the alcoves. Even though he couldn't imagine why the elves would single him out again, he couldn't help but feel uneasy after the attacks. He was nervous for Lornysh, too, and half-expected to come across his dead body abandoned in one of those alleys.

But the route was free of bodies and elves. Jev stopped at a bronze gate in a brick wall that surrounded a house offset from the others on the street. Fountains gurgled in the courtyard inside, and windchimes tinkled gently in the breeze. Statues of huge stone golems stood to either side of the path just inside the entrance, and Jev grimaced. Even though they were simple carvings, he'd seen enough of golems lately.

"This is it," he told Cutter.

The gate was locked, so he pulled a chain next to it. A gong sounded in the courtyard.

While they waited, Jev wondered if he should be direct or sit down and try to make friends with Veran Morningfar before asking about Zenia. He doubted he could muster the enthusiasm to make friendly overtures to someone who'd treated her so poorly, leaving her mother to die when a few coins would have won her treatment in a hospital. Would Morningfar remember the incident? It must have been close to twenty years ago. Jev remembered Zenia saying she'd only been about twelve when she lost her mother and went to stay at the Water Order Temple.

Jev touched his pistol, and he felt a twinge of nostalgia for the old days. As recently as in his father's youth, dueling had been legal and considered an acceptable way for zyndar men to settle their differences. It still happened from time to time, but it wasn't legal anymore, and it was a crime to kill another zyndar, even in a mutually-agreed-upon duel. Jev might have a hard time marrying Zenia from prison.

A silver-haired butler came out, his face stern. He met Jev's eyes through the gate, then looked pointedly toward the night sky, as if to let Jev know it was an unseemly hour for unannounced callers.

It wasn't *that* late.

"I'm Zyndar Jev Dharrow," he said without preamble. "I would like to see Veran Morningfar."

"Zyndar Morningfar is having his supper."

"I'd love to join him. Thank you."

The butler's eyes narrowed. "Please return in the morning at a more reasonable hour."

"I work for the king during reasonable hours. And often unreasonable ones. Please tell Veran that I'm here to see him and only need a few minutes of his time."

Jev was surprised his name wasn't getting him invited straight in. Even if he personally was the subject of spurious gossip right now, the Dharrows were an old and honored family, and most zyndar were careful not to irk them. Not to irk his old man, anyway. Jev admitted he was barely known after his ten years out of the kingdom. He suspected his *father* would have been invited right in if he had shown up. The butler had the mien of someone who considered anyone under forty an unruly youth best ignored or taught some manners.

"I will inform him that you are here, but I know his ways. He does not entertain after dark." The butler turned without waiting for a response and strode back inside, shutting the large front door with a thump.

"I wasn't planning on entertaining him," Jev muttered.

"What *are* you planning to do?"

Jev thought about mentioning his nose-punching fantasy again. "Negotiate with him. Veran Morningfar is Zenia's father. Her mother was common, but he's zyndar. If he were to acknowledge her as one of his children, it might make it easier to convince my father that she's good enough for his son to marry." He curled a lip at the notion that Zenia wasn't already *good enough*—any man would be lucky to have a woman who stood at his back in battles and helped him solve problems for the king.

"Human marriage customs are unnecessarily complicated," Cutter said. "If a dwarf woman wants a man, she simply tells him, after he's given her a suitable number of gifts to prove that his interest is true and unwavering."

"How many spice racks is considered suitable?"

"No more than one spice rack. It would be an uncreative mind that couldn't come up with more than one kind of gift."

"So, the woman instigates things in your culture?"

"Not always, but it's her decision in the end if she wants a man or not."

"Do status or bloodlines come into play? You've got kings, so you must have royalty."

"Not the way you do. You don't get to be king because of your blood. You battle the other contenders, and then the Crafts Council chooses based on who fought well and who they think has the superior head for leadership."

"Crafts Council?" Jev imagined a bunch of old dwarf maidens making doilies and knitting scarves while pondering a future leader for their people.

"The best engineers, metalworkers, and craftsmen in the tunnels. Master Grindmor was on the Council until she left for reasons known only to her to travel."

"It does seem a practical way to choose a leader," Jev said. "Merit rather than blood."

"Yes, you humans are terribly backward and strange. By the way, I don't think he's coming back."

Not only had the butler not come back outside, but he'd cut off the porch lamp that had been burning when they first arrived.

Jev gritted his teeth, tempted to climb the wall and let himself in. It wasn't as if his reputation could get much worse right now.

"Shall I open the gate?" Cutter wiggled his bushy eyebrows and pulled out his hammer.

Even though the tool had some heft—and would have probably required two hands if Jev were to wield it—it didn't look like it could break down the gate. Not that he would agree to that. Climbing would be much simpler. Though a little destruction *would* make a statement…

"How?" Jev asked curiously.

"Stand back." Cutter waved his hook at him.

Jev obediently backed out of his swing path.

"The good thing about being a fine craftsman is that it's easy to fix what one breaks, but I'll let you decide if you want me to do that." Cutter hefted the hammer and swung it sideways into one of the bronze bars of the gate.

Jev expected the ringing blow to dent the bar minutely. Instead, it bent it all the way to the next bar, partially dislodging itself from the cross bars above and below. Cutter swung again at the adjacent one. The blow rang louder than the gong had earlier, and the front door opened.

Whistling, Cutter stuck his hammer back through his belt and stepped through the sizable gap he'd made. The second bar creaked and toppled to the cobblestone walkway.

The butler rushed out. "What are you *doing*?"

Jev stepped through after Cutter, glimpsing a second man coming to stand in the doorway. He rested a hand on Cutter's shoulder.

"Do forgive me, good butler. I've got a wild dwarf here straight out of the Preskabroton tunnels. I'm afraid I can't always control him. He's a whirlwind."

Cutter cocked a single eyebrow at Jev.

The butler stared at the broken gate, too flustered to speak.

"Zyndar Dharrow," the man in the doorway said.

Veran Morningfar stepped outside, wiry arms folding over his chest. He was as rat-faced as Jev remembered, and far balder than he had been ten years ago. Jev had a hard time imagining him as someone beautiful young women had once flocked to. Had his title alone won him that attention?

"Your behavior is unseemly," Morningfar said. "Your father would be ashamed."

"He's busy being ashamed of me for other reasons this summer. Zyndar Morningfar, I only need a few minutes of your time."

"Since I fear you would break down my door if I said no, you have them." Morningfar stood on the path, as if he would block the way if Jev tried to go inside.

Jev decided the option of befriending the man was definitely out. "I'll get straight to the point so you can go back to your dinner. Do you remember a woman named Zenia Cham?"

"No."

"She would have been a girl the last time you saw her. A twelve-year-old girl asking you for assistance with her dying mother, a woman you once slept with." Jev watched Morningfar's dark eyes, hoping to see some recognition in there. With the lamp out, it was hard to see much of anything.

"I slept with hundreds of women in my youth. I remember few of them."

Hundreds? Jev barely managed to keep his mouth from falling open.

"That's a lot of women," Cutter observed quietly. "He must be better at making gifts than it looks like he would be."

"Surely, you remember the daughter of this one. She came to you personally, and you refused to help her. Her mother died of a disease that could have been cured if she'd had enough coin to afford a hospital stay and the attention of a good doctor."

"Commoners die. It happens."

Jev gritted his teeth. He couldn't tell if Morningfar remembered the incident or not. Maybe such things had happened often to him.

Hundreds of women, dear founders. Maybe it was hyperbole, but Jev supposed it needn't be. His wife was either an oblivious woman, a patient woman, or a long-suffering woman.

"You may not remember Zenia, but she remembers you, and she can prove that she's your daughter." Jev had no idea if she truly could, especially if she had only her dead mother's word for it, but he suspected that her dragon tear would allow her to see into Morningfar's mind and extract the truth. The problem was that she wouldn't want to and might be irked with Jev if she found out he had come here.

"Doubtful, whoever she is. Look, Dharrow. My wife is waiting for me to play Thuzen Lin for her on the piano while she reads. If you're done abusing my gate and my ears, I'll take my leave."

"Your wife?" Cutter asked. "You're married and you sleep with hundreds of women?"

"More like dozens now. I'm not as insatiable as I was in my youth." Morningfar quirked a lip.

Jev *curled* a lip, not wanting to hear about the man's insatiability.

"Your wife doesn't mind that you hammer in all those nails around town?" Cutter asked. "Or does she not know about all these mistresses?"

Morningfar squinted at him. "If you think you can threaten to tell her as a way to manipulate me, she is not unaware. We have an open relationship. When your parents arrange your marriage, what else can one expect?" He cocked his eyebrows while looking in Jev's direction.

Jev doubted Morningfar's wife was as accepting of his unfaithfulness as he implied. Otherwise, he wouldn't have rushed to have a young Zenia thrown out by the guards before his wife heard her pleas.

"Fidelity," Jev suggested. "Living by the Zyndar Code of Honor."

"Please. You're naive if you think that code was ever anything but a children's tale. When you're as superior as we are, with as advantaged a position in society, there's no need to be bothered by such trifling rules."

"Or when you're in an advantaged position, there's more need than ever to be scrupulous and honorable." Jev took a deep breath, reminded that he'd come to ask for a favor, not irk the man. "It's never too late to change one's ways, to do the right thing. If you were to acknowledge Zenia—"

"Your father wouldn't be on your back about plowing her field? Please, Dharrow. You dare come here talking to me about honor when the whole city knows you're trying to wheedle your way out of your arranged marriage? I'm not the unscrupulous one here. You are."

Heat rushed to Jev's face. The man's words made him furious, largely because there was so much truth in them. He wouldn't be here on Zenia's behalf—no, on *his* behalf—if he didn't want to marry her.

"Let's be reasonable men, Morningfar," Jev made himself say, unclenching the fists he didn't remember clenching. He noticed the butler had left and wouldn't be surprised if he had gone to get younger reinforcements. Given Morningfar's personality, he probably kept bodyguards on the premises to protect him from people he irritated. "Neither of us is perfect, but this is a chance for you to do something good. Something right. Zenia doesn't want anything from you. As you said, *I'm* the one who's life would be easier if she could put a zyndari title in front of her name. She doesn't even know I'm here. If you were to acknowledge her—"

"I'd have simpering twits from all over the city at my doorstep, claiming to be my children. And it's all dragon balls. Those common wenches sleep with every zyndar man they can in the hope of being able to get one of them to acknowledge their brats and thrust their way into a better life for themselves. If that wasn't their intention, they would drink their tea so they wouldn't get pregnant. It's *their* fault if our seeds find fertile soil. Yet they come at us and try to act like *we* were responsible. You have to watch them, Dharrow. And you'll find that out for yourself soon enough, if you haven't already. Your common girl is probably already pregnant, and that's why she's trying to wheedle her way into your marriage bed."

"I am positive that's not the case," Jev said stiffly. This was going nowhere, but he hated to leave, to give up when there might be some way to sway the man.

"Why? You haven't slept with her? She's got your prick leashed when she hasn't even shoved it between her legs yet?" Morningfar threw back his head and chortled.

Jev's face grew hotter, and his fists re-clenched. To the side, Cutter drew his hammer and slapped it in his palm.

"Then she's probably slept with someone else and wants to marry you and make you think it's yours," Morningfar said, still laughing. "Count the days back when the kid shows up, Dharrow. Common women are all sluts angling for zyndar titles and money. You think she's any different?"

Jev couldn't control his fists any longer. As he'd fantasized about doing ever since Zenia shared her history, Jev slammed a fist into Morningfar's nose.

Morningfar staggered back, grasping his face. "What the rot is wrong with you? Damn, that *hurt*."

"Good." Jev wanted to punch him again and again, but he wasn't a worthy opponent in any sense of the word. "That you'd call your own daughter a slut is beyond despicable. If it was in my power to revoke your zyndar status, I would. You're not worthy of your title."

Morningfar jerked his hands down to his sides, revealing a trickle of blood flowing from one nostril. He clenched his fists, as if he would launch a punch. Jev lowered into a crouch, curling his fingers into fists again. He would love an excuse to hit the bastard a few more times.

But Morningfar cooled and merely sneered. "Very little is in your power, boy. As you'll find out when I talk to your father. It's a shame he lost his younger boy and that you're his only option for an heir. It must keep him awake nights, imagining you in charge of his estate."

Cutter let his hammer slip out of his hand, and it flew to the side and cracked Morningfar in the kneecap. Hard. The man yowled and bent, almost crumpling to the ground.

"Oops," Cutter said. "I'll get that."

As he plucked his hammer up from the walkway, the butler returned, striding out with two pistols in his hands. He glanced at his master. Morningfar was gripping his knee and panting in pain. The magic in that hammer must have given it more heft than usual.

"Leave," the butler said, one weapon pointed at Cutter and one at Jev.

"We were planning on it." Jev waved for Cutter to back toward the gate and did the same himself. A window was open on the second floor, a lantern burning inside, and he couldn't help but call loudly, "May the founders bless the woman who has to live with this troll."

The butler glared, but his fingers didn't tighten on the triggers. He had to know he would be a dead man if he shot a zyndar, and Jev couldn't imagine Morningfar truly inspired that much loyalty. But he kept his eyes on the pistols and the butler until he and Cutter had backed through the gate and a stone wall separated them from the two men.

"You negotiate a lot like a dwarf," Cutter observed.

"Meaning ineffectively?"

"Meaning hammers and punches were involved. Most dwarven negotiating ends in blows. If it doesn't, then the topic in question wasn't worth the spit it took to bring it up."

"So you approved?"

Jev couldn't be surprised things had gone the way they had, and he hadn't minded punching that blowhard, but it would have been better if Morningfar had been willing to acknowledge Zenia. It wasn't as if it would have cost the curmudgeon anything. There weren't many precedents for women inheriting zyndar land and wealth, and none where daughters born to common mothers were involved. Zenia never would have wanted anything from him. She might have refused his name even if he'd offered. This had been a waste of time.

"I approved of you punching that orc-butt-licker. And I was pleased to try out my hammer on more than metal. I barely tossed it, and I think it cracked his kneecap. I heard a satisfying crunch, at the least."

"I'm glad you're on my side, Cutter."

"Dwarves make excellent friends." Cutter punched him in the arm.

It jarred his injured ribs and almost knocked him over, but Jev made himself respond with an agreeable, "Yes."

Zenia knelt in the corner of her room where she kept her small prayer rug, candles, and a statue of the Blue Dragon, trying to meditate. She longed to clear her mind of conscious thought and let her battered body relax.

She hadn't been hurled around the elven tower the way Jev had, but she'd been a conduit for the magical battle her dragon tear had fought against that creature. A shadow golem, Jev had called it. Zenia had seen rock golems before and knew there were other kinds of them in the world, but she had never seen anything like the strange shadowy entity. She was glad her dragon tear had known how to battle it, because she hadn't had a clue. The golem hadn't seemed to exist fully in this world, but it hadn't had any trouble throwing Jev around.

Onjiwa, she said silently, the mantra she'd been taught long ago at the temple by a monk instructing her in the ways of meditation. *Onjiwa, onjiwa, onjiwa...*

Every time her mind wandered, she brought it back to the mantra, three syllables that had no meaning, that merely existed to break up conscious thought, to let her mind relax. She was even burning pine and myrtle incense tonight to fill the air with calming scents. It wasn't the kind of incense the Temple mages used to encourage visions. She didn't want visions. And she especially didn't want nightmares. That was why she was attempting to relax her mind, in the hope that she might sleep well tonight. It had been so long since she had.

A soft knock sounded at the door.

Zenia sighed, opening her eyes to the dragon figurine resting on her makeshift altar, and debated ignoring whoever was out there. But it might be Jev. Maybe he'd heard something about Lornysh and needed her assistance.

She pushed herself to her bare feet and padded across the sheepskin rug to the door. Rhi stood in the hallway, nibbling on her knuckle. She wore the same clothing as she had in the office earlier in the day and didn't appear to have gone home at any point.

Rhi sniffed the pungent evergreen scents wafting out of the room. "Oh, sorry. Are you meditating? I can wait and talk to you tomorrow."

"Is something wrong?" Zenia asked.

"No." Rhi lowered her hand. "I'm just not sure how to respond to something and if there could be ramifications if I make the wrong response."

Zenia waved for her to come in. "What is it?"

"You know that friend of Jev's? Zyndar Hydal?"

"I met him for the first time this morning."

"Me too. But I've already met him again. And he gave me a book."

"A book?" Zenia had been more interested in recruiting Sevy than in chatting with her older cousin, especially since the topic had been women vying for Jev's attention, so she hadn't noticed much about the man, except that he had a bookish mien.

"On the history of the Water Order and the Blue Dragon. He said it had been on his shelf for ages, and that nobody in his family had been interested in it, so he thought I would like it."

"Maybe you should let him know your preferences lean toward murder mysteries and those stories about the dragon who longs to be human and helps an inquisitor solve crimes all throughout the kingdom."

"I read those as a girl."

"The whole collection was on the shelf in your room in the temple," Zenia pointed out.

"Because I enjoyed them as a girl."

"Including two volumes signed by the author."

Rhi propped her fists on her hips. "When did you root through my bookshelf?"

"When you were first assigned to work with me. I snooped. I'd seen you around the temple, and you seemed brutish and surly, so I had concerns."

"Did the presence of books on my shelf alleviate them? It's a shame there's that rule about no locks on doors in the temple."

"It did," Zenia said, amused that Rhi was more distressed at the idea of someone looking at her bookshelf than of thinking her brutish and surly. "I figured I could work with someone with whimsical tastes."

"They're not whimsical. They're normal. Listen, I have a question about Hydal. I think he wants to ask me on a date. You know where I ran into him? At the little eating house down the street from the farmhouse where I stay. He acted like it was a coincidence, but why would he have been carrying that book around if he hadn't expected to see me? And what was a zyndar doing in that part of town? It's a *poor* neighborhood."

"It sounded like their family isn't wealthy, but I concede your point about the book. Perhaps he wanted to bring it to you at the castle but, since he's supposed to be a secret informant, figured he shouldn't come up here twice in the same day."

"So instead, he found out where I live and hung out in an alley until I went out for dinner? Zenia, that's disturbing."

"Maybe he was going to go to your room, but you left and went to the eating house first."

"I fail to see how that's a vast improvement. Zenia, I don't want to date him. He's skinny and wears those goofy spectacles. You know I like a man with muscles and an ass you can grab when you're riding him like a stallion."

"Er." Zenia rubbed her face, trying to vanquish the image Rhi's words conjured.

Rhi didn't look apologetic for her sexual outburst. "Don't *tell* me you don't know what I mean. Jev has a nice ass."

Zenia rubbed her face again, in part because she felt the need, and in part to hide the rush of heat reddening her cheeks. "If he asks, can't you just say no? I've seen you turn down men before."

With Jev—and his anatomy—now on her mind, Zenia thought of the way he'd introduced Hydal to Rhi that morning. It had been awkward. Had he been trying to set them up? Jev was the last person Zenia would have expected to play matchmaker.

"Not *zyndar* men." Rhi walked in and sat on the edge of the bed. "Zyndar don't ask me out. They always want big-breasted vapid young things that will bat their eyelashes and make pouty faces with their kiss-me-now lips. Those are the kinds of women they take as mistresses."

"That seems like an overly generalized generalization, but even if it's true, I'm not sure how that changes anything. If he asks you to dinner, and you're not interested, just say no."

"Can I? Or will there be ramifications if I do? Commoners aren't supposed to turn down requests from zyndar for anything, you know."

"I don't think that extends to sex," Zenia said, surprised Rhi would worry about obeying such societal norms, even if they existed. "Not in this century. In the past… Well, thankfully we don't live in such ridiculously unfree times." She thought of Jev's arranged marriage and debated if the times were truly as free as she would like. An improvement over the past, perhaps, but… no.

"But he's Jev's friend, and I got the impression— Was Jev trying to get me to go out with Hydal?" Rhi frowned. "You don't think he promised Hydal a date in exchange for becoming a spy, do you?"

"I don't think Jev would presume to do that. Maybe he promised an introduction, but that shouldn't obligate you to anything."

Rhi grunted dubiously. "I don't know. Zyndar all know each other and all do favors for each other. I wouldn't want to lose this job because Jev got irked with me for not sleeping with his friend."

"That won't happen."

"Since I left Archmage Sazshen with cross words, my options are limited."

"Your job is safe, Rhi. But why did you throw cross words at her before leaving? The temple archmages aren't the best people to irk."

"I was defending someone who wasn't there to defend herself," Rhi grumbled, looking toward the sheepskin instead of Zenia.

"Oh. Thank you." Zenia walked over and patted her on the shoulder. "Just say no to Hydal if he asks you on a date and you're not interested. But maybe you shouldn't reject him based on his spectacles and backside. Weren't you telling me that you've been finding sex with random partners boring? Perhaps you would enjoy spending time with a man with some substance, not just some muscled pretty boy from the gymnasium."

Rhi curled her lip. "He looked up where I live and found me. That's intrusive."

"He looked up where you live to give you a gift he thought you might like based on what he learned about you. Don't you think that promises he would be attentive in a relationship?"

"It promises he's desperate."

"Or smitten." Zenia thought of Targyon's interest in the elven princess. Smittenness was going around.

"How can he be smitten? He just met me."

"Maybe he liked the way you wielded your bo."

Rhi's expression switched to one of exasperation.

Zenia had nothing invested in seeing them together, so merely spread her hands. "If you don't want to give him a try, I'm sure he can handle your rejection. There won't be ramifications from Jev or anyone else in the office."

This time, Rhi rubbed *her* face. "All right. Good. Thank you." She stood up. "I'll let you get back to your meditation."

"For what good it's doing," Zenia muttered, the words more for herself than Rhi.

But Rhi heard them and looked back, frowning. "Is everything all right with *you*? You seem tired every morning in the office. I would have assumed your weariness was due to riding the Dharrow stallion all night if you were also smiling and happy with life, but you've mostly been grumpy."

"I'm fine." Zenia couldn't help but glance toward the bedside table. She'd removed the dragon tear when she had changed into her nightgown, and it lay on the wood, the silver-and-gold chain in a spiral around it.

Rhi followed her gaze to the gem. "You sure?"

"Yes."

"So, you'll come into the office perky and well-rested in the morning?"

"I'll try." A part of her wanted to confide in Rhi, but she'd already confided in Jev, and it hadn't done any good. But Rhi truly looked concerned, so she admitted, "I've been having some bad dreams and not sleeping well since I got the dragon tear. It's a fair tradeoff, since it's helped us out of some tight situations—we couldn't have gotten those magically slumbering dwarves off their ship before it blew up without it."

"I've never heard of a dragon tear giving someone nightmares."

"This one is special." She smiled, meaning it as a joke, even if it was true.

"Yeah, I've noticed that. It's a good thing the king gave it to you and not Zyndar Garlok or some other twit in the office. *You* can handle it."

Even if Zenia hadn't intended to confide in Rhi, she found herself cheered by this simple statement of faith. "Thank you. And *you* can handle Hydal." She smiled.

"I would be a lot more interested in handling him if he had an ass."

"It must be difficult being a slim man."

"Scrawny. I don't believe Jev's claim that he has hidden ferocity."

"At least he brought you a book," Zenia said. "That suggests he's literate."

Rhi squinted at her. "I don't think we have the same requirements when it comes to men."

"That's very possible."

Rhi opened the door. "I'll bid you goodnight. Try rubbing your dragon tear before you go to bed. Maybe a massage will make it less likely to inflict dreams on you."

"I'll keep the suggestion in mind." Zenia waved as her friend shut the door, then went to the nightstand, picked up the dragon tear, and sat cross-legged on the bed. She didn't rub it, but she did hold it and gaze at the dragon carved into the front of the gem.

A feeling emanated from it. Sorrow? Lament? An apology?

Could it know it was causing her nightmares? If so, she believed the sharing was inadvertent. Despite Cutter's warnings that having a gem linked to a dragon, if that was indeed what had happened here, was dangerous, this soul had only tried to be helpful thus far. Not always in the most socially correct manner, but one could hardly fault a dragon for not knowing what was appropriate among humans.

"Thank you for the help with the golems today," Zenia whispered, touching her thumb to one of the carving's wings.

Even though she had come to dread bedtime, she didn't want the entity linked to the gem to feel bad. If dragons could feel. She definitely sensed that this one did. She wondered if it lived and breathed somewhere in the world or if it had died long ago and some portion of its soul had been embedded in the gem. Maybe it had even died in that cave she kept dreaming of. Was it possible she'd been reliving the dragon's last hours?

The gem grew warm in her palm, and she sensed that mournful sorrow within it again. She wished she could help, but it didn't speak to her, didn't give her any clues as to how she might ease its pain.

A few days earlier, Zenia had looked up dragon tears in the castle library, hoping to find information on the specific one she had—if it had been linked to a king of old, as Targyon had said when he gave it to her, it might have been written about in a journal. But she'd only found general information with few drawings of individual gems.

Would the elven princess have any knowledge of it? Zenia hadn't been in her presence since her return, but she'd heard Targyon had given her and her retinue suites in the castle. Zenia wouldn't presume to knock on her door to ask, but Yesleva *had* known all about the Eye of Truth, and elves had once been the keepers of dragon tears.

"I'll find out a way to ask her," she murmured.

A twinge of uncertainty emanated from the gem.

Zenia frowned. Because it knew something about the princess that she didn't? Or did it not want an outsider prying into its background?

She noticed the envelope on her dresser, the one with the avoid-the-elf note inside. Could the princess be the elf it was warning her about? Was it odd that Yesleva had shown up at the same time as these elven wardens?

When the note had first come, Zenia had thought it applied to Lornysh, since he was the only elf in the city she knew, but now she wondered.

"Maybe we'll do a little research tomorrow," she murmured.

This time, the gem seemed contented. Or was it all in her mind?

CHAPTER 7

J EV BORROWED ONE OF TARGYON'S steam carriages and a driver for the trip out to Dharrow Castle, hoping his bruised body might find a cushioned seat more comfortable than a saddle. The highway was as smooth as Targyon's chef's cucumber dip, but the rutted road leading up the hill to Dharrow Castle reminded Jev of a dip he'd once had with olive pits mixed in, poised to ambush unsuspecting teeth. At least the jostling kept him from thinking overmuch about this meeting. Or worrying about Lornysh. The night before, Jev and Cutter had visited three different cultural venues, but they hadn't spotted Lornysh at any of them.

They *had* spotted someone in a dark green cloak with the hood pulled up.

An elf, Cutter had been certain, and Jev had been tempted to confront the person, but the figure had disappeared into the shadows before they reached him. Perhaps it was just as well. Jev didn't think his ribs could handle being thrown against any more stone walls this week.

Jev peered warily out the window as the carriage reached the pond with its moat meandering around the castle walls. He half hoped the drawbridge would be up and nobody would be on duty to lower it.

"Right," he mumbled.

Not only was the drawbridge down, but an elegant steam carriage painted with the Bludnor family's red and silver colors was parked outside the castle. Jev had come up well before the lunch hour, intending to speak with his father, but it seemed Fremia had been eager to meet him. He grimaced at the thought, already uncomfortable at the idea of this lunch date.

As soon as Jev's carriage drew to a stop in front of the drawbridge, one of his cousin's sons, Teeks, ran out waving a dented wooden sword that looked like a favorite chew toy of the castle hounds.

"Hello, Uncle Jev," Teeks blurted, waving so hard his arm was in danger of flying out of its socket. "Are you here to tell stories? About noble battles? And the trolls in the swamp? We heard about them and that you single-handedly slew them all!"

Actually, *Lornysh* had single-handedly slain them. A lot of them. Jev and Zenia had taken down far fewer.

But Jev dared not bring up elves in the castle since it was a sore subject, and Zenia… He certainly hoped he could one day share stories involving her, but with Fremia's carriage here, this wasn't the day.

Jev ruffled the kid's hair. "Not until after I talk to my father and… the woman who's here visiting. Maybe there'll be time after lunch for a few stories and a battle—" he waved at Teeks's sword, "—if you go easy on me. I'm still recovering from injuries."

"From the trolls?" Teeks's eyes shone brighter than the sun in the clear blue sky.

"From the dwarven ship that exploded after we fought the trolls. I had healers work on me after that, but I'm bruised and battered again from a run-in with a shadow golem yesterday." He wriggled his eyebrows, certain Teeks would be interested in hearing about that.

"A shadow golem! What did it look like?"

"Shadowy." Jev made himself head for the drawbridge as he spoke. "You couldn't reach out and touch it, but it had powerful magic and knocked me across the room."

Teeks bounced at his side as they walked through the gate. "How did you defeat it?"

Jev appreciated his nephew's certainty that he *had* defeated it, even if he hadn't done anything. "Actually, I was with a mage, and she defeated it with the help of her dragon tear."

"It wasn't that inquisitor, was it?" his father asked from the side.

Jev jumped. He had expected to have to hunt down his father out on the property where he would be repairing a fence or laying new shingles on a roof. Instead, the old man stood next to the gate guard and wore a frown like a monsoon cloud.

"She's one of His Majesty's Crown Agents now," Jev said, "and, yes, she was the one."

"You remember what I said, and stay away from her until after you've planted your seed in your new wife's womb."

Teeks stared at the old man, his mouth dangling open and his sword drooping.

Jev patted him on the shoulder. "Why don't you go see if Mildrey has any snacks in the kitchen."

"It's lunchtime in an hour," Jev's father said. "Don't encourage the boy to ruin his appetite."

"I see you're in as cheerful a mood as ever, Father," Jev said, relieved when Teeks ran off. The kid did not need to hear about seeds and wombs for a long time. "But if you've been grumpy because you've been worried about me, have no fear. None of the battles I've been in lately have managed to permanently damage me. Or my seed planter." Jev quirked an eyebrow.

Maybe he should have been polite and circumspect around the old man, as he had been in his youth, but he'd lost his stomach for it. And it wasn't as if his father had set the tone for a friendly chat.

"Save your clever lip for your friends," the old man said. "We need to talk before you meet with your new lady. Follow me."

"Fine by me." Jev took a deep breath and braced himself. He had to get in what he wanted to say before his father launched into a lecture, though Jev didn't know why the old man felt compelled to do so. *He* was the one being an ass. First, he had promised that Jev could take the summer to find a wife, but then he'd arranged a marriage scant days later.

The old man stopped in front of the courtyard fountain, though he eschewed the flat stone lip and the shady bench to stand in the sun. He crossed his arms over his chest and glared at Jev.

"It's bad enough I've got gossiping women telling me you're cavorting around the city with that ex-inquisitor," Father said without preamble, "but now you've begged the boy king to interfere with our affairs?"

The boy king? Was that how he and his peers referred to Targyon? Damn, Targyon *did* have an uphill battle when it came to earning the respect of the old guard of zyndar primes.

"We haven't been cavorting," Jev said coolly. "We've been working together on assignments. We *are* colleagues now, you know."

"Which means you walk around the city with your hand on her ass and tongue down her throat?"

Jev frowned. "Whoever the source of your gossip is hasn't been truthful with you. There's nothing like that going on." Alas. "I wouldn't besmirch Dharrow honor by acting so, and it upsets me that you would believe such slander instead of simply coming into the city and asking me if it's true."

The old man didn't uncross his arms, but the pompous certainty on his face faded somewhat.

"I'm also disappointed that you didn't come to the Air Order Temple to visit me when I was injured," Jev said. "I would have come to visit you. I almost *died*. Did you hear about the trolls?"

"Yes. I didn't realize—Wyleria made it sound like you would be fine. And I've been busy here. You're never here, and your brother is gone, and all my remaining relatives are women. That doesn't leave many people to run the estate."

Jev thought about pointing out that his cousins Wyleria and Neama ran half the family businesses, and could certainly be trusted to hire people to fix things around the estate. It wasn't as if the old man *had* to personally oversee everything. But Jev didn't want to divert from the subject he'd come to speak about. Even though he ached to ask when his father had spoken to Targyon and what had been said. Jev had been certain, after the meeting the day before, that Targyon wouldn't say anything to the old man.

"Why did you say yes to the Bludnor marriage proposal, Father?" Jev looked around the courtyard, aware of a couple of white-coated butlers taking trays of beverages up the stairs to his grandmother's balcony garden. What *had* been her balcony garden, before she'd been sent into exile. Was that where he was to dine with Fremia?

"It made sense—I fought with her grandfather, so I know she comes from a brave and capable warrior line—and the girl is beautiful," his father said. "I figured she'd keep you entertained in bed so you didn't feel the need to stray."

Jev grimaced. He and his father had never discussed women, and he didn't enjoy doing so now. "The last time we spoke, out by the road fence, you agreed I could choose my own woman, and you gave me the summer to do so." That day, he'd thought it a ridiculously short amount of time, but it had been preferable to *this*. "Why did you break your word?"

He chose the blunt words on purpose and wasn't surprised when his father's eyes flared with indignation. The old man had grown up having the Zyndar Code of Honor drilled into him as surely as Jev had.

"I did not break my word. I simply accepted an excellent offer on your behalf to ensure you wouldn't do something foolish. I was acting for your own good, for the good of my future grandchildren, and for all those who will continue the Dharrow line for generations to come."

"You told me I could choose my own wife and gave me the summer. And now, you've chosen for me. How is that not breaking your word?"

Surprisingly, the old man's gaze flicked toward the burbling water of the fountain. "I never said I promised anything."

"You don't have to use the word *promise*. If you say something and then don't do it, that's breaking your word. It's implicit in everything you say you'll do. *You* taught me that."

Father's gaze snapped back to Jev's face, and he thrust a finger at his chest. "Don't you dare lecture me, boy. I know I'm doing the right thing. Sometimes, that's more important than words. And you forced it with your dishonorable actions with that, that *common* woman."

"Actions I've already informed you did not occur." Jev shook his head in frustration. Who had told his father he and Zenia had been necking in public? Fremia? It was hard to imagine a teenage girl walking up to his father and confiding anything to him. The old man was as approachable as a rabid badger.

Father squinted at him. "You deny kissing her?"

Jev hesitated. "In public, yes."

"You think dragging her off to your room in the castle and screwing her there is any more acceptable? How many hundreds of people work in that castle? Everyone will know when she gets with child that it's yours. And then what happens when she demands you legitimize it? Jevlain Dharrow, you will marry a zyndari woman and impregnate her with a son before you sleep with any others."

Jev's fingers clenched at the crude language and the insinuation that Zenia would do any of that. "We're not sleeping together, but I'll tell you what, Father. I damn well intend to sleep with her. I'm not going to marry some girl who was playing with dolls when I went off to war.

I don't care how many enemies her grandfather slew fifty years ago. Zenia slew a dozen trolls last *week*. At my side. While protecting my back. Not that this isn't the stupidest thing to base a marriage on, but she would make wonderful sons—and daughters. Of that, I have no doubt."

"She's common."

"So what? I'm going to marry her."

His father froze. He truly appeared stunned, like a stiff wind could have knocked him into the fountain and he wouldn't have noticed it.

Jev realized they'd been yelling—several staff in the courtyard were doing an admirable job of not looking in their direction while listening intently. Belatedly, Jev regretted his raised voice, especially if Fremia had heard it from the balcony garden. Even if the girl had manipulated his father, Jev didn't want to hurt her. He barely knew her, but the Zyndar Code made him feel he should protect women, all women, and not simply from physical enemies.

"You will *not*," Father finally managed to say. "If you do not marry that girl up there and do what's best for Dharrow blood, I will disown you. I'll choose another to inherit the estate."

"Promise?"

Jev hadn't meant it to come out so flippantly, but it did, and that seemed to shock his father further.

"I am prepared to do my duty and manage the estate to the best of my abilities when you pass on," Jev explained, "and to marry a woman and give you grandchildren, hopefully even the grandson that you want, but do not think that I want to be zyndar prime or have the sole responsibility over all of this." Jev waved to include not only the castle but the lands and the villages of tenant farmers and craftsmen that needed to be managed and protected. "It is only my honor that keeps me here."

"You would be penniless and have nothing from me," Father said, though he had lost all his certainty. He sounded like he was trying to convince himself that those things mattered to Jev.

"I am perfectly capable of working a job and earning a salary." Jev thought about pointing out that he was friends with the 'boy king,' as his father had dismissively called Targyon, but he didn't want to bring Targyon back into this, nor did he want to imply that he needed someone else's help to get by. "And you have nothing I truly want, Father."

This time, Jev crossed his arms over his chest as he waited for an answer.

As he'd said, he wouldn't walk away from his family—his honor would not allow that, even for Zenia—but if his father disowned him... by the founders, it would be such a burden lifted. Opening the door to his bird cage and letting him fly free.

The old man looked toward the balcony garden. The bushes and vines and dwarf fruit trees up there almost obscured the woman standing at the railing and looking down at them. It wasn't Fremia, as Jev had expected, but someone in her mid-forties. She had a large chest and wore a dress that revealed much of it. It took him a moment to place Fremia's mother, Zyndari Bashlari Bludnor. Before the war, Jev had seen her numerous times at the social functions he'd attended on behalf of the Dharrow family.

"Listen Jev," his father said, drawing his attention back to him. "I spoke hastily. You know I don't want to choose another heir. You vex me at times, as youth is meant to vex those older in age, but I do believe you are honorable and do what's right." His lined forehead creased more deeply than usual.

Jev couldn't read the thoughts behind the creases. One minute, his father was accusing him of acting dishonorably by kissing Zenia in public, and now, he agreed Jev was honorable? Jev was confused. His father was always obstinate and pigheaded, but one knew what to expect in dealing with him. Right now, he almost seemed wishy washy.

"Let's make a deal," the old man said. "Go up and have lunch with the girl. Talk with her. Tell me she doesn't stir your loins."

"Uh."

Loins? Dear founders, Jev had been less disturbed by this conversation when his father had been yelling.

"Give her a chance," his father went on. "Like I said before, you can take the other girl for a mistress later if you must, after you've given me a son from a zyndari woman. We cannot set ourselves up to be mocked or ridiculed or turned into the butts of jokes. We are Dharrows. We are not the type of men to be gossiped about at gatherings." His lips thinned, and Jev wondered again who had been feeding him all this gossip. Oh, he was aware it existed, thanks to Hydal, but it startled him that his father was aware. Usually, the old man stayed on the estate as much as possible and ignored the nattering of hens, as he called women *and* men who engaged in such behavior. Was young Fremia truly behind his current level of knowledge? Or...

Jev looked toward the balcony again. Bashlari was still there, blatantly looking down at them. He didn't believe she was close enough to hear them now that they were speaking in a normal tone, but she certainly was watching intently. Was she the one behind everything? That would make more sense than imagining a teenage girl having the gumption to speak with his father.

"Father," Jev said quietly. "Not her. Zenia has become a good friend. We are not—despite what the town gossips say—lovers, but I would like for us to be, and more. I don't want her to be my mistress. Even if that's considered acceptable, I've never found it to be honorable. I want Zenia to be my wife. I love her."

Father winced. "She's a manipulative witch with a dragon tear. She wants to get her clutches into you and our family—"

"She does *not*. I have no doubt she would marry me even if I were not zyndar. In fact, I'm positive she would prefer it if I weren't."

The wince turned into an expression that managed to be both confused and flabbergasted.

"Just talk to the girl, Jev. She's waiting patiently for you."

Maybe so, but the mother was the one up there glaring down at them. Maybe she *could* hear their conversation.

"I'll make a deal with you, Father. I'll have lunch with Fremia if you agree to have a chat with Zenia."

"We've already chatted." Father flung his hand toward the fountain.

"I believe you're thinking of the chat you had with her assistant, Rhi. Zenia isn't an inquisitor anymore. She works for Targyon, the same as I do. There's no reason to feel distaste for her."

"Except that she had her nose up in the air the whole time she was here, as if she was *equal* to us. Or better."

"Do you accept my deal or not? I'm prepared to leave you here to have lunch with them yourself."

"You wouldn't walk out on a woman expecting to meet you. I've taught you better than that."

"You made the date, not me."

"Don't be flippant with me," his father snapped.

Jev raised his eyebrows, not willing to budge. Maybe a part of him hoped his father would set him free of his obligations and that he could escape his duty. His destiny.

The old man sighed. "Fine. I'll speak with her."

Jev almost blurted a surprised, "Really?" But he didn't. He nodded once. "Your word on it?"

That indignation flared in his father's eyes again. He had to hate the insinuation that his implied word wasn't good enough, but he'd brought this doubt upon himself.

"My word. Send her up to speak with me when you wish." The old man didn't mention the possibility of a lunch.

Oh well. Zenia would probably find it torture to spend more than ten minutes with him.

"And now, your new lady is waiting for you." Father gestured toward the stairs leading up to the balcony.

The mother was gone.

CHAPTER 8

Z ENIA SAT DOWN AT A table in the library with a stack of books.

That morning, she'd sent an agent to get reports from her half-elf informant as well as the informant who worked in the port authority office. She wanted information on the elven princess and her ship—she was concerned Yesleva wasn't all that she seemed and might be an intentional or unintentional threat to the kingdom—but Zenia didn't feel she could walk up and interview her. Earlier that morning, Zenia had glimpsed Yesleva with Targyon, who had been giving her a tour of the gardens, a huge entourage of castle guards and elven bodyguards trailing them. No, Zenia couldn't simply walk up and ask questions.

While she waited for the reports, she was trying to find something that could help her with her dragon-tear problem. The books she'd selected from the shelves discussed dwarven and elven magic. Her earlier research on dragon tears hadn't been fruitful, but perhaps one of these more general texts would hold useful information. The others had all been from human points of view, but a couple of these had been translated from books originally written in Dwarfish or Elvish.

Less than a half hour into Zenia's reading, Rhi ambled in and found her.

Zenia had been distracted from her original research by a chapter about the magical swords that elven wardens were given and how the custom-forged gifts reflected the personalities of their owners. She stuck a bookmark in the book so she could come back to it. Since she and Jev kept getting attacked by wardens, it would be good to know as much as possible about them—and their glowing swords.

"You have reports for me?" Zenia asked.

Rhi wasn't the agent she had sent to gather information, but someone might have volunteered her to find Zenia in the library.

"As it happens, I do." Rhi plopped down in a chair and laid scraps of paper on the table. "Garlok was blustering about how things were done in his day, so I took these from Agent Yu and fled. Eventually, I found my way here."

"Eventually? I told Sevy to let people know I was in the library if they needed me."

"I might have taken the circuitous route through the stables."

"The stables aren't on the way up here."

"That's why it was a circuitous route. Have you ever chatted with that handsome young man with the floppy hair that works down there? He has lovely forearm muscles. I got him to agree to spar with me later. I must keep in tiptop form in case my boss decides to take me with her the next time she assaults an elven stronghold."

"Assaults? Jev and I went to snoop in desk drawers." Zenia picked up the scraps of paper.

"Do you deny assaulting happened?"

"I deny that we did it."

"Exactly why you should have had me along."

Zenia skimmed the message on the first piece of paper. "Jia reports that Yesleva is the fourth daughter and seventh child of the Taziir king Yvelon. She's held many positions in her two hundred years and often runs diplomatic errands for her father, but she's never been stationed long-term in another nation." Zenia turned over the note. "That's it. Nothing more than is publicly known, I'm afraid. I suppose you wouldn't expect a half-elf who has lived here her whole life to be an expert on the Taziir nation." It would have been convenient if she had more information, but Jia was still a good resource.

Rhi shrugged noncommittally. "Maybe you'll find the next note more enlightening."

Zenia picked it up, but it was nonsense.

"It's in code." Rhi smirked. "It's possible your port authority buddy has a lot of time on his hands."

"Maybe it's just so juicy that he feared it would be intercepted by unfriendly eyes."

"Uh huh. Ten krons says he's waxing nostalgic about some of the collections he started in his youth. Or enthusiastically talking about pressed leaves."

"I shouldn't have introduced you to him."

"Definitely not," Rhi said.

"Did he send a key along?"

"Not that I heard. This is all Yu gave me. Maybe he expects that you, in your crime-solving brilliance, will be able to decrypt it with one eye covered." Rhi leaned back in her chair and propped her sandaled feet on the table.

Zenia frowned, tempted to give it to Frankell, who handled secret communications, but Rhi's comment sounded like a challenge. Besides, the lengths of the words were normal, even if the letter combinations were gobbledegook. It was probably a simple substitution cipher. With an introduction at the top and a capitalized four-letter word? Her name? Cham?

Going on that assumption, she found the pattern quickly and created a key by shifting letters three places to the right in the alphabet. She grabbed a pen.

"That's it," she said as she started writing the shifted letters atop the originals.

"You already figured it out?" Rhi set her feet back on the floor and leaned forward.

"You doubted my crime-solving brilliance?"

"I didn't know it would help with decoding messages from loons."

"He's not a loon. He's a valuable informant."

"He's a loony valuable informant. What does it say?"

A lot. He was more verbose than their half-elf informant. "He describes the elven ship and mentions that they didn't send word ahead, that it was a surprise when it arrived. Two dozen watchmen and dock security officers ran out as the ship glided into the harbor because there was concern that it was a warship, here to start a fight."

"A warship? If you flicked a match at that thing, it would burn to a crisp."

"I'm sure magic protects it from that fate." Zenia held up a hand so Rhi would let her finish. "All two dozen of the men stopped and lined up, not reaching for their weapons. They stared with blank expressions on their faces as the elves—Princess Yesleva and several bodyguards—

walked past them. Our informant didn't hear what was said to his boss, but carriages soon arrived to take the elves to the castle. He notes that magic was definitely used to placate everyone, because people were suspicious of the ship's arrival."

"Comforting to know elves can use magic to stroll through the city and up to the castle any time they want," Rhi said. "You think she magicked Targyon too?"

"I'm not sure. He was smitten before she arrived at the castle."

"Smitten? Does that mean she magicked him last time she was here? This is the same elf that you gave that artifact to, right?"

"Yes. And I believe she did have a long chat with Targyon that night."

"A chat? Or a *chat*?" Rhi wriggled her eyebrows.

"I didn't ask."

"It's a little hard to imagine Targyon attracting a gorgeous elf princess, but maybe she has ulterior motives."

"Targyon is handsome. He's just young." Zenia, fearing her friend was about to comment on asses and stallions, held up her hand again.

Which was fortunate, because the main library doors opened and voices flowed inside. Zenia leaned out of the alcove that held her table to see Targyon stroll in at the princess's side with elven and human guards flanking them. Yesleva and Targyon weren't holding hands or walking arm-in-arm, but judging from the way he kept smiling at her, he would like them to be.

"Maybe you should hide," Rhi whispered to Zenia.

"Me? Why?"

"Didn't you blow a hole in the elven tower? What if she's planning to move in there?"

Zenia shook her head.

"This is my favorite room," Targyon said, gesturing expansively to the library. "I adore books of all kinds. I lament that my new job—life—doesn't leave me much time for reading for pure enjoyment. I get to read a lot of reports, but they're incredibly dry. I've been trying to decide if my uncle Abdor inculcated that tendency or merely chose extremely humorless men to serve under him."

Yesleva smiled. Zenia couldn't tell if she truly enjoyed Targyon's burbling or if she was being indulgent and diplomatic.

Zenia almost reached for her dragon tear, wanting a better read on her, but she paused, reminding herself that such tactics were for enemies, not guests of the king. Also, she suspected the princess would sense any such intrusion. She surely had magic of her own and wasn't like the simple elven embassy guards Zenia had once manipulated into answering questions.

As if sensing her thoughts, Yesleva looked over at her and raised her delicate blonde eyebrows.

Zenia lifted her chin. She had every right to be here and to want to protect her king and her kingdom.

One of Targyon's bodyguards veered toward them. "Captain Cham? You'll have to move your work elsewhere."

"Of course," Zenia said, though she wanted to object to moving all her stuff—or missing out on her chance to spy firsthand on the princess. This wasn't, however, a public or university library. Everything in this castle belonged to the king, and she worked here at his whim.

But as she reached for her books, Yesleva headed toward her.

"We don't need to interrupt Inquisitor Cham's research, do we?" Yesleva asked Targyon. "I'd hate for my presence to disrupt those working in your castle, Your Majesty."

Zenia was relieved she called him by title and not Targyon. Or Targy or some such. She didn't truly *want* Yesleva to be here for ulterior motives or to manipulate anyone. When she'd come to get the Eye of Truth, she'd seemed to have the good of humanity in mind. If not for that anonymous note, Zenia didn't know if she would suspect the princess.

"I'm honored that you remember me, Your Highness," Zenia said, hoping that was the appropriate honorific for an elven princess. She knew it worked for human princesses in this and two other kingdoms, but who knew what was proper in Taziira? "It's Captain Cham. I work for the king now instead of the Water Order Temple."

"Ah? That's good for him certainly." Yesleva turned her smile toward Rhi. "I also remember your comrade. And how effectively she knocks men into fountains."

"Yes," Rhi said. "Yes, I do." She curtsied.

"Were you able to return that artifact to a safe place?" Zenia asked.

Targyon stood back and clasped his hands behind his back, appearing content to let them have their reunion.

"It is in a safe place, yes," Yesleva said. "I've returned on an unrelated matter. Ambassador Shoyalusa no longer wishes to hold a position here. Even though you vanquished a number of troll scouts, he believes your kingdom may still be in danger and that our people should stay out of a potential war between humanity and the trolls and their allies."

Zenia grimaced, wishing *humanity* had more allies.

"Unfortunately, that war is still a valid concern," Targyon said. "We drove the trolls from our nearby swamps, but we're not certain if that alone will deter them from attacking our kingdom."

"It is true that once a troll gets a burr in his hide," Yesleva said, "he's disinclined to do anything except work it out."

Zenia thought that would be true for most species but suspected Yesleva was quoting some elven saying.

"Apparently, we need to figure out how to be less burry," Targyon said, smiling.

Zenia expected the princess to rejoin him—she and Rhi couldn't be that interesting to royalty—but Yesleva glanced toward Zenia's chest. The dragon tear was tucked under the yellow linen shirt Zenia wore today, but she had no doubt the elf sensed it.

"My father is working on convincing a new ambassador to volunteer for this assignment, but nothing happens quickly in Taziira." Yesleva smiled. "We are a slow and deliberate people when it comes to politics. I volunteered to come temporarily to your kingdom so there would be an elven presence in the city."

"To keep an eye on us?" Rhi arched her eyebrows.

Targyon cleared his throat and shot her a warning squint.

Yesleva's smile only widened. She did not appear offended, but Zenia suspected a two-hundred-year-old world-traveling elf would be experienced at wearing a diplomatic face.

"I believe the true reason she's visiting," Targyon said, "must be to hear me read my poetry."

"I'm sure that's it," Rhi said in a very bland tone.

Zenia took that to mean Targyon had taken Jev's suggestion about sharing a poem. Had it been well received?

"Had I known about the poetry, I would have been here weeks ago." Yesleva's green eyes twinkled.

If Zenia hadn't been looking at the king of Kor and a princess of Taziira, she would have been positive they were flirting with each other.

Targyon, she believed, was genuinely flirting, but Zenia had a hard time believing the elf wasn't up to more.

"Are you wearing a different dragon tear from the last time I saw you, Captain Cham?" Yesleva tilted her head. "What are you a captain of now? It's my understanding that most human nations do not allow women in their military organizations."

"I'm one of the heads of His Majesty's Crown Agents." Realizing she shouldn't allude to Kor having a spy network, especially when they spied on elves as well as every other people in the world, Zenia gestured at Rhi and added, "We solve crimes."

"Actually, she solves them," Rhi said. "I just thump people."

"Your Highness," Targyon murmured to her.

"I thump people, Your Highness," Rhi corrected.

Targyon sighed. Maybe thumping wasn't appropriate language to use with royalty. Zenia could think of worse.

Yesleva arched her eyebrows, not at Rhi's language but at Zenia. And her dragon tear.

Zenia had been thinking of asking the princess if she knew anything about it, but the fact that Yesleva had shown interest in it before Zenia had withdrawn it made her uneasy.

"The king lent it to me to use in his service," she said simply.

Yesleva opened her mouth, but a page burst into the library before she spoke.

"Sire," he blurted. "It's the elven embassy. Someone blew it up."

"Another hole?" Rhi asked.

"It's been completely annihilated." The page waved his hands expansively. "There's nothing but rubble left."

Targyon cursed, using far worse words than *thump*. He had the grace to look abashed when he recovered and glanced at the princess.

Yesleva didn't look surprised by the page's announcement. Had she already known? Or was she simply accustomed to masking her features? Right now, her face was impossible to read.

"My sincerest apologies." Targyon bowed to her. "I'll look into this right away. I assure you that you won't be in danger here in the castle."

"I'll come with you," Yesleva said as Targyon started for the door.

"Of course," he said, waiting so she could walk at his side. Their pace was far more rushed than it had been on their way into the library. The guards swept after them, their faces also masked.

"Why do people keep blowing up that tower?" Rhi asked when they were alone again.

"It wasn't blown up before," Zenia said. "The completely repairable hole in the outer wall was an inadvertent result of battling a golem."

"So... it was blown *out*?"

"Your wit will surely win that stablehand to your bedroom soon."

"It's not my wit he was looking at when I bent over." Rhi winked.

Zenia tidied her stack of books and swept them up to take to her room for further perusal, but that would wait for later. She wanted to see the tower for herself. If someone had truly blown it up, she was likely about to have a new case to solve.

Jev stepped onto the large balcony and did his best to smile at the young woman sitting at the decorative wrought-iron table in a cleared area surrounded by potted plants and small trees. Birds chirped from feeders dangling from branches, the feathered creatures too fat and indolent to flap away at his approach. Someone must have been refilling the seed since his grandmother left the castle.

"Jev Dharrow?" Fremia stood and stepped forward, reaching for his hands as she smiled at him. "You're even more handsome than the picture in that article I saw. I remember you from when I was a little girl, but that was a long time ago, and I wasn't sure..." She glanced aside to the other person on the balcony with them.

Zyndari Bashlari Bludnor leaned against the back of one of the other chairs, her tight smile far less sincere. She was an attractive woman, but all Jev could think was that she might be the one manipulating his father. Possibly with the large breasts that were not simply present but pushed up with a corset and on prominent display.

Fremia was similarly well endowed in the chest area, her dress also designed to draw attention to the fact. Her black hair hung to her shoulders in curly waves, and she had pale blue eyes that reminded Jev of the Taziir. Had some elf traveled through her bloodline in the past? Wouldn't the old man be shocked if that were the case?

"It's nice to meet you again, Fremia." Jev gave her the hand clasp she was reaching for. "What article are you referring to?"

"The one in the *Korvann Chronicle*. Haven't you seen it? It talks all about how you battled fifty trolls by yourself and stopped a huge invasion before it could start."

Jev tried to extricate his hands, but she gripped them more tightly and gazed raptly up at his face.

"I always thought I'd have to marry an odious old ogre because I'm the oldest girl and am expected to marry to further our family position. I'm so delighted to get you."

"Er." What was Jev supposed to say to that? All he could do was wish he were odious and ogrely so she would have objected to this marriage. "Yes. And may I say that you've grown into a beautiful woman?" A part of him wanted to be unpleasant—ogrely—but he couldn't bring himself to be rude or cruel.

"Thank *you*, Jev. May I call you Jev?"

"Yes," he said, while thinking that Zenia would squint at him if he ever complimented her beauty. She would be far more honored if he complimented her intelligence in solving a case. Had he done that? He should have, if he hadn't. *She* had been the reason they'd found out about the trolls in time to do something.

Bashlari shifted, and Jev nodded cordially to her. "And you're also looking lovely, Zyndari."

"Thank you, Jev." Bashlari smiled and looked him up and down, as if she were the one who would soon be marrying him. "I'll leave you two to get better acquainted while I have a chat with your father." She smiled cryptically and touched her chest.

It was only then that Jev noticed that more than skin was on display there. On a fine gold chain, she wore a dragon tear, its oval shape almost concealed between her breasts—they were wedged together to form a deep crevice that wayward jewelry might get lost in.

Jev couldn't see what was carved on its front but abruptly thought of inquisitors and their gems that gave them the ability to read minds. To read and *manipulate* minds.

"Of course," Jev managed to murmur as Bashlari sashayed around the table, swinging her hips like a pendulum.

He looked away, though he had no doubt that a lot of men didn't. Unfortunately, looking away from Bashlari only had him looking into Fremia's rapt face. Erg.

"Shall we have a drink?" Jev gestured at the table.

The staff had already filled glasses with tamarind lemonade, chunks of ice floating in it, the shards chiseled from one of the great blocks stored in the ice house behind the stable. There was also a tray of crudités with hummus and an olive dip. Appetizers. Wonderful. That meant someone had thought Jev should stay here for multiple courses.

"Of course." Fremia twirled, her dress floating out around her, then perched on the edge of the seat. She leaned her arms on the table, her chest thrust forward. Unintentionally? Or did she mean to flaunt her assets?

Usually, there were four chairs at this table, but someone had decided two would do for today. And they were arranged next to each other. Jev sat and adjusted the position slightly so he could see over the balcony.

Leaves partially blocked the view, but he spotted his father still down by the fountain. Bashlari headed straight for him, her hips still swaying. The old man watched, his gaze dipping toward her chest. Jev curled a lip. He had never known his father to fall for women's wiles, but if those wiles were enhanced somehow with a dragon tear...

"Your mother is still married, isn't she?" Jev remembered Zyndar Mahk Bludnor at functions, a sturdy man with a cane and countless war stories strategically deployed to bore the youth. Jev had once been among the bored youth.

"Yes, of course. She and my father have been together for almost twenty-five years." Fremia clasped Jev's hand under the table. "I know you must think I'm young, but I'll be a good wife, Jev. My mother insisted I remain a virgin for my future husband—" her lips wrinkled in distaste, "—but she also approved of me receiving suitable instruction on how to please a man."

The blunt talk of sex surprised Jev, perhaps because he'd grown accustomed to Zenia's shyness on the matter. However, he was fairly certain that when he'd left for the war, zyndari women had been more circumspect in discussing such things, at least to men they didn't know well. Sometimes, the ten years he'd been gone seemed a lifetime. He found himself uncertain how to navigate waters that had once been familiar.

"How thoughtful of her," he murmured.

Down in the courtyard, Bashlari reached his father and laid a hand on his forearm. Jev shifted, trying to see better through the foliage. Zenia's dragon tear often glowed blue when it was working its magic, but he hadn't seen many others give off such telltale signs. He supposed Bashlari's chest wouldn't start to glow.

"I understand the Dharrows own several businesses," Fremia said, squeezing his hand.

"Yes."

He had the impression she was trying to draw his attention back to her. Manners drilled into him in his youth forced him to face her with an apologetic smile. But he resolved to have a chat with Zyndari Bashlari later. Maybe with Zenia and her dragon tear at his side. He hated to rely on her that way and wondered if he should have taken Targyon up on his offer of a dragon tear of his own to wield. As a boy, Jev hadn't shown any aptitude for magic, but it was said that anyone who was willing to work at it could learn to rudimentarily access the power within the gems. Patience hadn't been his aptitude in his youth, but perhaps now…

"Jev? Did you hear me?"

So much for his manners. "I'm sorry. I have a lot on my mind right now."

"Something related to the Dharrow businesses? I was wondering about your mines in the mountains. We have property up there, too—it was left in my name specifically—but we're not sure if there's any ore in there. Perhaps, after we're wed, your workers could bring some exploratory mining equipment over for a while. If my land turned out to be profitable, we could both benefit."

"You have older brothers, don't you?" Jev asked.

"Three, yes."

Meaning, they would inherit the majority of the family's assets when their father passed away. Fremia's land in the mountains might be all that had been left to her, so it made sense that she would want to see if it could be made profitable. Of course, if she married a wealthy zyndar prime—or future prime—she wouldn't have to worry about money. But maybe she hoped to have money independent of her husband. Her husband who would not be him.

Jev took a deep breath, smiled, and returned her hand clasp. "Fremia, I would be happy to lend you some of our resources to explore your land, but I need you to know that I won't marry you. I know our parents want this, but my heart belongs to another." He tried to make his expression as gentle as possible. He didn't know her well enough to guess if she would be crushed or outraged by his rejection.

"Oh, Jev. Is this about your common woman?" Fremia patted his hand and gazed up at him as if he were some wayward and mentally challenged toddler to be pitied. "My mother said you might say this but not to worry. We *will* be wed, Jev. You'll soon see that I'm the best choice."

That wasn't the response he'd expected. A servant brought lunch then, so he wasn't able to answer. Maybe it was for the best. It was her mother that he would have to deal with—and his own father—if he wanted to cut this weed down before it went to seed.

Jev suffered through lunch, during which Fremia chatted amiably about his mines and how she could help him find people to run his various businesses so they could travel the world together. It sounded as idealistic and unrealistic as expected from someone young, and by the end of lunch, Jev definitely had the impression that the Bludnor family was purely interested in him because he was his father's heir. It wasn't surprising—many zyndar marriages were arranged for financial and political gain—but it did make him long to run back to the woman who loved *him*, not his family or his money.

As soon as lunch was over, Jev pardoned himself and evaded an offered kiss by pretending to need to rush back to work.

His father and Bashlari were no longer in the courtyard, but when he strode to the stable for his horse, he found the old man there, directing the stacking of hay for storage, as if the hands couldn't handle that on their own. One of the hands brought Jev his horse, and he thanked the boy.

"I'll be bringing Zenia by to meet you soon, Father," Jev said. "As we discussed."

The old man's eyes narrowed. "Fine, but as Zyndari Bashlari and I just discussed, we've planned the eighteenth for your wedding."

Jev rocked back on his heels. "That's less than two weeks away."

Didn't women need longer than that to prepare for a wedding? For that matter, didn't all those who helped with the ceremony and inviting guests need longer?

"Bashlari offered to handle all the planning."

Jev had no doubt she had.

"All you need to do is get an appropriate suit for the ceremony and show up. I trust you can manage that, but if not, I'll send Wyleria or one of your aunts to help."

"I'm not marrying her, Father," Jev said, forcing himself to meet the old man's eyes and look as stern and determined as he could.

He was surprised to realize he was a couple of inches taller than his father. How had it taken him so many years to realize that? The old man had always seemed to tower over him, but maybe that was a mental illusion.

"You will—"

"Further," Jev interrupted, not caring that it was rude and the Zyndar Code ordered children to be respectful and obedient to their elders, "I believe Zyndari Bludnor is using a dragon tear to manipulate you into doing her bidding."

Fury flared in his father's eyes like an inferno. "I'm not some weak-minded child that can be manipulated by a mage."

"You're not acting like yourself. Anyone can be manipulated by a mage. I'll have Zenia check when she meets with you."

The old man clenched his hands. "You keep that inquisitor witch out of my mind."

"All she'll do is fix things if someone's controlling you."

"Dragon shit, she will. If she shows up here, I'll—"

"*Talk* to her." Jev fought the urge to clench his own fists. "You gave your word. Or are you going to break it again because that manipulative woman is diddling your head?"

"Damn you, Jev. You show respect for me and your elders or I'll—"

"Are you sleeping with her? Because she's married, I understand. Where's your vaunted honor, Father?"

Caught up in his anger, Jev almost didn't see the punch coming. Instinctively, he whipped a hand up and blocked it.

His father, blood rushing to his face, threw a second punch. This time, Jev caught it out of the air, his fingers wrapping around the old man's fist. It surprised him that he'd been able to do so, to thwart the attack.

Father snarled and jerked his hand away. "You get out of my castle. You're not welcome until you can show me the respect I deserve."

"Fine by me, but you better stay away from Bashlari when she's wearing her dragon tear. She's controlling you like a puppet."

"Get out!" Father roared and looked around the stable, like he was thinking of grabbing a rake and beating Jev with it.

He could try, but Jev wasn't the boy he'd once been, and he wouldn't stand still for a beating.

Maybe his father realized that. The old man stomped out of the stable without another word.

Jev noticed the stablehands had disappeared during their argument. A black gelding stood blandly, chewing on a piece of hay. The king's carriage hadn't waited after dropping Jev off, so he saddled up the horse to ride back to Alderoth Castle.

As much as he didn't want to ask Zenia to use her dragon tear to help him—or to ever speak with his dyspeptic father again—he didn't have time to learn to use one of his own. And he feared that confronting Zyndari Bashlari on his own might only end up with him also under her spell.

CHAPTER 9

A CROWD MILLED IN THE STREET outside the walled compound of what had been the elven embassy. Zenia, riding side by side with Rhi, arrived before the king's carriage and his entourage, and it was clear from several blocks away that the tower wasn't just damaged. It was completely gone. Whatever remained wasn't visible above the wall.

The wrought-iron gate was closed when they arrived, as if nobody had been inside the compound since Zenia and Jev left. But the devastation inside promised otherwise.

Zenia and Rhi struggled to guide their horses to the gate due to the density of the crowd.

"Step aside," Zenia called to the people gawking while they elbowed each other and whispered with speculation. "We are agents on the king's business."

She knew the crowd would disperse instantly when Targyon's carriage and platoon of bodyguards came into sight, but she wanted to get a look before he arrived. More specifically, before the princess arrived. She doubted Yesleva had ordered her own people's tower destroyed, especially less than a day after she'd arrived, but Zenia wasn't sure if she could count the elf as an ally or not. It continued to unnerve her that Targyon was so clearly smitten with her.

"My captain said step aside," Rhi roared when nobody moved or did more than glance at their horses.

Rhi poked people in the backs with her bo to achieve compliance. People glowered but backed away, clearing a path.

"I knew there was a reason I hired you," Zenia said.

"For my wit and my charm and my big stick, eh?"

"At least one of those things."

The hint of a feeling came from Zenia's dragon tear. Indignation? Had the gem wanted her to use it to clear the crowd?

Her old dragon tear wouldn't have been able to manipulate numerous minds at once, but this one definitely had greater range. How great? Zenia wasn't sure she wanted to find out. She was glad Rhi was able to do the job with her bo.

When they reached the gate, Zenia joined the crowd in gawking at the pile of rubble inside the courtyard. What had been a tower of more than ten stories was now a two-story rock heap. Chunks larger than horses had tumbled all the way to the courtyard wall. What kind of explosion could have so completely obliterated the structure? It seemed strange that they hadn't heard anything up in the castle. It was a couple of miles away, but sound traveled up the hill, and she'd often heard foghorns from ships approaching the harbor as she prepared for bed.

"Did someone set explosives?" she wondered aloud. "Or is it possible magic did this?" After her experience with those two elf wardens, she had no problem imagining their shadow golem tearing down the walls.

"We could take a look, but someone left the gate locked." Rhi pointed her bo at the padlock, which had been secured again since Zenia opened it the day before. "It wasn't noticeably effective at securing the compound."

"Someone from the watch might have come by and relocked it to make sure people don't snoop before an official investigation can be put together."

"But we're going to snoop, right?" Rhi raised her eyebrows.

"We're His Majesty's officially appointed Crown Agents. We don't snoop, we investigate." Zenia chose not to remember that she'd used the word to describe her activities with Jev the day before.

"Wouldn't official investigators have a key?"

"It's not necessary." Zenia touched her dragon tear and envisioned the padlock snapping open. She might not like the idea of manipulating masses of people, but iron and steel were different matters.

The lock opened promptly and tumbled to the cobblestones. A smug sensation came from her dragon tear.

More and more, Zenia had the feeling that the soul linked to her gem was young. But how some young dragon had come to be tied to a dragon tear that had been in the royal family's possession for centuries, she could not guess. She knew dragons were reputed to live for centuries and maybe even millennia, but after living for a few hundred years, surely even a dragon wouldn't be considered youthful.

"I'll take that as an invitation." Rhi used her foot to push open the gate, then guided her horse through.

A couple of teenagers in the crowd looked like they wanted to head in—maybe these people had looting on their minds?—but Rhi glowered at them and waved her bo. The young men backed off. Sometimes, Rhi could be as menacing as a guard dog.

Zenia followed her in, closing the gate behind them, and dismounted. They found a few skeletal trees with charred trunks that were still sturdy enough for them to tie their horses to.

"It's the king," someone outside blurted.

"Come on." Zenia picked a quick pace through the rubble, hoping to investigate before Targyon and the princess arrived. "Let's see if we can figure out if magic or black powder was responsible."

"How would we know the difference?" Rhi asked.

"When the Fifth Dragon Guild blew up a corner of the Water Order Temple, Jev said he saw the remains of the kegs that had been holding the black powder."

Zenia peered through the wreckage, but she realized it would be hard to pick out wood from kegs. All manner of furnishings had been in the tower, and the floors themselves had been wooden. Everywhere she looked, smashed tables and beds and snapped floorboards lay among the rubble.

"Would Iridium have done this?" Rhi asked. "I can't imagine why the guilds would pick a fight with the elves."

"Nor can I."

Zenia circled the main mass of rubble, what had been the location of the tower, and spotted a bunch of greenery on the far side of the pile. The remains of some garden? No, the foliage was on top of the rubble, not buried under it.

"What is that?" she murmured, climbing over slabs of rock for a better view.

Finally, she stopped atop a pile and faced the greenery. Dozens and dozens of vines were woven together in a flowing pattern that lay atop the rubble. Whatever they were, they had definitely been placed *after* the tower fell. And, assuming people's reports of the explosion had reached the castle promptly, this had been done under the bright, revealing light of day. Who would have taken the time for this elaborate setup after blowing up the tower?

"Are those words?" Zenia asked as Rhi scrambled to the top of the pile with her.

"You're asking me? To my eyes, it looks like an infestation of weeds."

"A very ordered one in a sweeping pattern." The vines themselves seemed to shift and flex slightly as Zenia looked upon them. They reminded her of the sword that warden had used, the one that had grown vines to wrap around Jev's limbs. She took a couple of steps back. "Unfortunately, we need someone who can read elven."

"That can be arranged," a woman said from the other side of the courtyard. Princess Yesleva.

She and Targyon walked in, bodyguards trailing them. Two of the bodyguards started toward Zenia and Rhi, wearing the determined expressions of bouncers, but Targyon said something quietly and waved them toward the main gate.

Zenia lifted her head, mollified. She was one of Targyon's agents. It was her place to be here, investigating a crime.

"May I offer you a hand, Highness?" Targyon asked when the princess came around the pile and looked like she would climb up beside Zenia and Rhi for a better look.

Zenia scooted to the side to make room, and Rhi hopped down.

Yesleva smiled at Targyon but jumped lightly from perch to perch on her own. She gripped her chin and gazed at the vines.

"It is a warning," she said.

"I had a feeling it wasn't a dinner invitation," Rhi grumbled.

Targyon frowned at her.

"Your Highness," Rhi added.

"It says that there can be no peace between the Taziir and the savage humans of this kingdom. Any elves who attempt to make overtures will be considered traitors and punished accordingly." She clenched her jaw, her eyes blazed with indignation, and she spat a stream of words in her own language.

Zenia had no idea what they meant, but they did not sound ladylike.

Targyon blinked a few times. Maybe he understood some of them.

"I think if it *had* been a dinner invitation," Rhi whispered, "she would have rejected it."

Zenia held a finger to her lips. She didn't want to be ordered to leave because Rhi was irking people.

But Yesleva paid her no heed. She finished her tirade and looked at Targyon.

"King Targyon," she said formally, "I wish to have this facility rebuilt. One of my attendants has architectural experience." She waved in the direction of the harbor and her ship. "I will have him draw up blueprints. Do you have someone who can assist me in overseeing the construction? I will, of course, pay for the labor."

"I can provide numerous assistants, Your Highness," Targyon said. "But I refuse to let you pay for anything. It is my fault this happened."

"It is not. My people are responsible for this sabotage." She thrust a hand toward the vines. "They used elven magic to destroy an elven structure. This is unforgivable."

Zenia felt a warning tingle from her dragon tear, and a second later, the foliage spelling out the warning withered and turned brown, then turned to dust. An unnatural breeze kicked up, smelling of earth and rich foliage rather than of the sea and the city, as one would expect. It blasted the dust into oblivion.

Zenia stirred uneasily, not heartened by Yesleva's display of power. It meant the princess, should she ever turn against them, had strong magic of her own to call upon. Maybe she could also conjure up golems from the bowels of the earth.

"I am my father's chosen representative in this matter," Yesleva said. "I will not be scared away by unprincipled rogues who work at odds with the king's will and take the law into their own hands."

Zenia was a little encouraged to hear that those wardens hadn't been sent by the king, but she didn't know if it mattered. They were here, and the elven king was a continent away. Did his daughter have the power to stop them?

A boom rang out in the harbor, and Zenia jumped.

"What now?" Targyon groaned.

Frowning, Yesleva leaped from the small rubble pile to the main one. She ran up it as if it were the smoothest of slopes, and from her perch, she looked over the wall and toward the harbor.

Zenia, Targyon, and Rhi climbed up after her. The rubble pile was just tall enough for them to see over the tavern across the street and to the part of the harbor where the elven ship was docked. Where it *had* been docked. Wood and bits and pieces of green foliage floated among the wreckage of the pier. They were all that remained of the ship. The vessels around it were all damaged, as well, but only the elven ship had been obliterated. Like the tower.

Yesleva whispered something in her own language and then added, "They go too far." She shook her head. "They go too far."

Targyon's expression vacillated between rage and horror.

Zenia mostly felt numb. Had elves been aboard that ship when it had blown? The very architect the princess had spoken of? An entire crew?

Zenia didn't know if the same party of elves had been responsible or if some human coalition had decided the Taziir weren't welcome in the city. If it was the latter, her people could be in a lot of trouble. And if it was the former... she wasn't sure that was much better. The princess might not blame Korvann for events happening on kingdom soil, but would her father be as understanding? What if he believed Targyon had allowed this to happen? Or had even colluded to assist the elves?

Targyon looked at Zenia. "Meet me in my office in an hour. Find Jev and make sure he's there too."

Though Zenia didn't know where Jev was currently—still out at his family's castle?—she nodded and said, "Yes, Sire."

She had a feeling the Crown Agents were about to get a new mission.

The sun was setting as Jev dismounted in front of the king's stable, feeling guilty that his personal business had kept him away the majority of the day. It wouldn't be so bad if Dharrow Castle were closer to the city, but after a thousand-odd years, he doubted the rest of the family wanted to change addresses.

A stable boy came out to take his horse as Zenia rushed out of the castle and jogged straight at Jev.

"I need you," she said, gripping his arm.

The stable boy snorted and smirked. He was old enough to understand the possible connotations of such a phrase and young enough to find it highly amusing.

"Actually, the king needs you," Zenia added, not glancing at the boy.

"You had me excited there for a moment," Jev said, heading toward the closest door to the castle. He wasn't sure if Zenia's mind was as randy as that of the stable boy's or if she would fail to catch the innuendo.

She quirked her eyebrows. "The addition of Targyon makes the offer less exciting?"

"Decidedly so, yes. How did you know I was coming?" He hoped Zenia hadn't been waiting by the door for long.

"My dragon tear did."

"Ah."

"Targyon needs us in a meeting. Three minutes ago. That's why I was waiting for you. The elven tower was blown up, and so was the elven ship. I'm not sure if any of the princess's crew were aboard or if they were staying in the castle, but either way, it's egregious."

The startling news took a moment to digest.

"Do we know who did it?" Jev remembered Iridium blowing up one corner of the Water Order Temple.

"The princess seems certain it was those elven wardens."

"I thought they were just after Lornysh."

Not that wanting to kill him wasn't bad enough.

"Apparently not."

Since Zenia was running, Jev had to hurry to keep up with her. He lamented that they were late for a meeting he hadn't known about. He suspected this wouldn't be the best time to ask Targyon for a dragon tear.

"My father agreed to meet with you," Jev said as they climbed the stairs toward Targyon's office.

"What?" Zenia threw a startled look over her shoulder.

Maybe it wasn't the best time to bring that up either. But he was rattled that his father—or more precisely that conniving Zyndari Bludnor—had already set a wedding date. A *close* date.

"I'll explain more later. I was hoping that he'd warm up to you if he met you, but now I'm hoping you can tell if a zyndari with a dragon tear is manipulating him."

"All right. I'll go up after this situation with the elves is under control."

Jev thought about mentioning the wedding date, but it could wait.

The bodyguards outside the office waved them through the already-open door. The secretary was standing at the open inner door. He also waved them through. It was more of a hurry-up shooing motion.

Inside, Targyon paced back and forth in front of his desk. Princess Yesleva, whom Jev had only met briefly when she had retrieved the Eye of Truth from his castle, sat in a chair next to a low table. Two male elves that Jev hadn't met stood behind her, their faces carved from stone.

"Did you bring something to write with?" Targyon asked Jev and Zenia without preamble.

"Uh," Jev said.

Zenia withdrew a small notebook and pen from the compact purse she carried. "I'm ready, Sire."

Targyon nodded curtly, then faced the princess. "Please begin whenever you're ready, Your Highness."

Jev didn't speak, not with Targyon so tense, but he touched Zenia's shoulder, wanting her to know he appreciated that *she* was always far more prepared that he was. If his family duties ever required him to step down from this job, he knew she would be fine without him. That made him feel superfluous, but he silently resolved to find an opportunity to work harder for Targyon as soon as his marriage problem was resolved.

"As I'm sure you're aware," Princess Yesleva said in her beautiful lilting voice, "there is a faction within Taziira that has always had isolationist tendencies and that wants nothing to do with humans. They were extremely vocal during the war, and it seems, that hasn't ended. If anything, they've escalated their tactics. As was clear today. They are making their wishes known." Her lips pursed. "Dramatically."

"The Zsayon." Targyon nodded.

"They've been here for several days at least," Jev said, also familiar with the faction and not surprised the wardens were affiliated with it. "Four of them. But we thought they came for Lornysh since your people aren't overfond of him."

Yesleva hesitated. "He chose a path that led to that, and he knew the consequences when he started down it."

Jev fought the urge to defend his friend since Lornysh had fought against and killed his own people during the war. It had benefited Kor and it had benefited Jev and his unit, but he could grasp why a Taziir princess would condemn him.

"I understand," Jev said, "but my point is that I thought he was the sole reason these wardens came. Is that not correct? Is Lornysh a side mission, and *you're* the reason they're here, Highness?"

Yesleva rubbed her chin thoughtfully. "As far as I know, the Zsayon did not deliver any threats or ultimatums to my father about this journey I've chosen to undertake. But then, we did not announce it publicly, since even non-Zsayon Taziir want nothing to do with your kingdom right now. There would have been vehement objections from the population in general."

Targyon winced.

"It is my belief that it wasn't until they saw my ship arrive and learned that we intend to reestablish an ambassadorial team that they chose to act."

"Who told them that's your agenda?" Zenia looked up from her notepad—she had already scribbled several lines. "It hasn't made our newspapers yet."

"They are powerful enough to learn what they wish to know without reading the news," Yesleva said.

"No doubt," Jev murmured and rubbed his arm where that strange sword-vine had gripped it the day before. "So they came all this way for Lornysh? And then this attack on your ship and the embassy was an opportunistic thing? I'm confused as to why they would harm their own people and destroy elven things to make their point."

"They believe violence is an effective way to make a point." Yesleva shook her head. "They are young and angry. Many of them lost friends and family during your invasion."

Targyon winced again.

"If you try to rebuild the embassy while they're here," Zenia said, "won't they blow it up again?"

"No," Targyon said firmly. "Because my Crown Agents are going to find them and stop them. Capture them. Take all their magical artifacts away and put them on a ship sailing away from our continent."

Jev tried not to feel daunted. If not for the help of Zenia's dragon tear, he would have met his end simply battling one of those elves. And Targyon expected them to get rid of all four? Who knew what else besides a shadow golem they could conjure up?

"Though I'm sure your human agents are capable," Yesleva said, glancing not at Jev but at Zenia—or maybe the dragon tear resting under the fabric of her dress, "they aren't a match for elven wardens. I will send my people to deal with these rogues."

Her two bodyguards exchanged nervous glances, and one whispered to her in urgent Elvish. He spoke quietly and rapidly, and Jev struggled to hear and translate, but he caught the gist. They had lost a couple of their best people in the explosion of their ship, they had only one warden among the elves they had brought, and her small escort wouldn't be a match for the might of their enemies. He urged her to consider returning to Taziira and asking her father to send trained wardens loyal to him to deal with the Zsayon elves.

The princess held up a hand. "We will not run fleeing with our tails between our legs," she spoke in the kingdom tongue. "They will believe they've won, and it will only bolster the Zsayon and those silent elves who support them. We—" She broke off with a frown and faced one of the tall windows behind the desk.

Twilight had descended outside, and Jev couldn't see anything except the reflection of Targyon's lamps in the glass.

But then the window opened, and a breeze whispered in.

"Intruder," one of the bodyguards barked in Elvish.

He and his colleague drew their blades and sprang toward the desk as Targyon jumped to the side.

Lornysh hopped down from the window sill and lifted open hands, showing he held no weapon. A fresh gash marred his left cheek, and his usually tidy silver hair was tangled, as if he'd been sleeping in shrubs. Maybe he had.

Jev lunged forward and caught one of the elves by the back of the tunic, afraid they would attack him. They had no more reason than the Zsayon to love Lornysh.

The elf tried to jerk away as the other one sprang onto the desk, raising his sword.

"Stop!" Yesleva shouted.

The guards froze so quickly Jev wondered if she'd added a magical compulsion to the command. They did not, however, lower their weapons. They glared at Lornysh, and he gazed calmly back at them.

"My desk," Targyon said, "is not the appropriate place from which to launch attacks." He also sounded calm, but Jev knew him well enough to spot the worry in his eyes.

"This *traitor* could be here to assassinate you," the guard on the desk said, his sword point aimed toward Lornysh's chest.

"Or he could be here to offer his assistance," Jev said. "Let him stand with your warden, and that'll make two of them against the Zsayon's four. Two is better than one, right?"

Lornysh's silver eyebrows arched. Whatever he'd come for, it hadn't likely been to offer assistance, at least not to the princess's party.

The second bodyguard, the one Jev still gripped from behind, sniffed. "Salyishan will never stand with that traitor."

"Put your weapons away," Yesleva said firmly, and Jev twitched, experiencing an urge to sheath his own weapons even though he hadn't drawn any.

The guards sheathed their swords. Yes, that was definitely a magical compulsion.

At Jev's side, Zenia frowned and narrowed her eyes.

"I came to speak with King Targyon," Lornysh said, facing him and making a point of ignoring the guards. "Actually, to bid you farewell. And you, too, Jev. It's too dangerous for me to stay here, and I believe my presence led to the princess's ship being blown up. If they hadn't come for me, they wouldn't have witnessed her arrival."

Targyon exhaled slowly.

"Lornysh, you can't just leave," Jev said, hoping his second time making the argument would be more effective than the first. "Targyon just assigned Zenia and me to find those elves and kick them out of the kingdom." He smiled and dropped a fist in his palm, though he still doubted they could handle the wardens, even with every agent in the office and a couple of platoons of soldiers at their backs.

"I see," Lornysh said. "You've irked Targyon, and he's sacrificing you so he can hire new agent captains."

"I am confident that Zenia and Jev can find a way to deal with them," Targyon said, not reacting to Lornysh's sarcasm.

"I'm not."

"Thanks, buddy," Jev said.

"Is there a leader?" Zenia asked.

"What?" Lornysh asked.

All eyes in the room turned toward Zenia.

"You all keep talking about sending people into battle against these four powerful wardens, but if there's a leader that we can negotiate with, wouldn't it be better to try to find a peaceful resolution?"

"I know the Zsayon," Yesleva said as Lornysh shook his head. "They never accept peaceful resolutions when they believe they are in the right."

"For me, this fate was inevitable," Lornysh said. "They believe I deserve death, and no words from a human will deter them."

Zenia frowned. "That's a fatalistic attitude. Is there a leader, or not? Even if he won't negotiate, perhaps we could put all our resources into capturing him, and then the rest of the band would disperse."

Lornysh looked skeptical.

"It's not a bad idea," Jev said, "if someone truly is spearheading this and the others are just going along with him. Lornysh?"

Lornysh's lips pressed together.

"You know the leader," Jev stated, certain he was reading his friend correctly.

"Vornzylar," Lornysh said.

The princess nodded. Maybe she'd known too.

Jev thought the name sounded familiar, but maybe only because he'd heard it mentioned in association with the faction before. He would ask

Hydal and see if his former Gryphon Company lieutenant remembered more than he did.

Of course, judging by the expression on Lornysh's face, he knew plenty about the elf.

"Vornzylar?" Zenia was writing again. "What do you know about him? Do you know what motivates him?"

"Yes. Killing me." Lornysh backed toward the open window. "Do not seek him out. He's the most dangerous of those wardens. He's stronger than I am." Lornysh looked toward the princess and her bodyguards. "And he's far stronger than your warden. I've faced them both before. I know. Just leave them alone. I'll depart before morning, and they won't have a reason to harass you anymore."

Lornysh sprang to the window sill.

"Wait," Jev blurted, releasing the bodyguard and stepping around the desk. "You can't just leave without…" Without what? Saying goodbye? Hadn't he just done that? "You have friends here, Lornysh. You don't have to handle everything by yourself."

Frustration welled in Jev's throat, but Lornysh didn't look back. He sprang down to the gardens below and disappeared into the night.

Targyon sighed. "I'm not sure he's right."

The princess shook her head. "I'm not sure either. Vornzylar may have come for Lornysh, but now that he knows I'm here… he and his team may take more drastic measures to ensure an embassy isn't reestablished."

"More drastic than blowing up your ship and the tower?" Jev asked. "What else is there?"

She gazed bleakly at him.

"They wouldn't dare attack you personally, Highness," the bodyguard on the desk said, finally leaping down. He'd spoken in Elvish, but he wasn't whispering this time, and Jev had no trouble understanding him. "Your father would order the most powerful mages in the kingdom after this vigilante to destroy him."

"He may have already done that," her other bodyguard added.

"We can't count on that." Yesleva continued to speak in the kingdom tongue, determined to include everyone. "Targyon, thank you for your hospitality and allowing us in the castle. I will confer with my people about all of this. But in the meantime, it is an elven matter. Do not get your people involved. It's too dangerous."

She waved for her men to follow her, and they glided out of the office without another word.

As soon as the door shut, Targyon faced Jev and Zenia.

"We're getting involved, aren't we?" Jev asked.

"Yes," Targyon said. "These elves blew up a ship in *my* harbor and a tower in *my* city. I don't care if they went after elven targets. It's happening here, on kingdom land. It's our problem, and I intend to fix it. I intend for you to fix it." He met Jev's eyes and then Zenia's. "With all the resources you need. I already sent a message to Krox in the army compound. He will ready men to assist you in the hunt."

"We may need magic more than we need soldiers," Jev said. "Mages from the Orders are more likely to make a dent in elven defenses."

"I can't as easily command the Orders to send people to help, but I will speak with the archmages in the morning and do my best to have mages with dragon tears at your disposal by midday tomorrow. In the meantime, I suggest you find out where this Vornzylar and his men are staying. It must be in the city or nearby. They reacted quickly to the princess's arrival." Targyon clenched his jaw.

"Yes, Sire." What else could Jev say?

Zenia had Vornzylar's name written in block letters on her notepad with two lines under it. She looked more determined than daunted, as usual.

"I'll see if I can dig up anything on Vornzylar tonight," she said.

Jev almost said that he already planned to speak with Hydal, but maybe she would find something else in the library. It was possible the elf was hundreds of years old, had been to Kor before, and was written up in some old newspaper.

"Thank you," Targyon told her. "Dismissed. Jev, wait a moment, please."

If Zenia minded being dismissed while Jev was kept for something else, she didn't show it. She strode out, flipping through her notepad, probably heading straight for the library.

Jev was eager to look for Hydal and also to try and catch up with Lornysh before he disappeared forever.

"Yes, Sire?"

Targyon clasped his hands behind his back and paced in front of his desk. "Am I doing the right thing, Jev? With getting involved? I don't want these elven rogues to think they can blow things up in our city, but…"

"I don't know, Sire. How much of your desire to help stems from your longing to read poetry to the princess? In bed?"

Targyon's cheeks flushed, but he said, "It's not *only* that. And I know that's unlikely to happen, regardless. Our people would riot in the streets if we were seen holding hands, and her people… I'm sure her father doesn't want some dirty human touching his daughter. I just want to do my best to mend our relationship with the Taziir. I know it's early to hope that's possible, but don't I have to help if I can?"

"I'll do my best to help you help, Targyon. I think Zenia already has some ideas."

Targyon smiled faintly. "Yes. Good. Thank you."

CHAPTER 10

A FTER SPENDING THREE HOURS IN the library, Zenia gathered the notes she'd scribbled about the Zsayon faction—unfortunately, she'd found nothing about Vornzylar specifically—and went searching for Jev. She checked his room first, since it was getting late, but he wasn't there. An attentive page directed her to the gymnasium and baths in the basement of the castle. It was late, but a few thumps and grunts came from the large wrestling and boxing room. She wondered who Jev had found to spar with at this hour.

Gas lamps burned on the walls and posts of the spacious room, shedding enough light to reveal two bare-chested men trading punches on a mat. When Zenia recognized Jev as one of them, she started toward the pair, but she paused when she spotted Rhi leaning against the wall by the door, a towel draped over her shoulder.

"Training hard for our upcoming confrontation with a pack of elven wardens?" Zenia asked, though she didn't see Rhi's bo.

"Actually, I was on my way to take a bath, but if you're not joking about that confrontation, maybe I should go throw sandbags around for another hour." Rhi frowned at her.

"It may not be a joke, I'm afraid. Jev and I have to locate them first, but the king wants them booted out of Kor before they cause more trouble, He's going to try to recruit Order mages with dragon tears to help."

"Mages from *which* Order?" Rhi looked back toward the men as a flurry of smacks and thuds sounded.

"Whichever one will help, I imagine." Zenia cocked her head. "Are you hoping to be invited to join in?"

"No, I heard their noise and came to see who was sparring so late. Now, I'm assessing them for hidden ferocity."

Zenia realized Jev's sparring partner was Hydal. He was more compact and wiry than Jev but more muscular than she would have guessed after seeing him in clothing. Though the bespectacled Hydal didn't appear to be a natural athlete, he was holding his own on the mat. He darted in and out quickly, throwing tricky combination attacks before dancing out of reach.

Jev blocked the attacks with impressive speed, and Zenia caught herself watching him. She hadn't seen him often with his shirt off, and her cheeks warmed as she remembered Iridium's lair and the first time she'd seen him naked. The *only* time.

His muscular form hadn't been slick with sweat then, damp skin gleaming under the yellow lamplight. He wasn't pulling any punches, and she wondered if he was working out his frustrations from the week. She hadn't had a chance to ask him how his meeting with his father—and his supposed fiancée—had gone. But she could guess that dealing with his father had left him annoyed. And dealing with the young woman? Zenia had no idea what she was like, but she had an urge to tug Jev off to a private corner and remind him that *they* were meant to be together. Maybe with a kiss that would leave them both breathless with longing. Or maybe with *more* than a kiss, so they wouldn't be left longing for anything. She could put her vow to herself aside for Jev. He wouldn't—

"He's better than I expected," Rhi commented.

Zenia jerked her gaze from Jev, embarrassed that she'd forgotten all about Rhi and had probably been licking her lips while she ogled Jev.

Fortunately, Rhi was watching Hydal and didn't seem to have noticed.

"I admit I'd dismissed him, but maybe you were right," Rhi said. "Maybe dating a man with substance would lead to a deeper and more meaningful relationship."

"If you're referring to the beads of moisture on his chest, that's sweat, not substance."

Rhi shot her a dirty look. "*You're* the one who said he has depths. So what if he's not as handsome as some? He might be more appreciative if a woman chose to spend time with him. More eager to please."

"Are you looking for a man or a hound?"

"Don't worry." Rhi clapped her on the shoulder. "I'm sure Jev is eager to please too. All those years at war probably left him lonely and grateful for a female touch."

Not wanting to discuss it—or the fact that she'd offered Jev scant few touches—Zenia looked down at the notebook she gripped and remembered she'd had a reason for coming down here.

"I need to talk to him about work," she said and headed toward the men.

"Uh huh, sure you do. I'll distract his friend so you two can work in private." Rhi raised her voice. "Hydal, I need a hand in the bath. Are you busy?"

Zenia gawked at the brazen offer. She couldn't imagine suggesting sex—and she could only assume that was what Rhi was doing—to a man she'd only spoken with twice.

Hydal stumbled back from Jev so quickly he almost tripped over his own feet. The quick grace he'd shown a moment before disappeared, and he lifted his fogged spectacles to squint in Rhi's direction.

"Did you say...?" he started uncertainly and glanced toward Jev.

"Yes, but the offer isn't open for long," Rhi said. "If you're not interested, I'll find a castle steward to soap the parts I can't reach."

"Can we be done?" Hydal asked Jev.

"Did you tell me everything you know about Vornzylar?" Jev looked amused.

"Yes."

"Then we can be done."

"Good." Hydal sprinted off the mat and toward Rhi. "I'm excellent with soap, Ms. Rhi Lin. My mother insisted on cleanliness when I was growing up."

"Glad to hear it." Rhi clasped his hand and led him into the corridor and toward the baths.

Zenia knew there was a public steam room and pool where both sexes could mingle before going to the segregated baths, but she'd never seen couples there engaging in soap sharing. It was late at night, so maybe they would have privacy.

"That's an unexpected turn of events," Jev said as Zenia walked up.

"Seeing a sweaty half-naked man being athletic and aggressive puts thoughts into Rhi's mind."

"Just Rhi's?" Jev smiled at her, and she made herself hold his gaze, because otherwise her eyes would lower to *his* sweaty half-naked parts, and that would definitely distract her from her work. Not that his smile wasn't distracting enough. And the warmth in his dark brown eyes.

"My mind needs to be focused on work. Until…" She spread her hand, not wanting to bring up his engagement and definitely not wanting him to think of the woman he'd met that day, but it was hard to forget those things existed. Even if she was sad she hadn't kissed him far more often, she shouldn't contemplate it while he was promised to another.

"Of course," he said, then looked away, disappointment replacing the warmth in his eyes.

She stepped closer, immediately regretting causing him disappointment and likely adding to his frustrations. The world was piling enough of those on him without her help. And she wanted to make him feel better, wanted to make him relax, to make him smile. Make him enjoy being with her, not dread it because she kept saying no to him.

"I am having thoughts," she whispered, resting her hand on his side and letting her gaze drop to his chest, to the curvature of his pectoral muscles, the skin gleaming through his dusting of short hair. What would it be like to kiss his muscles? To let her tongue slip out and taste him?

"Oh?" He lifted a hand, touching the side of her face, then pushing his fingers through her hair to cup the back of her head. They were warm and strong, his short nails grazing her scalp and eliciting a tingle that heated and tightened her entire body. "I suppose it would be inappropriate to act upon them."

"Definitely." She gave in to her urge and leaned down to kiss his chest. He tasted warm and salty, and she breathed in his masculine scent, surprised how much she enjoyed it, enjoyed *him*. She let her lips explore further, both for her own pleasure and because she longed to drive any thoughts of the woman he'd seen earlier out of his mind.

His fingers tightened, and his head fell back. His body tensed, his muscles hardening beneath her lips, but she sensed that it had to do with building desire rather than stress or tension.

"Let's go to my room," he whispered. "We can share our thoughts. I won't—we don't have to do anything that would break your vow to yourself." He wrapped his other arm around her, his strong hand finding her back and kneading her through her dress.

Her notepad fell from her grip, but she barely noticed. She had decided when she'd almost lost Jev in that explosion in the harbor that she would trust him in a relationship. They would do their best to keep from conceiving a child, but if that happened, she knew he wouldn't abandon it. Or her. He wasn't the asshole her father was. He was an honorable man.

It was *his* father and all the people who wanted to manipulate him into the marriage they desired that bothered her now, the fact that he could be engaged against his wishes. She didn't want him manipulated into anything. She wanted him to be his own man and free to choose. To choose her.

She slid both hands around to his back and over his muscles as she ran her lips up to his throat, kissing and nibbling the tendon there. She pressed her chest against his.

"Zenia," he whispered, his mouth close to her ear, his breath tickling her sensitive skin. "I want to be with you."

"Good," she whispered and kissed him.

He seemed surprised, but he recovered instantly, pulling her tight against him and kissing her hard. She returned it eagerly, molding her body to his. In the back of her mind, she knew they should go to one of their rooms. Even though it was late, this was too public a place. As long as he was engaged, he shouldn't be seen—

A startled gasp came from the doorway.

Zenia broke the kiss and glanced over, expecting a maid with a mop bucket and hoping she could be bribed not to spread any gossip. But it was a zyndari woman, one she unfortunately recognized. The wife of one of Targyon's brothers, Dominqua. The week before, she'd stopped Zenia in the courtyard, irritated Zenia hadn't kowtowed to her noble highness sufficiently. Maybe Zenia would get lucky, and the woman wouldn't remember her. Just another commoner she'd stepped on recently...

But Dominqua's lips curled into a smile. "Well, well, Captain Cham. I'd wondered how a common wench had gotten such a lofty position working for the king, but I suppose it should have been clear. I assume you screw Targyon too?"

"Mind your own business, Dominqua," Jev growled, his arm tightening protectively around Zenia.

As much as she appreciated his arm and his protection, it might have been better if he'd pushed her away and pretended they had been in the middle of sparring. Though Zenia supposed the woman had seen too much to believe that.

"Jev, dear," Dominqua said, giving him a long brazen look that included a deliberate study of his crotch. "I can't blame you for falling prey to a woman's wiles. She's a beauty despite her inability to match shoes. I understand she's manipulating you. But perhaps, if you were to join me in the baths tonight, I could be convinced to forget that I saw you about to shove the tramp up against a post."

Hot anger rushed through Zenia, and she lunged away from Jev, wanting nothing more than to slam her fist into the woman.

"I'm sure your husband would prefer to be the one to help you in the baths," Jev said, his tone icy instead of hot.

"He's out late tonight, leaving me all alone." Completely ignoring Zenia, Dominqua batted her eyelashes at Jev and touched her breasts.

"A shame." Jev clasped Zenia's hand, not commenting on the fact that it was balled into a fist, and nodded toward the exit. Maybe he meant to mow over Dominqua if she didn't move out of the way so they could leave.

"If you don't entertain me, I'll be certain to let Zyndari Bludnor know you've been sleeping with this common filth."

Zenia gritted her teeth, reminding herself that she would only end up making trouble for both of them if she punched a zyndari woman— Targyon might not be able to look the other way if one of his agents did that. But the founders knew she wanted to.

A surge of indignation emanated from her dragon tear, and unease replaced Zenia's anger. If the gem acted on her behalf...

She clasped a hand to her chest, willing it to be good. An instant later, flames appeared all around Dominqua.

Zenia's unease turned to sheer terror. She sprinted to the woman, imagining they would have to heft her up and throw her in a bath to put the fire out.

But the flames disappeared as rapidly as they'd appeared, leaving Dominqua standing naked in front of them, her dress and shoes having turned into a pile of ashes at her feet.

She shrieked, nothing seductive this time as she pressed a hand to her breasts. She sprinted out of sight. A sense of smug contentment came from Zenia's dragon tear.

Zenia slumped in relief, glad she'd somehow ended up with a soul more prone to practical jokes than death and destruction. Not for the first time, she wondered if her gem was truly linked to a dragon. None of the legends of dragons spoke of senses of humor.

"I wish it had done that before she looked through the door," Jev said dryly, his own sense of humor returning.

"Me too."

Zenia shook her head as she stared at the ashes, knowing a little magic wouldn't keep the woman from tattling on Jev. As if his unpleasant father needed any more reasons to hate Zenia and want to keep her away from his son.

"I'm sorry I made more trouble for you, Jev. If we didn't need to work together, I'd say we should completely avoid each other until..." She groped in the air with her hand, not sure how to articulate herself. Until after his engagement was called off? But what if it wasn't called off and he was married?

"Absolutely not." He stepped up behind her, wrapped an arm around her waist, and bent his head to rest his temple against hers. "And you have nothing to apologize for. *I'm* sorry I'm not some simple castle clerk that nobody would gain anything from by manipulating."

She leaned back against him and closed her eyes. "Is it wrong for me to fantasize about that?"

"No, I've started to." He kissed her temple. "I told my father I'd walk away from him and my position as his heir if he tried to force me to marry that girl. And I will. I want to be with you, Zenia, and I'm not going to let anyone tell me I can't be."

A rush of happiness went through her, but she tamped it down immediately. It was selfish of her to want him to give up his birthright. She knew he would be a good zyndar prime for his family and all the tenants on his land when the time came. And she knew he considered it his duty to be that person. If she asked him to give up his heritage, it would be like asking him to break a vow.

"Jev, I want to be with you, too, but I don't want you to have to give up everything."

"Too late. I already told him I would. You'll still love me when I'm a simple castle clerk, right?"

"You don't think Targyon will let you keep your Crown Agent job? If you were a clerk, you'd have to follow me around dutifully and hold my books."

"I'd happily do that now." He squeezed her waist and kissed her again. "Alas, my father didn't disown me when I made the threat. A wishful part of me hoped he would. I got the impression he might be willing to deal, but like I told you, Zyndari Bludnor—Fremia's mother—has a dragon tear. I'm almost positive she's manipulating him. That may be why he agreed to the marriage in the first place, after he'd promised me I could at least have the summer to find someone."

"But you said he agreed to meet with me, right?" Zenia shifted in his grip to face him.

"Yes. You don't have to charm him. But if you and your dragon tear could check to see if some kind of spell is over him, I would appreciate it."

"I could do that."

"Good. Thank you." He smiled at her.

The gesture took away some of the misery she felt over the night's turn of events. If she wasn't careful, she would end up wanting to kiss him again. She made herself pat his shoulder, not noticing its appealing nakedness, and step out of his grip.

"I came down here to share my research with you." She glanced to where she'd dropped her notepad.

"Ah, of course. I actually brought Hydal here to ask him if he remembered anything about Vornzylar."

"Did he?"

"A little, yes. He also overheard Zyndar Garlok talking to some other zyndar over drinks and sharing gossip about *us* like some teenage girl. It sounds like Garlok is behind some of the stories circulating about us."

"I'm more concerned about Vornzylar right now."

"So am I, but that doesn't mean I don't want to punch Garlok."

Angry raised voices drifted up the corridor from the direction of the baths. It sounded like Dominqua had found someone to rant to. Not Rhi, Zenia assumed. Rhi would have thumped her, with a bar of soap if her bo wasn't close at hand.

"Maybe we should go to my room," Jev said dryly.

The suggestion sounded innocent enough, but Zenia feared she would find reasons to be distracted again if they ended up sitting together on his bed. And she already worried what the backlash would be for this indiscretion. By the founders, she had finally found a man she cared for and could see marrying, and the world was determined to ensure it wasn't a possibility. Unless he gave up everything. Her heart ached at the notion.

"How about the library?" she suggested.

Jev smiled a little sadly but said, "I'll wash off and meet you up there."

He jogged over, picked up her notepad, and brought it to her. The small thoughtful act made her want to kiss him again. She didn't.

CHAPTER 11

J EV SCRAPED HIS FINGERS THROUGH his damp hair as
he hurried into the library. He hadn't wanted to keep Zenia waiting,
but he also hadn't wanted to plop down in one of Targyon's padded
leather chairs while sweaty and unwashed. And he thought he should
smell good for Zenia, too, just in case she had the urge to lick his chest
again. Founders, where would *that* have gone if that dreadful zyndari
woman hadn't shown up?

He wanted to solve the city's new elf problem as quickly as possible,
if only so he could set things straight with his father and get the freedom
to date Zenia. One way or another.

It had crossed his mind that she might be able to use her dress-
incinerating dragon tear to manipulate his father into changing his
mind about her, but the idea impinged upon his sense of honor. He also
couldn't see her agreeing to it. She might not be zyndari, but that didn't
mean she didn't have honor of her own that she held close. She had a lot
more than many zyndari he'd met lately.

Zenia sat at a table near the door, her notepad and a thick book open.
She'd chosen a public location rather than a private alcove. This late at
night, the library was probably empty of other visitors, but it seemed a
clear statement that she had work on her mind rather than anything else.
Understandable, even if his chest was disappointed.

"Do you share first?" Jev sat in a chair beside her.

"Sure. As I said, I wasn't able to find much about Vornzylar
specifically—nothing, I'm afraid—but the Zsayon are mentioned so often
that there's a whole shelf devoted to them in the elven history section."

"Did you read every book on the shelf?"

She snorted. "Not in three hours."

"*Half* the books?"

"I may have skimmed half of them."

"I thought so." Jev smiled at her. "We had a lot of information on their current activities come through Gryphon Company but not much about historical stuff. They mostly seemed to stir up their people and incite them to attack our camps, but I'm not aware of them having stepped foot in Kor or the other human kingdoms during the war. I'm actually surprised this Vornzylar lured three other wardens to his side, as the elite warriors of the Taziir have traditionally considered Zsayon methods less than honorable." He stopped talking and extended his hand, remembering he'd invited her to go first.

Zenia nodded. "Most of the historical texts suggest they've acted behind the scenes rather than on the open stage. They were supposedly considering an infiltration of Kor ten years ago, which may have prompted King Aldor to preemptively start the war. Their mission seems to be to protect their forests and their people from the other intelligent races in the world. It's not just humans. They've taken actions against ogres, trolls, and orcs too. Interestingly, they don't seem to have worried about dwarves."

"Maybe because dwarves largely keep to themselves and don't start wars. They're pleased enough to finish them, but they're not expansionists. And they tend to claim land—underground land—that other races aren't interested in. I think it's against elven religious beliefs to live in caves, much less underground tunnels."

"I have more notes on them, but I spent more time perusing some of the weaponry typical of elven wardens, so we would know what we're up against." Zenia pushed the open book over to him, revealing a diagram of a familiar sword, the one that had sprouted vines to grab him. A paragraph of description lay under the drawing. She flipped a few pages to show him other magical swords, including one that looked a lot like Lornysh's, with flames appearing to leap from the blade. "The swords are typically the main and often only source of ancillary magic they carry. They're gifts granted to the elves after they complete fifty years of training to become a warden."

"Is that all? Such a short time."

"They study swordsmanship, wildcraft, and magic during those years, and they're not given swords and granted the title of warden unless they can pass tests on all three."

Jev had heard of the extensive training before, so he merely nodded. "Any tips in there for how to defeat the swords?"

"A few dragon tears over the years have been powerful enough to permanently nullify the power in them."

"Break them, essentially?"

"Destroy their magic. The blades themselves weren't necessarily broken. Each one is created by a dwarven master and then infused with elven magic."

Maybe that was why the Zsayon had never picked on dwarves. Elves and dwarves had been allies for so long that it would be foolish to do so. Had either of those races had the expansionist tendencies of humans, they could have worked together to take over the entire world millennia ago.

"Do you think *your* dragon tear can break them?" Jev had never met anyone with a more powerful gem.

"Possibly? It sounds like it takes an hour of intense and uninterrupted focus to do so." She pointed to text on a page that showed a sword and an oval gem. "So, you'd have to disarm the elf and then steal the sword away for me so I could spend some quality time with it."

"*I* would?" Jev touched his chest.

"You've built a rapport with the wardens. You could slip in close."

"They tried to kill me. That's not as rapport-building as you would think."

She smiled, but only briefly before frowning thoughtfully at the page.

"I'll do my best to steal this Vornzylar's sword so you can tote it off to your room to commune with it. Violently." Jev ran his fingers over the sword in the picture. "Though it would be a shame to break such beautiful weapons. I suppose there's no chance any humans have successfully wielded them?"

"There was a chapter early on about that. A prince of Kor managed to acquire one in noble battle once—I read between the lines that he stole it—and it lay dormant for him. Apparently, humans can use them as regular swords, but the magic won't come to life for us. It's tied to elven blood, which is inherently magical." Her eyebrow twitched.

He didn't know if that signified skepticism or envy. Or distaste.

"Here's what Hydal remembered about Vornzylar." Jev withdrew a folded paper with sweat stains on it. He and Hydal had decided to spar in the gym while they spoke since Zyndar Garlok had been in the Crown Agents office, and Jev didn't want the man knowing Hydal was working for them now. Just in case Garlok was doing worse than gossiping about Jev. Who knew if he was feeding important information to some outside source?

"Sorry my notes aren't as neat as yours." He pressed the paper on the table, doing his best to smooth it so it lay flat. "At first, I wasn't going to write anything down, since my memory is as powerful as those elven blades. Then I realized I was asking Hydal for information because I'd forgotten it, and I grabbed the closest pen and paper I could find."

Zenia turned the page over and saw a gymnasium equipment repair diagram on the back. "I see." She scrutinized Jev's notes on the front. "He's only been prominent in the Zsayon faction for five years?"

"As far as Hydal learned from our intelligence operatives. Vornzylar was on a mission on Taziira's northern shoreline, defending the villages up there from frost orcs, and making quite a name for himself as a warrior of renown. Then some family matter drew him back to their capital. Shortly after, he joined the faction and soon became one of their leaders. Interestingly, and I remembered this after Hydal brought it up, an assassin tried to get to Lornysh about a year ago when he was in our camp. Someone reported seeing a glowing white sword—Vornzylar has a magical ice blade—so it's possible he was the would-be assassin. Of course, Lornysh was tight-lipped about everything. As usual."

"Is he just a private person or is he ashamed about something in his past?" Zenia asked.

"More bitter than ashamed is the sense I've always gotten."

"Hm." Did she disagree?

"Have you ever tried to read him with your dragon tear?" Jev asked.

"No. I haven't spoken directly to him that many times." Zenia tapped her chin thoughtfully. "A glowing white sword like one of the elves we faced in the tower had? Was that Vornzylar?"

"Neither of them introduced themselves."

"Rude."

"I thought so."

A breeze touched Jev's cheek, and he frowned and looked around. Maybe someone had left a window open.

The shadows stirred down a dark aisle, and Jev sprang to his feet, reaching for a weapon that wasn't at his waist.

"It's me," came a soft voice in elven.

"Lornysh?"

He walked out of the shadows, his hood down and his silver hair spilling around his shoulders and his backpack. He carried his blade, his bow and quiver of arrows, and everything he'd brought with him after the war.

"You're leaving," Jev said with certainty. He couldn't be surprised. Maybe he ought to simply be pleased Lornysh had come to say goodbye. He must not have wanted to earlier with the other elves watching.

"Yes." Lornysh stopped and looked at Zenia.

She was still sitting at the table, but she gazed back at him, not looking like she intended to leave. Jev didn't want to have to ask her to, but if Lornysh wanted to speak in private…

"If I tell you something in Elvish, will you simply tell her everything later?" Lornysh asked.

"It depends on if it has something to do with her or our case." Jev rested a hand on Zenia's shoulder, not wanting her to feel uncomfortable that they were talking about her, though he wasn't sure how to include her.

"Your case." Lornysh sighed and closed his eyes. "That is what I wish to warn you about before I go. It is my hope that Vornzylar will leave you and Princess Yesleva and all other elves in the city alone after I go, but it's possible he won't. He seems particularly upset that the Taziir king is making this overture toward Kor. Given all that's happened between our two peoples, it does seem premature."

"Maybe your king sees Targyon as a more reasonable ruler than Abdor and hopes he can avoid further hostilities with humanity by forging a peace with him."

"Perhaps." Lornysh looked toward the double doors of the library.

Zenia and Jev had left them open. A breeze stirred again, and the doors closed with soft thumps.

"Have you spoken to this Vornzylar?" Jev thought it sounded like Lornysh had.

"I've done my best to avoid him since I can't kill him."

"Care to explain that? I've never noticed you hesitating to kill people who try to kill you."

"It is difficult to explain him without explaining everything." Lornysh smiled sadly.

"Which you won't do?" Jev had asked a few times over the years about why his friend had left his people, but Lornysh had always refused to answer or pretended he hadn't heard the question.

Lornysh clasped his hands behind his back. "It has nothing to do with you or your people. He—"

He spun toward the far wall of the library, squinting in the direction he had come from.

Jev frowned, turning an ear that way to listen, but he knew Lornysh had superior hearing. He glanced at Zenia, wondering if she had detected anything. She touched her dragon tear and closed her eyes. Asking it, perhaps.

"I heard—" Lornysh started, but then he grabbed his chest and gasped.

Startled, Jev reached for him.

Lornysh's knees buckled, and he dropped to the tile floor, his face contorting with pain. Jev gripped his shoulder, alternately glancing at his friend and at the shadows in the aisles. Nothing stirred except for that faint breeze from the window Lornysh must have left open. Or *had* he left it open?

Zenia's chair scraped on the tiles as she stood. Her eyebrows drew together in puzzlement.

"What is it, Lornysh?" Jev whispered. "Some kind of magical assault?" He had a hard time believing his hale elven friend was having a heart attack.

Lornysh nodded his head jerkily. "Get out of here," he gasped. "He only wants me. Don't... put yourself... risk."

"Well, he doesn't *get* you." Jev released Lornysh and looked at Zenia again. "Can you detect someone using magic? Tell if Lornysh's attacker is in here?"

Her dragon tear glowed a soft blue, the light leaking between her fingers as she gripped it.

"He's not in here," she whispered, her eyes distant. "He's crouching on the wall surrounding the castle. The guards don't see him. Them. There are two."

Jev grimaced, remembering the battle in the tower.

"Wait, the guards are unconscious." She grimaced. "Or dead. I can't—"

A *clink, clink, clank* came from deep within the library. Jev snatched a lamp off a wall and ran down an aisle of books toward the noise. The lamplight barely pushed back the deep night shadows.

A sweet and acrid scent tickled his nostrils. It reminded him of his aunt grilling limes for her honey-lime shrimp recipe. He held his breath, worried it was something far more nefarious than citrus.

At the end of the aisle, Jev spotted one of the tall windows standing open to the night. A faint smoke hazed the air in front of it, the grilled lime scent growing stronger. Something glinted on the floor, reflecting his lamplight. An odd eight-sided canister with rounded corners. It was the source of the haze—a steady stream of blue smoke wafted from a small aperture.

Jev snatched it up, the sides icy cold in his hand, and ran to the window. As he drew his arm back to throw it, he spotted a figure crouched atop the wall on the far side of the courtyard. A figure with a bow drawn and aimed in his direction.

"Intruder!" Jev yelled as he threw the strange canister toward the archer.

Hoping enough guards were awake to hear the cry and investigate, he leaped aside. An arrow blurred past, almost shaving his jaw. It thudded into a bookcase, the fletching quivering.

Jev put his back to the solid stone wall between two windows and did his best to shout again from behind cover. "Intruder in the castle!"

His voice was hoarse, and his throat hurt. He realized he'd released his breath to yell, and that smoke still hung in the air.

"Zenia, Lornysh," he called. "Are you all right?"

He was surprised Zenia hadn't followed him, but maybe she'd wanted to stay with Lornysh since he was defenseless as long as that magic gripped him. Jev slammed the window shut—not that the glass would stop an arrow—and ran back toward them.

"Here," came Zenia's voice from the table where he'd left her. It was strained. And hoarse.

Worrying the smoke had also reached them, Jev tried to sprint the rest of the way back, but his legs felt oddly rubbery. He stumbled, his feet numb, and his shoulder smashed against shelves. The case shuddered, and several books fell to the floor.

He growled, shaking off the strange ennui, and stumbled the rest of the way down the aisle. He passed another wide open window, but that was the least of his problems. An elf in green and brown leathers and a dark green cloak faced Zenia, a glowing silver sword held aloft.

Jev almost barked a warning, but Zenia already faced the elf, her hand raised, blue tendrils of light emanating from her dragon tear. The magic curled up her arm and spread from her fingers toward her adversary. The elf himself was frozen in tableau.

Lornysh was on his hands and knees on the floor between them, struggling to rise. The elf warden was poised, not to attack Zenia but to cleave him in half.

Jev threw his knife at the intruder's back.

He expected some magical shield to appear around the elf and deflect the blade, but Zenia must have commanded his full attention. The knife landed point first and sank into the back of his shoulder.

The elf screamed in surprise and pain, almost dropping his sword.

As if the knife attack had broken some spell, Lornysh sprang to his feet, yanking his own sword free of its sheath. He barked a word in Elvish, and magical flames sprang to life along the blade.

The intruder snarled, reached over his shoulder, and managed to grab Jev's knife and yank it free. He threw it at Zenia.

"No," Jev shouted and sprang at the elf.

The bloody knife hurtled toward Zenia's chest, and at that range, she didn't have time to dodge. But a shimmering blue shield flashed in the air all around her. The blade bounced off instead of hitting her.

That didn't keep Jev, fury flushing his body with strength, from slamming into the elf and taking him to the floor. He slammed a fist into his foe's jaw before an icy cold power wrapped around his heart, and pain sprang from his chest.

Jev gripped the elf and tried to stay on top of him, tried to smash him against the floor and knock him out, but the pain was too much. Numbness flooded his body, and his grip loosened. It felt like his heart was being ripped from his chest.

The elf flung Jev off and rolled to the side an instant before Lornysh came in, aiming his sword at their foe's head. Though Jev was in too much pain to help, he noticed Lornysh used the flat of his blade. As if he didn't truly want to hurt the elf. What in the founders' hells was stopping him? This elf wanted to hurt *him*.

"Jev!" Zenia rushed to his side and gripped his shoulder.

Such pain filled Jev that he couldn't reply, couldn't do anything except gasp, "Wall," and wish he could telepathically convey that the elf outside was the one applying magic to him. He was certain the warden inside was too busy to be the one responsible.

Swords clashed, the warden leaving silver streaks in the air as he swept his blade to meet Lornysh's again and again. Lornysh defended himself, his eyes set with determination, but he never took the role of aggressor. He wasn't the deadly killer Jev was accustomed to.

Zenia sprinted toward the window. Jev tried to rise to follow her, but blackness was creeping into his vision. Fear followed— Was it possible this magic would stop his heart and kill him?

"Arrows!" he blurted, reminded that the elf on the wall had a bow. "Watch out... for them."

A horn blew in the courtyard. Jev hoped that meant the guards were awake and would fight off the elves.

The pain around Jev's chest stopped so abruptly he almost blacked out. He gasped in air, his entire body trembling.

Zenia stood at the open window, that blue shield around her again as she thrust her arm outward, more magic flowing from her fingers. Jev hoped she was knocking that elf off the wall and all the way back to Taziira.

He grabbed the table and pulled himself up. Lornysh cried out in pain as his enemy's blade slipped through his defenses.

The double doors to the library banged open, and a cadre of guards charged inside. The elf hesitated, then cursed and sprinted toward the open window.

"Look out," Jev rasped, afraid Zenia wouldn't see him coming up behind her.

She turned in time and flung the window shut. The warden swung his sword at her head.

"No!" Jev yelled.

The silvery sword halted in midair as it struck her shield, but her dragon tear's visible barrier disappeared as the blade collided with it.

Zenia stumbled back, fingers tightening around her gem and alarm flashing across her face.

The guards fired at the elf. He turned around long enough to fling a canister identical to the one Jev had seen earlier. Then he sprang through the window, glass shattering.

He disappeared into the courtyard below. The guards charged toward the window, almost knocking Zenia aside.

Jev snatched up the canister and ran to another window. He jerked it open and flung the smoking projectile outside. Then he rushed to Zenia, worried she'd been hurt when her barrier fell.

Next to them, the guards fired through the broken window, aiming downward, but then shifting their aim upward, as if the elf was scaling the wall to escape. Maybe he was.

"Are you all right?" Jev wrapped his arm around Zenia.

"Yes, but Lornysh." She pointed back toward the doors.

Lornysh lay crumpled on the floor, blood pooling on the tiles around him. Cursing, Jev ran to him, chagrined that he'd worried about Zenia first and hadn't noticed his friend had been so badly injured. By the Air Dragon, what if the warden had finished his mission before fleeing? What if Lornysh was dead?

Jev dropped to his knees, resting a hand on his friend's shoulder. The amount of blood on the floor terrified him.

"Lornysh, are you still… awake?" Jev spotted a dagger sticking out of Lornysh's stomach.

He cursed again and pulled his shirt over his head. He wadded it up and did his best to staunch the flow of the blood without disturbing the dagger. A trained healer would need to withdraw it.

"I need a healer!" Jev hollered toward the hallway, fearing nobody would hear him.

But the guards had stopped firing, and his voice rang out, the castle having gone disturbingly quiet.

"Tell your king," an accented voiced called from the courtyard, or perhaps the wall opposite the library windows, "that he harbors an assassin, a criminal, and an enemy to the Taziir. If he doesn't send Lornysh the traitor out of your castle and your city by dawn, we will use our power to raze your kingdom to the ground."

"He's going to do that with four people?" Zenia asked.

"You have no right to be here, Vornzylar," a feminine voice answered from somewhere below the library windows. Jev imagined the princess standing on the front steps of the castle and yelling up at the elf—or elves—on the wall. "Return to Taziira, by the king's will. Leave this human land without doing more harm."

"Your will is not the king's will. We go where we please. We are free Taziir. Hear my words, human king, wherever you are cowering. You have until dawn!"

Rifles fired outside. Jev shook his head, knowing the guards wouldn't hit the wardens.

Lornysh's eyelids fluttered but then squeezed shut again, his lips curling in pain.

"Lornysh," Jev said. "Why in all the world were you using the flat of your blade?"

Zenia came up to them but took one look at the blood and said, "I'll get a healer."

"Thank you," Jev said as she raced out of the library. "Hold on, Lornysh," he whispered. "We'll get you fixed up. You're not leaving the city yet."

Jev thought of the warden's threat but was certain Targyon wouldn't give in to a bully or dump an injured friend onto the street outside the castle to fend for himself.

The courtyard fell silent again. Jev had a feeling the elves had disappeared without being captured or seriously wounded. No, at least one had taken a knife in the back. Jev hoped that would slow the elf down for a while.

"Amuzhara?" Lornysh whispered, his eyes opening, though they were pained and unfocused. "Is that you, Amuzhara?"

"It's Jev." Fresh worry thrummed through his veins. "Are you with me, Lornysh? A healer is coming to help you."

"I thought it might be Amuzhara," he whispered, sounding devastated that it wasn't. His eyes closed again.

Afraid that his friend neared death, Jev was relieved when one of the castle healers arrived with two assistants carrying a stretcher.

"It's an elf," one of the assistants blurted.

Jev stood up, bracing himself to argue for his friend's right to aid.

"Get him to my infirmary," the healer said, waving her helper to silence.

The man clenched his jaw.

"Help her," came Targyon's stern voice from the corridor. He stood there with Zenia at his side.

The assistant jumped and blurted, "Yes, Sire."

The trio shifted Lornysh onto the stretcher and carried him out. Targyon strode after them, as if he meant to personally see to it that Lornysh was cared for. Good.

Jev started to follow them but paused when Zenia stepped forward to hug him.

"He'll be all right," she whispered.

"Yes," Jev said, returning the hug and glad for her support. "Thank you for helping."

"I wish I could have done more." She grimaced, and Jev had a feeling she had, for the first time, encountered people with power that was equal to or greater than that of her dragon tear.

"We'd probably all be dead if you hadn't done what you did," he said.

She didn't appear comforted.

CHAPTER 12

AFTER ZENIA WASHED AND APPLIED bandages to the small wounds she'd received from shards of glass flying when the elf leaped through the window, she went to the castle's infirmary. Targyon, the princess, her two bodyguards, and Jev were all in there, standing back as the healer worked on Lornysh, her dragon tear glowing a soft yellow on her chest.

Lornysh lay shirtless on a bed with his arms at his sides as one of the assistants finished tying a bandage around his abdomen. His pack and weapons leaned against the wall by a window. The shirt draped atop them was so saturated with blood that Zenia couldn't imagine it ever being clean again.

Jev looked at her when she walked in and lifted an arm in offering. He stood off to one side, not joining in whatever quiet conversation Targyon and Princess Yesleva were having.

Zenia joined him, leaning against his side as he wrapped his arm around her shoulders. Before coming up here, he'd put on a pistol belt with two holsters and an ammo pouch. Zenia never would have thought they would be in danger inside the castle walls, but now she knew better. And she knew how powerful their adversaries were. The more times she ran into these elf wardens, the more amazed she was that humans had survived for a month, much less ten years over on their continent. What idiot had thought it a good idea to make war on the Taziir?

Targyon left the princess's side—she looked tired and sad as she stood with her hands in the voluminous sleeves of the sage-colored robe she wore—and crouched beside the healer. He murmured a few words.

Zenia didn't hear them all but got the gist, that he was asking to be kept notified of changes. Then he rested a hand on Lornysh's arm before standing and heading for the door.

"I don't think he's going to be better by dawn," Jev said quietly.

"So long as he gets better," Targyon said. "We're not kicking him out."

Jev nodded, probably not surprised by Targyon's statement, but Zenia sensed relief from him. Maybe he had been a little worried that their king would decide it was too much of a risk to keep Lornysh here. Zenia hoped none of Targyon's guards had been killed by the elves.

She rubbed her face, hardly believing there had only been two of those wardens. There were at least two more out there somewhere, waiting to add their skills to the fight to destroy Lornysh. And what if there were even more than that? Her informant had seen four at the tower, but that didn't mean more couldn't be in the city.

The princess walked out after Targyon, taking her bodyguards and leaving only Jev, Zenia, the healer, and her assistants in the room. Though her eyes were still closed, the healer murmured something to the assistants, and they also left.

She looked over at Jev, her hair in a long gray braid that hung over one shoulder. She was the same woman who had tended to Lunis Drem a few weeks earlier. What was her name? Neena.

"He will return to consciousness soon," Neena told Jev. "I've sealed the internal organs that were punctured by the blade, but it will still take time for his body to heal. Not as long as a human body, I believe, but he'll need to stay largely immobile for a few days. I gave him some pain potion—" she pointed to a dark brown glass bottle of Grodonol's Pain-No-More on the bedside table, a dagger with a red X over it on the label, "—but you can give him more if he needs it. It'll make him a little woozy, but that's better than being in horrendous pain."

"Are you telling me all this because I've been volunteered to be his nurse?" Jev asked.

"My assistants *are* afraid of him." Neena smiled. "Most of the staff is on edge at the presence of the elf entourage, but a beautiful princess is somewhat less alarming to them than a surly elf warrior."

"How do you know he's surly?"

"He woke briefly when I removed the dagger. And he spoke."

"A dagger being pulled out of one's gut does have a tendency to make one snippy," Jev said.

Zenia was amused that he was defending Lornysh's surliness. She had spoken to the elf enough times to believe the adjective applied well, even without daggers and injuries involved.

Neena rose to her feet, poured water from a pitcher into a glass on the bedside table, then headed for the door. "My room is just down the hall." She pointed in the direction Targyon and the others had gone. "Second door there. Please come get me if he's in pain or needs anything."

She yawned, no doubt drained from healing Lornysh. As Zenia well knew, the dragon tear held the power, but it was funneled through its human handler, and it was a tiring experience. She inadvertently mirrored the yawn, but she turned it into a smile when Jev looked at her.

"It looks like you have a new roommate," she observed.

"There's only one bed in my room."

"Then I hope you two grew very close during the war."

Jev's mouth twisted. "Not *that* close."

Zenia patted him on the stomach. She was about to ask if he would mind if she went to bed—it had to be after midnight by now, and they still had an assignment, to find where those elves were staying. She doubted the two who had come to the castle had left address cards.

"But he can have my bed," Jev added. "I can sleep on the floor."

"Not under the window, I hope," Zenia said. "That seems to be the preferred method of entry for elves."

Jev snorted. "I'll have to talk to Targyon about bars for the windows. Magical elf-proof bars."

"Do such things exist?" Zenia had no trouble imagining those magical swords slicing through metal bars like butter.

"Maybe Master Grindmor can make some. I sent word to her shop that Lornysh was injured. I think Cutter has been sleeping there. If he's sleeping at all. She's quite the slave driver. But he seems to like it."

"Maybe he's sleeping on her floor under a window."

"Possibly. Dwarves think mattresses are too soft and squishy. A good slab of stone keeps one's back healthy, Cutter tells me."

"Jev," came a wan whisper from the bed.

Jev released Zenia and stepped up to Lornysh's side. "I'm glad you remember who I am, my friend. Earlier, you were calling me some woman's name."

Lornysh sighed, his eyes barely open. "Amuzhara. She no longer lives."

"I'm glad I'm not her then."

"For a moment, I thought I might be going to join her in the Eternal Garden."

"You're too young and surly to take up an afterlife of gardening." Jev dragged over a stool and sat on it.

"Surly?"

"The healer assured me of it."

"Mm."

"Want some pain potion? The healer said you could have another glug."

Lornysh's lips twisted. "Is that why my head is fuzzy?"

"Maybe. Or it could be that you lost a couple of gallons of blood on the floor."

"There is no need to be melodramatic. The average elven body contains only approximately five-point-three liters of blood in its entirety."

Zenia thought about slipping out and leaving the men to their banter, but Jev smiled over at her, rolled his eyes, and mouthed, "Surly."

"Your female is here," Lornysh said. "I sense her dragon tear."

"Yes, she is," Jev said. "If she and her dragon tear hadn't helped, we might both be dead."

"I know."

Jev raised his eyebrows, as if he expected Lornysh to say something else, but he fell silent.

"That was Elvish," Jev told her. "It translates to he appreciates your help and he's relieved you're in my life."

"Ah," she said. "That's good to know since I don't speak Elvish."

"I'm a good translator. Have no fear." Jev looked at Lornysh, as if he hoped his friend would crack a smile.

Zenia hadn't seen him smile yet, whether he was injured or not, so it would have surprised her.

"Amuzhara was the love of my life," Lornysh said, his eyes closed.

Jev's eyebrows flew up. Zenia assumed that meant this was new information to him. Or perhaps that it was shocking that Lornysh was sharing it.

"She was also Vornzylar's twin sister," Lornysh said. "They were very close."

Jev digested that a moment before asking, "What happened?"

"There was a fire. The tree in which her house was built burned down, and she didn't get out in time. She died."

"That's awful," Zenia whispered, then clasped a hand over her mouth. She hadn't meant to butt into their conversation.

"Vornzylar believes I did it. I did not. I adored her, even after she rejected me. I investigated all around the tree and questioned everyone, in case it wasn't an accident. But several people saw the lightning strike that started the fire. It seems it was a freak accident of nature. Or, for some unfathomable reason, the will of the gods."

The Taziir, Zenia recalled, believed in gods that lived in the natural world and dismissed the dragon founders as mere dragons that had died long ago.

"Why did she reject you?" Jev asked.

"For the same reason they all did."

Jev looked toward the bottle of painkiller, maybe wondering if another slug of the stuff would make his friend more likely to keep sharing. Zenia suspected the initial dose was the reason he was speaking now. Maybe he would have shared with Jev anyway, but she had a hard time believing Lornysh would, in his typical mind state, reveal anything of his past in front of her.

"Princess Yesleva is my half-sister," Lornysh said.

Zenia frowned at the change in topic.

Jev's eyebrows flew up again. "Yesleva is King Yvelon's daughter."

"Yes. And I am his son."

Jev's jaw dropped.

Lornysh opened his eyes, but not to look at either of them. He gazed at the ceiling and continued on in the tone one might use to recite a passage from a book. Or perhaps to recite a piece of history.

"He was only Crown Prince Yvelon at the time I was born. After his wife died, he abandoned his duties for a time to mourn her. He walked the forests of Taziira for years and eventually crossed the sea and found one of the colonies of elves in Shangdalor, one believed to have been lost, but its inhabitants had merely chosen to adopt an insular existence and work on their art away from the politics of the Taziir nation.

"There, on a small wooded island with a single mountain at its core, he found love again in the arms of an elf female. He talked her into returning to the mainland with him. Historians there researched her lineage and discovered she was a descendent of Simora, the bard and great warrior of our third century after founding. Simora was the firstborn to Emperor Hy-marishon, back when we were an empire and the rest of the races were little more than clans of people living in hide huts. The descendants of Hy-marishon were all thought to be long dead, so when it was learned that this woman—my mother—was of that line, our people decided that any offspring born to her and my father would have a greater right to rule than those born earlier to my father and his first wife. She had been his loyal love but had also been the equivalent of a commoner in your land."

Zenia listened intently, almost wishing she had her notepad with her. She knew little of elven history and was hearing many of these names for the first time.

"I can't imagine the king's firstborn liked being replaced as heir," Jev said.

"Not his firstborn, second born, or third born, no," Lornysh said, his gaze still toward the ceiling, a distant and unfocused aspect to his silver eyes. "It was actually his third born who thought to do some more research on my mother and see if it was possible the genealogists had been mistaken. By this time, I was a grown elf in training to become a warden and your people had sent their first armies to our southern shores.

"Since my father, the king, was a mere four hundred years old, I didn't expect to become king any time soon, nor did I even want to be his heir. I'd always thought rule should be decided based on a person's merit and aptitude rather than blood, in a similar manner as to how the dwarves do it, but nobody cared much what I thought. At the least, few in my family listened except for my mother. My half-brothers and half-sisters were grown and traveling the world when I was a youth, so I barely knew them, but I knew they all resented me. Even my sisters, who would never have become rulers, resented that my father had taken another woman after their mother passed."

"So, you and Princess Yesleva aren't close," Jev said.

"No. She occasionally deigned to speak with me when we crossed paths when I was young, but that was infrequent."

"All this means you're a lot younger than I realized," Jev said. "I always thought you were one of those crusty old elves of at least five hundred."

Lornysh snorted softly.

"I had no idea you were a prince—the *crown* prince? Should I be kneeling to you? Arranging a better healing spot for you than the bed in my room?" Jev was smiling and joking, but his eyes seemed troubled when he looked over at Zenia. Maybe even bewildered. This was definitely new news to him.

"I am nothing now." Lornysh closed his eyes again.

"Because you attacked your own people during the war?" Jev asked.

Lornysh was silent again, and Zenia feared he would stop talking. Now that he'd started, she wanted to hear the whole story.

"That came after they drove me out," he finally said.

"Your people kicked you out?" Jev asked. "Because of the fire?"

"Because of what my half-brother dug up. My mother is indeed a descendant of Emperor Hy-marishon, but she is also the descendant of a half-elf traveler who visited the colony in her grandmother's day."

Jev leaned back on the stool and twitched when he realized his seat didn't have a back. "You're part human?" he asked when he recovered.

"My mother is one-eighth human. I am one-sixteenth."

"One *sixteenth*. Lornysh, who could possibly care about such minor dilution?"

"My people. And you know the word they use for it." Lornysh met Jev's eyes. "It's not dilution."

Jev grimaced. "*Sythok.*" Jev looked at Zenia. "Somewhere between infection, parasite, and taint. It's not literal. Elves like to take poetic license."

"The revelation made for quite an outcry, and my father was horrified. He looked at me as if he'd discovered I were three-quarters orc. My mother, the last I heard, fled back to her colony and isn't speaking to my father. The Council of Elders revoked my right to be my father's heir and asked me to leave."

"Because you're one-sixteenth human," Jev said, disbelief in his tone.

"Because they deemed me unclean. You are aware that those of mixed blood are not welcome in Taziira. They are permitted to travel through the forests, as humans were before the war, but they may not live in our cities and become subjects of the king. They have no rights to inherit belongings or dwellings or hereditary positions."

"I knew half-elves weren't allowed, but I didn't realize... by the founders, Lornysh. One-sixteenth. Do you even have any human traits? I've certainly never noticed any."

"Thank you." Lornysh sounded genuinely pleased, though it was short-lived. He closed his eyes again. "I was angry and felt it unjust. I didn't care about being the king's heir—I was even relieved when that announcement was made."

"I can imagine," Jev murmured, and Zenia knew he was thinking of his own situation.

"But when they ordered me to leave by the end of the year, I knew it would mean leaving Amuzhara. Her work was there, all her business, her gallery. I asked if she would consider giving it up and moving with me, but she said no." Thus far, Lornysh had been delivering the story in a matter-of-fact, even grudgingly accepting, way, but bitterness crept into his tone now. "I believed—she'd led me to believe—that we would wed. But as soon as she learned about my unclean state, she began distancing herself from me. Looking back, I should have realized that it was over before I even suggested moving. But I wasn't that wise then.

"I left in anger with red hazing my vision, and when I stumbled across your army—fell into the hands of your scouts, as you'll recall—I was still furious. I wanted to hurt my people. The people who were no longer my people. I was happy to be your king's assassin."

"Actions which turned you from an exile to a hated enemy," Jev said quietly, certainly.

"Yes."

"And Vornzylar wants to kill you to punish you and avenge those you killed."

"And because he believes I, in my anger, burned Amuzhara's home. The three of us had been close once. He taught some of my classes when I was training to be a warden."

"That's why you can't kill him," Jev said.

"That is why."

"Well, that doesn't mean *I* can't kill him."

Lornysh turned his head away. "I am tired, Jevlain. I do not want to see him killed, but I also do not want to fight him anymore. I *never* wanted to fight him."

"You won't have to. You just stay in the castle and rest." Jev touched his shoulder, then stood up. "Healer Neena has already decided you should get my room. I'd have a guard push the armoire in front of the window, if I were you. Castle windows are like catnip to elves, apparently."

Zenia thought that might evoke a hint of a smile from Lornysh, but he only stared at the far wall, as if he hadn't heard.

Jev patted his shoulder again, moved the pain potion closer to him, and headed to the door. Zenia followed him out. Once they were out of even elven earshot, he stopped and faced her.

"Can you use your dragon tear to track down Vornzylar?" he asked intently.

"I…" Could she? She hadn't considered it, but those elves all carried magical swords and her dragon tear could sense other sources of magic. Could it do so across many miles?

"He's the one who attacked us in the library. Your dragon tear will be familiar with his sword, and I'm sure that wherever *it* is, he is."

Zenia clasped her dragon tear and closed her eyes, formulating the request through thoughts rather than words. She hadn't gotten a good look at the elf's face, but she could envision the glowing silver sword well enough. She imagined racing through the streets of the city with a leashed dog, on the trail of the elf and his magical blade.

The dragon tear imparted a somewhat different image to her.

She was running along the highway east of the city, miles away from Korvann and the castle, and instead of a dog, she was accompanied by a magnificent green dragon flapping its wings as it flew over her head on the trail of the elf. A wistful sense of longing accompanied the vision, and she didn't quite grasp what the dragon tear meant. Did it feel it couldn't quite track the elf? Or maybe it wanted to be in dragon form and out there flying free?

The equivalent of a nod of agreement came to her.

Before she could formulate a response in her thoughts, elves came into view in the vision. Four of them rode on horses headed away from the city. Vornzylar, a bloody bandage wrapping under his armpit and over his shoulder, led the way. His sword was sheathed, but the pommel glowed its distinctive silver. He glanced over his shoulder and squinted straight at Zenia, as if he could somehow sense her watching him through these magical means.

She shrank back, and the vision faded.

"He's heading away from the city, following the coastal highway," she said, growing aware again of Jev. He was still watching her intently. "To the east."

"Toward Dharrow land?"

"That direction, but I have no way to know his final destination. I think I can check again, but I better wait. He seemed to sense me."

"Understood. Thank you. I'll tell Targyon and find out if he's sent word to the archmages yet. We're going to need magical help if we're going to take on those elves."

"I agree."

Zenia thought of how her dragon tear hadn't been enough tonight even though it was the most powerful one she'd encountered in the city. Even if Targyon *could* convince the Temple leaders to send mages, would it be enough?

CHAPTER 13

S HORTLY BEFORE DAWN, JEV WATCHED from the castle
courtyard as Captain Krox, the current garrison commander for
the troops that had stayed on full-time after returning from the
war, marched a platoon through the gate. Jev tried to look attentive, and
grateful that help was coming, but he had only slept a few hours, and he
kept yawning.

"Platoon, halt," Krox called after the fifty-odd men had entered.
"Form it up!"

They hustled to divide themselves into four squads facing him. Jev
recognized some of the men and was glad Krox had brought veterans
to help with the elves. He would be even more glad if Targyon was able
to convince the archmages to send trained mages with dragon tears. It
seemed unfair that they needed such forces to go after four elves, but
four elves with magic almost equaled the might of a dragon.

Expecting Zenia at any moment, Jev kept glancing over his shoulder
as Krox barked orders at his men, running them through push-ups and
other calisthenics while they waited. The exercises were awkward since
the soldiers all wore short swords or daggers at their waists and had
rifles and packs strapped to their backs.

Someone jogged out the side door of the castle nearest the Crown
Agents' office, but it wasn't Zenia. Their new secretary, Sevy, hurried
toward Jev, her dark hair clasped behind her neck and a set of fat books
under her arm.

"Zyndar Jev," she blurted. "Captain Cham is having a—a—I'm not
sure. She gripped her desk, and her eyes are all glazed as if she's in

a trance. We'd been talking about the new batch of reports, and she went rigid in the middle of a sentence. Uhm, her dragon tear is glowing through her shirt."

Jev cursed, barked a, "Thanks," and rushed for the door.

He almost crashed into Zyndar Garlok, who was heading up the walkway with his mug and satchel.

"You need help finding the office, Dharrow?" he asked, deliberately planting himself in Jev's path. "It's in the basement in case you've forgotten because you're never there."

Jev, remembering Hydal's words that Garlok had been behind at least some of the rumors circulated about him and Zenia, stopped long enough to punch him in the nose. Garlok reeled back, dropping his mug and satchel.

"You're fired, jackass," Jev growled, then raced around him and toward the door.

"I was appointed by Targyon," Garlok snarled after him. "You can't fire me."

"I just did. Go gossip about it to your cronies."

Jev ran inside, not waiting for a response, and sprinted down to the office. Numerous lamps burned on walls and desks, but nobody was in there except—

"Zenia!" Jev yelled, spotting her kneeling on the floor between their desks, clenching the edge of the closest. Her other hand gripped her dragon tear, and a sickly bluish-green light leaked between her fingers. "Zenia, what happened?"

He cracked his hip on a desk as he ran down the center aisle, but he didn't slow down. He dropped to his knees in front of her and gripped her shoulders.

Zenia's eyes were open, but she didn't react.

"Is it the elves?" Jev whispered. "Some attack? Or is it your gem?"

She didn't seem to see or hear him, or even be aware that he was in front of her.

"Dragon tear, let her go," Jev ordered, though he had no idea if the thing could understand.

He gently gripped her hand and tried to peel her fingers away from the gem. Maybe if he could break her contact with it...

A magical wall slammed into him, knocking him away with such force that he skidded on his ass along the tiles until his back cracked into one of the desks. Papers and knickknacks rained down on him.

"Jev?" Zenia asked uncertainly, her voice weak.

He rushed back to her side, dropping to his knees, but he hesitated to touch her again. "Zenia? What is it? What's wrong?"

"I—" She swallowed and looked down at her chest. The dragon tear had gone dark. "Nothing. Just a dream."

"People don't dream with their eyes open. Sevy said you fell into a trance."

"It was one of my nightmares about being a prisoner in a cave." She frowned and touched the dragon tear. "I can't sense it. It's cold. Something happened."

"Yeah, it knocked you to the floor and took over your mind." Jev's fingers twitched with the urge to pull it over her head and toss it to the other side of the room where it couldn't influence her.

"No, I mean something happened to it. To the soul the gem is linked to. Him. Or maybe her. I've never been certain."

"Because little oval gems don't have genitalia, Zenia." Jev rested his hands on her waist, prepared to help her to her feet if she was ready. "Can you stand? Krox has brought some troops. We're going to have to meet with them and give them what intel we have on the elves. I don't suppose you could check on them again and see where they holed up for the night?"

"I can't check on anything." She held the dragon tear out on its chain, the gem still dark. "I don't sense it anymore, and I don't think I can call upon any magic."

Dread filled Jev. Thus far, her dragon tear was the only thing that had been effective against the powerful elf wardens.

Zenia's eyes held similar dread, and concern, as well. "I'm worried about it. And without it... I have nothing to offer."

"You have *plenty* to offer." Jev helped her to her feet and wrapped her in a hug.

Light flared between their chests. Startled, he released her and backed away.

The gem pulsed with a strong blue light, the hue appearing healthier than the green-tinted blue from before.

"It appears to be back," he noted dryly.

Zenia wrapped her fingers around it again. Jev was tempted to grab her wrist and stop her, lest she be pulled into another trance.

Her mouth twisted. "It's refusing to tell me what happened."

"Rude."

"I think when it shares the dreams with me, it's unintentional. I wish I knew how to help it. The soul linked to it."

"At the risk of being rude myself, could you check on the elves again? It concerned me that you detected them heading east last night." Toward his family's land. Other zyndar families held land out in that direction, but the Dharrows had a lot of it and close to the city. Jev worried they would find out those elves had been taking refuge in the forest on the back half of his family's acreage.

"Yes, I will." Zenia took a deep breath. Was she shaken from that dream or trance or whatever it had been? "Give me a moment, please."

"Can I get you anything? Something to drink? To eat? The kitchen staff was awake and cooking when I went by on my way out."

"Maybe after this." She smiled at him, but it seemed wan.

Jev felt guilty for asking her to use the dragon tear again so soon after she'd experienced something that had disturbed her. "Never mind. We'll ride out in that direction and look the old-fashioned way once we hear back about those mages."

"It's all right. It won't take me long to check again." Zenia smiled again and touched his jaw. "Besides, I like having you hold me."

"Oh? I'm willing to do that anytime, you know. Just come up and lean on me, and I'll wrap my arms around you."

"Good to know." Zenia took another deep breath, as if she were bracing herself for something painful, then closed her eyes.

He frowned, wishing he hadn't asked at all. He didn't want her risking pain or discomfort simply to help him.

"I sense them," she whispered. "The dragon tear is familiar with Vornzylar now and can find him quickly. I just have to make sure he doesn't sense *me*."

Jev's frown only deepened. He feared the elves might be able to attack her somehow through her link with—

Zenia gasped and stiffened in his arms. Her lips rippled back in pain.

Damn it, why had he asked her to use the thing again?

"Zenia?" Jev stroked her hair. "Come back to me. Forget it, all right?"

Her knees buckled. If he hadn't been holding her, she would have crumpled to the floor again.

ELVEN FURY

Zenia's eyes flew open. Her hand jerked up, found his arm, and gripped it tightly. Her breathing came rapidly, as if she'd run a race.

"I'm sorry," he whispered, knowing his request was the reason for her pain.

"He sensed me."

"Vornzylar?"

"Yes. He looked right at me, the same as last time. He touched his sword and—I'm not sure what exactly he did. Some kind of mental attack. Somehow, he was able to hurt me even across many miles."

"Then no more searching for him. Not that way. We'll get some hounds if we need to find him."

"No need," she whispered. Her face had grown ashen. "He and his three friends were on your property, standing in some trees across the pond from your castle and looking at it."

A harsh chill hammered Jev's spine. "Why? What could they want there?"

He had the urge to sprint to the stable, snatch the first horse, and gallop out to Dharrow Castle. Was there some reason the elves would target his family? Because he'd befriended Lornysh and they hadn't been able to kill him? Would they hurt Jev's kin in order to get to him, and through him to Lornysh? His mind balked at the twisted logic, but that didn't keep him from fearing for his family.

"I'm not sure. I couldn't tell what they were thinking. I just saw them, as if I were a bird flying above them." She tilted her head, a touch of wonder entering her voice as she added, "Or a dragon."

"I wish we *did* have a dragon. I hear they're faster than horses."

She snorted softly, patted his arm, and released it. "We better take your friend's men and go out there right away. I don't think we can wait for Targyon to sweet-talk the archmages."

"No." Jev grimaced at the idea of fighting those elves without more magic at their backs—especially if something was going on with Zenia's dragon tear and it might not be reliable—but he had to check on his family and make sure they weren't in danger. As soon as possible.

"I wonder if they could be looking for that magical stone on your property," Zenia mused. "Didn't Lornysh say it was for communicating with other elves?"

Jev swore. "I'd forgotten about that." He released Zenia and thumped a fist against the nearest desk. "I bet that's it. I bet they're calling in reinforcements."

"More wardens?"

Jev envisioned more powerful elves with powerful magical swords appearing to come after Lornysh and any elf tying to befriend Kor. "By the founders, I hope not."

The steam carriage hissed and rattled as it turned off the kingdom highway and charged up the bumpy road toward Dharrow Castle.

Zenia, Rhi, and Jev sat on a bench opposite two army officers, everyone's shoulders and knees knocking together as the vehicle jostled them about. The rest of the soldiers were coming in steam wagons requisitioned from the king's vehicle house. Rhi had almost missed arriving at work in time to join the caravan, and she'd had a few snippy words about Zenia trying to leave for an epic adventure without her.

Jev sat with his elbows on his knees, his fingers threaded together, and his chin resting on them. His jaw was tense, his eyes tight. He definitely didn't see this as an *adventure*.

Zenia wanted to rest a reassuring hand on his back, but she didn't know Captain Krox or the other officer—a zyndar lieutenant who'd fought with them in the war. The last thing she and Jev needed were more rumors spreading about their relationship.

"Dharrow Castle ahead," the driver called back from the bench outside the carriage.

"Maybe they'll have breakfast prepared for us," Rhi muttered. "Since we had to leave before eating."

"You didn't have to come." Zenia didn't mind having Rhi along, but she worried physical strength and weapons would be a poor match for the elves. She hoped Targyon had arranged for some mages to follow as soon as possible.

Jev pressed his forehead against the window in the door. He looked like he might open it and peer out, no matter that they were flying along an uneven road at close to thirty miles an hour.

He glanced at Zenia, a question in his eyes, and she thought he would ask her to check on Vornzylar again. Zenia would if he made the request, but she was afraid of what would happen to her if she did. By now, the elf knew she was spying on him. The first time, he'd only looked at her. But last time, his mental attack had been like a dagger driving into her brain. Even hours after the dragon tear had broken the link, the pain lingered, a stabbing headache behind her eyes.

"There's no smoke or anything like that, Zyndar Dharrow," the driver called back.

Jev didn't appear reassured, but he looked back out the window without asking for anything from Zenia.

"Elves assassinate people," Krox grumbled. "They don't burn down buildings."

"These ones do," the lieutenant said. "They blew up the elf tower and that weird tree ship. Not that I care about those things as long as they leave *our* buildings alone. I don't know what the problem is if they're just fighting their own kind."

Jev glared at the officer, his hand tightening into a fist.

Krox slapped his man on the chest. "They're doing it in *our* city, and they're intruders we didn't invite. *That's* the problem. Besides, the men need a training exercise." He grinned. "After the beatings we took in the war, I'll be *happy* to run these bastards out of Dharrow Castle."

Zenia didn't think they were in Dharrow Castle, but she didn't mention the magical meeting stone. She doubted Jev wanted everyone to know there was a special elven communication device on his property.

Rhi opened her mouth, but Zenia gently nudged her with an elbow, and she kept her thoughts to herself.

The carriage swung around and stopped in front of the drawbridge. It was raised. When Zenia had been up here before, it had been lowered, and that had seemed its normal state.

Jev threw the door open and jumped out, hollering a worried greeting.

Krox and his officer stepped out too. Zenia hesitated, questioning whether she would be welcome. She had no trouble imagining Jev's father stomping out and yelling at her, no doubt believing her some vile influence seducing his son and leading him astray.

Rhi shifted, as if to get up, but paused to look at Zenia, her eyebrows raised.

"Is he out there?" Zenia murmured, touching her dragon tear. Checking on Jev's father shouldn't cause any problems. He wasn't some magical elf who could hurl an attack from afar.

The gem responded by showing her an image of the drawbridge lowering and Heber Dharrow riding out with five other men, all on horseback and all carrying weapons.

"Are we hiding from Jev's surly relatives?" Rhi asked when Zenia didn't climb out.

"For the moment."

"You sure? I wouldn't mind kicking his father in the fountain again."

"You seem extra grumpy this morning." Zenia scooted over so she could see out the window. "Didn't your soap-sharing adventure with Hydal go well?"

"It took an unexpected twist. I had an itch I needed scratched, and he seemed like an available itch-scratcher, but he wouldn't look at me when I was naked in the bath. He was blushing, so I know he wasn't unaware of my lush nudity, but kept trying to *converse* with me while politely handing me soaps and sponges that I could use on myself. He recited a poem about some zyndar of old singing ballads to a zyndari daughter trapped in a tower by her horrendous mother who insisted she wait for marriage to see men."

"The Tale of Chastity Chroma, yes. I remember it."

"I didn't know if he was trying to tell me something or just babbling nervously. I was clearly available. It wasn't as if he had to woo me. Are all zyndar this confusing?" Rhi looked out the window toward where Jev was walking up to his father's horse.

"I'll hazard a guess that he wants to court you like a gentleman, not simply scratch your itches."

"What kind of man doesn't want to scratch a woman's itches?"

"I'm sure he *wants* to, but maybe he wishes to get to know you better first."

"That's so weird."

Zenia held up a hand to still the conversation for now.

"What's going on, Father?" Jev's voice carried through the open door of the carriage.

"A girl from one of the villages came up at dawn and reported seeing elves while she was out milking. Elves. On our land. *Again*." Heber growled like a rabid dog.

"We're here to handle them. Why don't you stay and watch the castle? I don't think they have a reason to threaten our family, but we believe these are the elves that blew up the embassy and a ship in port. Did that news make it out here?"

"Filthy savages." Heber spat noisily. "We're not hiding while they cavort on our land."

"I didn't say to hide. I said to protect the castle. I've brought fifty men up, and the king is going to send mages soon."

Or so he hoped, Zenia thought. Jev didn't mention that they weren't certain about the mage reinforcements.

"You had better be here to direct them," Jev added.

"You want me to cower in the castle while others fight for me?"

"Others who are young, muscular, and experienced at battling elves. Krox, show my father some muscle."

"You know I only do that for the ladies, Jev."

"Not *that* muscle," Krox's lieutenant said.

A couple of men laughed. Heber did not. Neither did Jev.

"We'll handle it, Father," Jev said. "You can help look if you like, but..."

Jev trailed off, and with the help of the dragon tear, Zenia saw why. A woman in her forties and wearing a robe stepped into the castle gateway. That wasn't Fremia, was it? No, Jev had said she was a teenager.

In the courtyard behind her, a boy with a wooden sword peered out at the gathering. A portly woman in an apron swooped in and pulled him away.

"So nice of you to give me permission," Heber growled.

"What is *she* doing here?" Jev asked, his voice growing icy.

"None of your business," Heber said.

Zenia, through her dragon tear, sensed someone using magic. It wasn't unusual to find other people with dragon tears, especially among the zyndar, but she found it suspicious and reached out to pinpoint the source. It was the woman. She was wearing a dragon tear *and* using it.

"Zenia is here," Jev said, startling her.

Zenia hadn't minded staying out of sight in the carriage.

"You promised to talk to her," Jev added.

Now? Surely, they had more important things to worry about. Unless he believed that woman was a threat?

"Not while there are elves crawling all over our property," Heber said.

"I think now is the perfect time. Krox, your men are going to have to go on horseback. The fields are too rough for the wagons, and I wager the elves are in the trees. Bhraykok, show these officers to the stable, please. Father, which village was it? We can have some of the men start the search there. And Morlok, take one squad and check the other side of the pond. Zenia saw them there earlier."

Since her name kept coming up, Zenia felt cowardly for staying in the carriage. She eased out, though she lingered near the door, not wanting to intrude on what was turning into a military operation.

Heber spotted her right away and glared at her from atop his horse. At first, the woman in the robe—she looked like she belonged in a bath or bedroom, not wandering around a castle courtyard—only squinted curiously at her. But something must have helped her recognize Zenia, for the squint turned into a chilly glare.

Zenia still had no idea who she was, but her dragon tear sensed hers and did the magical equivalent of raising its hackles. It didn't usually do that when it encountered other dragon tears. It was almost as if it believed the woman and her gem were enemies.

The daylight faded, and Zenia's vision grew hazy. She winced and gripped the carriage door, afraid she was going to experience that walking nightmare again.

Instead, she continued to view the men speaking in front of her, but she also saw something more. A faint lavender line in the air, running from the woman and her dragon tear to Heber's head. It reminded her of a leash.

It's manipulating him? she silently asked.

Her dragon tear gave the mental equivalent of a nod. A very firm nod.

Zenia sensed it was doing more than manipulating Heber. Almost controlling him? She wished she were close enough to see the engraving in the woman's gem. Was it the eyetooth of justice? The same as she'd had when she'd been an inquisitor? Zenia had never used that gem to attempt to control anyone, but she'd read minds and occasionally manipulated enemies for the good of the temple. She knew it was possible for such dragon tears to be used in less scrupulous ways.

"Zenia?" Jev touched her arm, and the light returned to normal. "Lieutenant Cark and I are going to take men out to locate the elves. I know we'll need your help eventually, but I'd like you to stay here for a while and talk to my father and Zyndari *Bludnor*." He emphasized the name so she wouldn't miss it. Fremia Bludnor's mother, of course. "I'll fire shots in the air if we find the elves and need you to come out."

"Don't you think it would be useful if I came with you now?" Zenia asked quietly. Rhi had also stepped out of the carriage and was eyeing Heber speculatively. "I could talk to them later. After this issue is resolved."

She sensed that Jev wanted to prioritize his issue—their issue—but he sighed and nodded. "You're more logical than I am." He lowered his voice and turned his back to the others as he faced her. "But I'm right, aren't I? That she's manipulating him?"

"Yes. And it's illegal since she's not a watchman or inquisitor."

"Nobody's going to arrest a zyndari woman," Jev said.

Zenia snorted. "Tell me about it. I—"

A little tingle emanated from her dragon tear, and she received a brief vision of newcomers heading up the road on horseback. An elf and a dwarf. Ah.

"Cutter and Lornysh are riding this way." Zenia pointed down the road, though a few trees and a bend hid them from sight.

"What? Are you sure? Lornysh shouldn't be out of bed, much less riding." Jev frowned as the pair appeared around the bend, riding on two horses Zenia recognized from the king's stable.

"Is that an elf?" Heber asked, his voice dangerous, his hand tightening on his rifle.

Some of Krox's men stirred uneasily too.

"A friend." Jev held up a hand to stay everyone, giving his father a particularly hard warning glare, and ran down the road to meet his friends.

Heber didn't appear subdued by Jev's glare, and he exchanged a long look with a couple of the men at his side. Dharrow Castle staff, Zenia suspected. Men who would be quick to obey him.

She thought about staying to make sure they didn't defy Jev's wishes, but her dragon tear created a protective barrier around her and, with a quick flash of a vision, conveyed that she could share the protection with Jev and his friends.

"Watch those men, please, Rhi," Zenia whispered.

"Gladly." Rhi had brought her bo, and she thumped it in her palm.

Zenia jogged after Jev. She was glad she had chosen boots, trousers, and a tunic today rather than a dress. She'd belted on a pistol holster, too, though she would be in trouble if she lost her dragon tear and had to rely on the firearm against those elves.

"...doing here?" Jev was asking when Zenia came into earshot.

"I will not allow you to battle my people on my behalf while I cower in Targyon's castle."

"It's not cowering if you lost half your bowels the night before and you're convalescing," Jev said.

"My bowels are still intact," Lornysh said, though it was clear from the stiff way he sat in the saddle that he was in discomfort.

"Just slightly perforated," Cutter added.

"You were not there," Lornysh told him.

"I can tell when you're looking perforated."

Jev pushed a hand through his hair and glanced back. To make sure nobody was aiming at Lornysh?

Zenia had placed herself in the way, confident in the barrier around her. Sometimes, the dragon tear made it invisible, but it was shimmering a faint blue now, letting everyone know it was there and large enough to protect Cutter and Lornysh.

"You can't go into battle like that," Jev said. "And you've already proven you won't raise a blade against your countryman. Country-elf."

Cutter hadn't been there to see it and must not have heard, because he arched his bushy eyebrows in surprise. Lornysh didn't deny the statement.

"Use me for bait, then," he said. "I am what they want. What *he* wants."

"Bait?" Jev asked. "You want me to dangle you from the castle wall by your wrists until they show up?"

Lornysh touched his abdomen, his tunic hiding the bandage that had to still be there. "That sounds uncomfortable. Perhaps I could lie on a floating mat in your moat."

Jev looked at Zenia, shook his head to himself, then turned back to Lornysh. "Can you sense if they're nearby now? Watching us? Zenia saw them on Dharrow land this morning, standing over there and spying on the castle from the opposite side of the pond, but that was several hours ago. And she can't keep checking, because Vornzylar is capable of attacking her magically through the visions."

Lornysh gazed at their surroundings. "It makes no sense that they would be interested in your castle. I assumed they came out here to use the communication stone."

"We've had that thought too," Jev said, "but that's not where they were standing."

"Maybe they were simply on their way across your land to that hidden valley." Lornysh pointed toward trees in the distance off to the side of Dharrow Castle.

Zenia was roughly aware of the location of the stone, thanks to Rhi telling her what had happened that night she'd followed Jev and Lornysh out to it, but Zenia had been busy stalking Jev's grandmother at the time and hadn't been out there herself.

"Possibly," Jev said. "But that wouldn't have been the most direct route for them."

"You don't have any more desirable artifacts that elves would be interested in over in your castle, do you?" Zenia asked.

"I hope not. But it *is* an old castle with a lot of secrets." Jev scratched his jaw and looked around thoughtfully. "We'll split our resources just in case."

"Are you referring to those soldiers?" Lornysh's lips thinned, and Zenia suspected he didn't consider them resources worth mentioning.

"Yes. I'll leave half of them at the castle with Zenia. Zenia, is that all right with you?"

"I thought we decided it would be more useful if I stayed with you and confronted the elves. That's where you plan to go with the other half of the men, I assume."

"I want to take them and Lornysh to the communication stone, yes, because that seems the most likely reason they would have come out here, but... I don't know. It makes me uneasy that they were eyeballing my castle. Even if they weren't, Targyon's mages should—with luck—be on their way out. Someone will need to lead them to the stone if we haven't come back. Rhi can stay with you. She should remember the way."

Zenia still thought it would be better if she went with Jev, as she couldn't imagine what in Dharrow Castle would interest elves who had, by their own words, come here to kill Lornysh. She hoped he wasn't trying to keep her out of the way to protect her. Thus far, he'd seemed to accept that she was, with the help of her dragon tear, as capable of surviving trouble as he was. Maybe he truly believed there *was* something that would interest elves in the castle. Or maybe he just had a hunch.

"I'll do as you wish, Jev," she said.

"That's a good woman right there," Cutter said. "You should make her something else, Jev."

"She's wearing the necklace you helped me make."

"I see that. It's pretty. But does she have a spice rack yet?"

"She hasn't requested one," Jev said.

"A woman shouldn't have to request gifts. You have to be thoughtful and anticipate her needs."

"Is that what you're doing for Master Grindmor?"

"Yes, it's why you haven't seen me much since I started my apprenticeship. She requires a lot of anticipating."

Lornysh sighed noisily at the direction the conversation had taken.

"You two, meet me in the trees over there." Jev pointed. "I'll talk to Krox, get some of his men, and ride over to join you."

Lornysh looked toward the soldiers glaring down the road at him. "I'll take a circuitous route."

"Always advisable," Cutter said.

After Lornysh and Cutter turned off the road, Jev waved for Zenia to walk back to the others with him. He looked like he might touch her shoulder, but he must have noticed the shield. Zenia willed the dragon tear to lower it. Heber and his men were glaring at Lornysh as he rode across the field. Apparently, an elf irritated Jev's father more than a former inquisitor did.

"I'm not trying to get you out of the way, Zenia," Jev said. "If we find the elves first, I'm hoping your dragon tear will know, and you can rush out to help us. I'm just not positive there isn't some old artifact in the bowels of Dharrow Castle that the elves believe might be useful. After all, my mother had that tie to elves. As did some of my ancestors."

"It's fine, Jev. I'll stay. Just don't get yourself killed without me."

"I wouldn't dream of it. I definitely want you there if I'm going to get myself killed. So you can hold my head and kiss me as I lie dying."

"We already did something like that. I appreciated that you lived."

"I'm amenable to living. And finding a way to marry you." He smiled, even though Heber had shifted his glare back to them. The woman—Zyndari Bludnor—was watching them and glaring too.

They weren't doing anything except walking shoulder to shoulder and speaking, but maybe they looked like a couple as they did it. Zenia refused to step away from Jev. She had the petulant urge to clasp his hand, but she refrained. He did pat her on the shoulder before trotting over to speak with Krox.

Zenia's stomach knotted at the idea of talking to Bludnor and Heber. Maybe that was the real reason she'd been so eager to go with Jev, to avoid that confrontation.

"I don't feel particularly welcome here," Rhi said when Zenia joined her.

"Then you'll be excited to hear that we're staying here while Jev takes half the men to that elf stone you visited."

"No, I won't."

"What if I let you kick Heber into the fountain again?" Zenia smiled, though it was a joke. She would feel she had failed utterly if she and Rhi ended up in a fight against Jev's father, verbal or physical.

"That might be somewhat exciting."

Zenia watched as Jev, the lieutenant, and twenty-five of Krox's men headed across the field toward the trees where Cutter and Lornysh had already disappeared. Aware of Heber and the zyndari woman continuing to glare at her, Zenia wished she were going with them.

CHAPTER 15

C AN YOU TELL IF THEY'RE nearby?" Jev asked quietly.
He, Cutter, and Lornysh were leading the way through the tree-filled
and undergrowth-clogged gully, the twenty-five soldiers crunching
and snapping foliage as they tramped behind them. Grunts and curses flowed
from the men's mouths. If the elf wardens were here, there was no way this
group would sneak up on them.

"I can't sense them anywhere within miles," Lornysh said, "but
they're powerful enough that they could be camouflaging themselves
from me. They are…" He spread a hand, the sunlight making it through
the leaf canopy dappling his palm. "I told you my story. I didn't finish
the warden training. I was making good progress and was awarded my
sword, but I had another five years left to achieve mastery over the
magic that wardens are taught."

Now that Lornysh had shared his background with Jev, he was more
open about discussing his past—and his failings. Jev had half-expected
Lornysh wouldn't remember that he had, under the influence of that
painkiller, spoken of it all. Jev was still reeling from the revelations. He
never would have guessed that Lornysh had a tiny amount of human
blood flowing through his veins or that such a small amount would truly
matter to his people. Jev could see it disqualifying someone from taking
the throne, but for them to kick him completely out of their city over it?
He shook his head.

"I haven't seen any fresh prints." Lornysh waved to the rocks and
mossy earth they were walking over, most of it a dried creek bed.
Water had been flowing the last time Jev had been this way, but spring

had shifted to summer, and it hadn't rained much lately. "But it's also possible they could pass without leaving trace."

"I do so love dealing with elves."

Lornysh headed up an animal trail that led away from the dried creek, and the trees grew higher, the canopy blocking out more of the daylight. Jev spotted the ancient stone up ahead, almost like a ten-foot-tall mushroom with an umbrella-like structure that flared out at the top. It glowed a soft yellow, gently warming the mossy ground with its light.

Lornysh stopped and frowned at the stone.

"It wasn't glowing the first time we walked up on it," Cutter said. "Not until you started fondling it."

Jev remembered it glowing, but he also remembered that Lornysh and Cutter had found it on their own before bringing him to it. They had to be referring to that experience.

"It's possible someone was already here." Lornysh trotted toward the stone.

"And sent a message to your people?" Jev asked. "To other members of their faction? Do you think they would have called for reinforcements?" Jev almost fell over as the thought came to mind. How many more elven wardens might Vornzylar be able to bring to Kor?

"There's no way to know who they spoke to or what they said." Lornysh walked slowly around the structure.

The soldiers caught up to them, muttering and touching their weapons as they stared at the blatantly magical stone.

"What does it do?" Lieutenant Cark asked.

"As far as I know, it's for communication," Jev said. "Wait here, please. And have the men keep their ears open. It's possible our elven enemies will show up to try and finish off Lornysh while he's wounded." He waved for the men to stay back, worried Lornysh wouldn't speak as openly if they were within hearing range.

Jev and Cutter walked up to the stone and waited. Lornysh was looking at the ground around it, seeking evidence that someone had been here earlier.

Jev eyed the stone cairn beyond an ancient bench facing the communication stone. The last time he'd been here, he hadn't known who was buried under it. It chilled him now that he knew his mother's bones lay under the rocks and that she'd been shot by her *own* mother, to keep her from running off with some elf lover.

Somehow, Jev doubted the humans of Kor would be any more understanding than the Taziir if they learned that their king's heir had elven blood. For Targyon's sake, Jev hoped he wasn't falling in love with the elven princess, for nothing could ever come of it. Nothing open, anyway. Jev couldn't imagine Targyon having an elven mistress while he married an appropriate zyndari woman for the public. Nor could he imagine the noble Princess Yesleva engaging in some secret relationship against the wills of both their nations.

"Sometimes, I wonder why people make everything so complicated," Jev said, feeling morose.

Cutter looked like he would respond, perhaps by suggesting more people should make spice racks for each other, but Lornysh returned, and he held his tongue.

"I found sign of several animals that have been through recently," Lornysh said, "and there's a faint indentation over there by the bench that may have come from an elven moccasin."

"Recently?" Jev asked.

"Yes. The fact that the stone is activated means it either anticipated our approach or... someone was here less than an hour ago."

Jev looked sharply at him. "How likely is the former?"

"It didn't activate the first time I showed up, not until I touched it."

"And nobody has touched it yet."

"No."

Jev eyed the runes carved into the glowing stone. "Is there any way to ask *it* if it was used? And by whom?"

Lornysh smiled sadly. "It's not that sophisticated. Zenia's dragon tear might have been able to ferret out the information." He tilted his head. "Why did you leave her behind?"

"Most of my family is inside that castle. My father's being an overbearing jerk, especially right now, but the staff, and my cousins and aunts and their children, they're all good people. I want someone there who can protect them. I also want someone who can keep an eye on my father since he's being manipulated right now."

"Manipulated?" Cutter asked.

"By a zyndari woman, the mother of the girl my father agreed to engage me to. Bludnor probably only wants to make sure the wedding goes forward, and that's why she's here, but—disgustingly—I think she's sleeping with my father too. One wonders what *her* husband thinks of that."

"While I sympathize with your domestic problems," Lornysh said, "I fail to see how it's relevant to the elf problem. *My* problem."

"It's probably not, but I could see her urging my father to do something stupid like shoot at you." Grudgingly, Jev admitted he could see the old man shooting at Lornysh whether Bludnor was around or not.

"I'll avoid them."

"If those wardens already showed up—" Cutter prodded the stone, "—is there any point in staying out here?"

"Bait." Lornysh eyed Cutter's finger, as if offended that he'd poked the stone without proper reverence. "As I said before, they're after me. I may not know where they are, but it's likely they know where *I* am."

"So we should prepare to make a stand?" Jev asked.

Lornysh gazed into the surrounding brush, though there wasn't a breeze and the leaves weren't stirring. "If you prefer this to the castle. We can stand with our backs to the stone and hope we have enough men to overcome whatever magic they throw at us."

"Seems like a castle would be a better place to be ensconced if there's going to be a siege," Cutter said.

Jev blew out a slow breath, again thinking of all his family living inside, including at least a dozen children. He didn't want to bring a battle to the castle, especially not a magical battle. Those elves had raised a shadow golem in the middle of the embassy, and there was no reason they couldn't do the same thing in Dharrow Castle courtyard.

"Let's wait here for now," Jev said. "Can you set some traps that they might stumble into?"

Lornysh's eyes brightened. "I did attend all three years of woodland crafts during my training."

"Is that the class where you learn to make traps?"

"It is."

"Let us know how we can help." Jev pointed at his chest and waved at the milling troops.

"Stay out of the way." Lornysh jogged off, disappearing into the foliage.

"Cutter," Jev said, "can you make any special dwarven traps?"

"Good dwarven traps rely on metal and forges, not twigs and leaves, but I'll see what I can do."

"Thank you."

Jev looked around the clearing, hoping the elves would indeed be lured to this place—and hoping his team had resources enough to battle them. He also hoped Vornzylar hadn't used the stone to request reinforcements. Jev tried to reassure himself that, even if he had, it would take days for more elves to arrive.

The drawbridge of Dharrow Castle was raised after Zenia, Rhi, Captain Krox and his soldiers, and Heber Dharrow and his men entered the courtyard. Guards walked along the ramparts, hands on their weapons as they peered out over the cleared fields around the castle.

"Are you going to talk with the woman glaring at you now or after she does something nefarious?" Rhi asked, joining Zenia near the fountain.

Zenia had chosen the spot so she would be out of the way. Dharrow Castle was a large rambling structure of several stories, but it wasn't as large as the king's castle, and the courtyard felt busy with all the soldiers and many of the local men milling around.

"I'm hoping to ignore her." Zenia was aware of the zyndari woman—she'd gone to put on a dress and had returned recently—standing in a doorway and watching as Heber discussed who knew what with Krox. Judging by the way they were gesturing toward the castle walls, they disagreed with Jev's suggestion to stay put.

"She looks like she's plotting something," Rhi said. "Want me to thump her?"

"She's zyndari."

"So? I'm only allowed to thump commoners?"

"Technically, you're not supposed to thump anyone without provocation."

"That glare is definitely provocative."

Zenia wrapped her fingers around her dragon tear. She would talk to the zyndari woman eventually, but she was more worried about those elves, especially now that Jev had gone off without any magical protection, other than what the injured Lornysh could call upon.

She closed her eyes and thought of the vision her dragon tear had shared that morning, of the elves watching the castle from afar.

Do you know what they wanted? she asked silently, hoping the gem would understand.

But she received the mental equivalent of a shrug. Hm.

Is there anything in the castle that could interest elves? Something magical?

The dragon tear showed her the hidden vault in Jev's grandmother's crafts room. It was dark and dusty, apparently not having been disturbed since the woman had been exiled. The vision shifted, showing her the inside of the vault and the dragon tears inside.

Thanks, but I knew about those magical items. Anything else?

Zenia tried to envision glowing artifacts. She had no idea what type of magical item might be here, but she needed to communicate in a way the dragon tear would understand. It didn't seem to speak the kingdom tongue. It never responded with words, only with emotions or images, so she assumed it responded to *her* emotions and the images she conjured in her mind.

A triumphant feeling came from the dragon tear. Because it understood? Or because it understood and had something for her?

She rose onto the balls of her toes and tightened her grip on the gem, hoping for enlightenment.

Rhi elbowed her. "Trouble coming."

Zenia shook her head, keeping her eyes shut, not wanting to pull her attention from the dragon tear. In her mind's eye, she left the courtyard, her point of view again from above, as if she were flying. She swept through familiar stone passageways toward the kitchen and laundry rooms in the back of the castle, but then she descended stairs she hadn't been down before. She passed a wine cellar, storage rooms, and a dungeon and interrogation chamber with tools far dustier than anything in the grandmother's suite. She hoped that meant that the Dharrows hadn't needed to interrogate anyone for many, many generations.

A hidden door opened in the back of the dungeon, cobwebs falling to the ancient stone floor. Her vision took her down dark stairs caked with dust and through passages built at the beginning of the thousand-year-old castle's history, or maybe before. A rockfall lay ahead, but somehow the vision pushed between the rocks and into more dark passageways beyond it. A dark chamber lay ahead, and she sensed something magical lay within it.

"What can we do for you, Zyndari? Zyndar?" Rhi asked loudly, elbowing Zenia again. "Wake up," she hissed.

Zenia hadn't yet seen what the dragon tear wished to show her and didn't want to push away the vision, but Rhi gripped her shoulder and shook her. The vision dissipated, and Zenia growled in frustration as she opened her eyes.

Heber Dharrow and Zyndari Bludnor stood in front of her.

"What magic are you employing, woman?" Heber demanded.

Bludnor squinted at Zenia. Her fingers were wrapped around her own dragon tear, and once again, Zenia saw a faint tendril of energy tethering Heber to her—to *it*.

"I'm trying to figure out what the enemy elves may be seeking inside your castle. And my name is Zenia Cham." She made herself curtsey and add, "It's good to meet you again, Zyndar Dharrow."

"I know your name. I will speak with you in private." Heber glared at Rhi and at the fountain gurgling beside her, maybe fantasizing about kicking her in as payback. "Now."

"Zenia?" Rhi asked, not budging.

Did "in private" mean with his zyndari puppet master standing beside him? Zenia gave Bludnor a pointed look.

"My son asked for this," Heber told the woman. "Leave us for a few minutes, please."

He was much more polite with her than with Zenia and Rhi.

Bludnor didn't look like she wanted to budge any more than Rhi did.

"I'll be right over there if you need my help," she said.

Heber sniffed and jerked his chin up. "I do not need anyone's help to talk to a woman."

Bludnor's elegantly plucked eyebrows twitched, but she did not respond otherwise. She ambled to the other side of the fountain and sat on it with her back to them. The water splashing into the pool ought to ensure she couldn't overhear them, but Zenia had no doubt her dragon tear would help her spy.

You're more powerful than her dragon tear, right? she asked her gem, starting to follow the silent words up with thoughts that would convey the same. But there was no need.

Her dragon tear understood perfectly and shared an image of Bludnor's gem exploding under a surge of power. Then it shared a hopeful feeling, like a dog eager to be let off its leash.

Zenia had faith that her dragon tear truly was more powerful, not that it was overconfident. Good.

"Give us a few minutes, Rhi." Zenia touched her friend's arm. "Thanks."

"Fine. I'll just go stand over there." She pointed her bo at a flagstone mere feet from Bludnor.

"What's your price, woman?" Heber asked when they were alone.

Zenia blinked. "What?"

"To leave my son alone. Look, you're a beauty. I'm not blind. I see why he wants you, but you will not wed him. I'm not going to have common children that wouldn't be suitable heirs for Dharrow Castle and all that it oversees. A lot of people depend on us. I won't have them abandoned to inferior children after Jev and I are gone."

Zenia clenched her teeth. She wanted to go back to investigating whatever lay beneath the castle, but she had to deal with this prejudiced bastard first. But how? If she treated him like an enemy and responded to his comments the way she wanted to—the suggestion that she would birth inferior children infuriated her—it would do nothing to help their cause. As much as she loathed the idea of kowtowing to him, she had to try to win him over, or at least win his grudging acceptance. If she was a jerk to him, he would never let Jev marry her.

"How much do I have to pay you to leave him?" Heber added. "I'm sure you have some dream of being made zyndari and living the noble life, but it won't happen. With money, you can still buy a life of ease and some townhouse in the city." His lip curled, and she sensed how much it galled him to make this offer, how startled he'd been when Jev had been willing to give up his inheritance and his title for her.

"I don't want your money, nor do I wish to be zyndari," Zenia said. "I love Jev because he appreciates me and makes me laugh. And he brings me flowers even though he's colorblind and struggles to pick out ones that go together." She smiled at the memory—and Rhi explaining

199
ELVEN FURY

how hard that task had been for Jev—even though she was as tense as a ramrod standing before Heber. "Honestly, I wish he wasn't zyndar because then we could simply get married without having to deal with your... with zyndar politics."

Heber's eyes narrowed. "You asked him to give up his birthright? His duties?"

"No, I wouldn't do that. I know how much his honor and duties mean to him. But that doesn't mean I don't fantasize about how much easier it would be if we were both common and nobody cared about the *quality* of our children." She tried not to clench her jaw again, and she reminded herself once more to be polite, but it was hard.

"He is not common. No amount of fantasizing will change that. He is my heir, my only son now, and it is his duty to marry a zyndari woman and have children who will take care of Dharrow land and its people after our passing. I want what's best for him and for the family's future."

Zenia wished she could see that tether of control now, hinting that Bludnor was manipulating him into speaking this way, but it wasn't there at the moment. These were Heber's genuine thoughts.

"Is that why you're letting that woman manipulate you with her dragon tear?" Zenia asked. "Because you think it's best for him?"

Heber rocked back on his heels.

Zenia was surprised by *his* surprise. Had he truly not had any idea? Bludnor couldn't be with him every moment. In the times when she'd been gone, he must have wondered if all the ideas she was giving him were truly his. Or were they in such close alignment that her manipulation didn't matter?

"She's the one you should be worried about," Zenia said. "Not me. I don't want anything from you or your estate. I'd be happy to sign paperwork to ensure I never get anything if you wish. I just want Jev to be happy, and I'd like to be happy with him, but if I had to choose his happiness over mine, I'd like to see him..."

The magical tether reappeared as Zyndari Bludnor squinted over her shoulder at them.

Heber didn't seem to notice it—it was only because of her dragon tear that *Zenia* noticed—but his lips tightened, and she saw an objection leap into his eyes.

Stop it, please, she silently said to her dragon tear, while envisioning an axe chopping the magical tether.

The gem warmed against her chest, and she sensed a substantial burst of magic rush out of it.

Bludnor yelped and sprang to her feet.

"Ow, ow!" she shouted and tore her dragon tear away from her chest, breaking the thin gold chain that held it. She cried out again and threw it in the fountain, then looked at her hand. A scorch mark was visible on her palm.

A smug satisfied feeling came from Zenia's dragon tear.

"You attacked her!" Heber lunged forward and snatched Zenia's arm, startling her.

"No. I was defending you."

Rhi ran toward Heber, raising her bo.

"No, don't," Zenia barked, trying to shift to stand between them as she raised her free hand.

But Heber held her too tightly. Anger flared in Rhi's dark eyes, and she looked like she would shove Zenia into the fountain if she had to in order to crack Heber over the head.

Her dragon tear flared with blue light, and a wave of power blew outward. Rhi, Heber, and Bludnor were flung backward, along with a couple of nearby soldiers. They sailed several feet and landed on their hips or butts with startled cries.

A rumble sounded, and the ground shook. Hard.

Zenia wobbled, bumping against the lip of the fountain, and almost ended up in the water.

"What are you doing?" she blurted to her dragon tear as the ground continued to shake.

She grabbed the gem, but it had cooled off, and she sensed surprise from it. It may have flung the people threatening her away to keep her from harm, but it wasn't the reason the ground was shaking. And continuing to shake.

Zenia gripped the lip of the fountain for support. The soldiers in the courtyard spread their legs and arms, trying to keep their balance and remain upright.

Heber rose to a sitting position, his eyes like chips of ice as he glared at Zenia. He thought she was responsible for this.

"It's not me," she blurted.

A vision encroached, and she saw that dark chamber under the castle again. The magic that her dragon tear had sensed was growing stronger—coming to life. A crimson glow pushed back the shadows as it grew brighter and brighter.

By the founders, were the elf wardens responsible for that? She remembered the golem from the tower. Were they raising some other magical creature? Something that would threaten all of Dharrow Castle?

"Get her!" Heber roared and pointed straight at Zenia. "Guards!"

Rhi leaped to her feet and stood protectively in front of Zenia. She raised her bo, but guards with rifles ran down from the ramparts and toward them.

Zenia wanted to explain, but she sensed the magic growing stronger down below, the threat increasing. "Rhi, come with me."

She sprinted for the door that led to the kitchen. Thank the founders, Rhi didn't argue. She raced after Zenia.

Without being asked, the dragon tear created a barrier around them. Zenia half-expected the guards to fire, to treat her like a known enemy invader. She lamented that the progress she'd started to make with Heber had likely been destroyed and that he now believed her a threat, not only to his son but to his entire castle.

The ground quaked harder, tossing her against a stone wall as she ran. A thud sounded behind her, and Rhi cursed.

Zenia made herself keep going. She remembered that she'd seen a rockfall blocking the way and worried she wouldn't be able to get down to the source of the magic in time. Even if she could, would one dragon tear be enough to thwart whatever powerful elven magic or creature was down there?

CHAPTER 16

J EV PACED WHILE CUTTER AND Lornysh set traps, occasionally going over to hold something when they asked for assistance. The soldiers were playing chips and smoking, the scent of their cigars pungent and out of place among the earthy vegetation of the woods.

"I'm beginning to think you're not as enticing a piece of bait as you thought you were," Jev said to Lornysh's back.

His friend was crouching, tying branches together in a loop.

"We haven't been here that long," Lornysh replied without glancing back.

The light grew dimmer. Jev looked up, thinking a cloud had passed over the sun, but so little light filtered down through the leaves that it wouldn't have mattered. He realized the massive magical stone had stopped glowing.

Lornysh frowned over at it.

"Does that mean something?" Jev asked.

"It's gone inactive," Lornysh said.

"Does *that* mean something?" Cutter asked, his beard dusting the grass as he worked on some trap of his own.

Lornysh stood and considered the stone. "Assuming it was used shortly before we arrived, enough time has passed for it to go back to its dormant state."

"So the elves came, used it, and left already?" Jev knew Lornysh had implied that before. What he didn't know was if his friend's presence would lure the elves back again.

Lornysh spun away from the stone as if he'd heard something. He stared into the trees. Jev dropped a hand to his pistol.

"Someone coming?" he whispered.

"All of a sudden, I sense a great deal of magic," Lornysh said.

Cutter stood. "I feel it too."

Jev felt nothing, but humans didn't have any innate magic or senses for magic. "Where?"

Cutter and Lornysh gave each other a long look. A long *knowing* look.

"Where?" Jev repeated, his stomach sinking.

"The castle," Lornysh said.

Jev almost asked if it might be Zenia using her dragon tear, but if she had a reason to call upon that much magic, something was wrong. Very wrong.

"Back to the castle," he barked to the soldiers, then raced toward the gully, not waiting for Lornysh to lead the way. He felt like an idiot for having come out here in the first place.

Foliage crunched under heavy boots as the soldiers followed him back down the gully. Men cursed as they slipped on the rocks in the dry creek. Despite the injury that had to be hampering him, Lornysh glided over them and passed Jev. His face was grim with determination, and Jev thought he glimpsed a flash of guilt in his eyes.

As they turned into the wider valley that led back to the spot where they had left their horses, Jev wanted to tell his friend that he'd chosen to be a part of this fight, that he still wanted to make sure these vengeful asses didn't kill Lornysh.

But Lornysh halted before they came out of the trees and threw up his arms in an abrupt gesture.

The horses were gone, their tethers all cut, but it wasn't until Lornysh drew his sword and spun toward the valley slope that Jev saw the real threat. The elf with the icy silver sword stood up there. Vornzylar.

He wasn't wielding his sword; he gripped a drawn bow. Leaves stirred around him—the rest of his buddies?

"Find cover!" Lornysh yelled.

He sprinted toward the opposite valley wall and dove for a boulder.

Vornzylar loosed an arrow. It spun into the ground, missing Lornysh by inches.

"Cover," Jev repeated the order, scrambling up the same slope, hoping the tree trunks up there were thick enough to protect the soldiers from arrows.

Some of the soldiers returned fire, the reports from their rifles filling the valley. It was a mistake. The elves were shooting from the high ground and from behind cover. They loosed arrows relentlessly while the soldiers' bullets thudded harmlessly into wood.

A man cried out as Jev ducked behind a tree. He glimpsed the soldier grasping an arrow sticking out of his chest and winced.

"Cark, get your men behind cover!" Jev yanked out his pistol and leaned out from behind his tree, hoping for an opening to fire at Vornzylar.

Arrows continued to rain down from the opposite side of the valley, but the elves were so well hidden that the projectiles seemed to come from the trees themselves.

Three soldiers lay on the valley floor, arrows in their chests or eyes, the deadly precision terrifying. The rest of the men had reached the trees, but Jev didn't know if it would be enough.

He glimpsed movement, an elf leaning out to shoot. One of the males he'd battled in the tower.

Jev fired as the elf did, but his target was already leaning back. His bullet clipped the tree trunk beside where the elf's head had been and bark flew. Jev growled in disgust. Beating up *bark* wouldn't help with anything.

"Brace yourselves," someone—Cark?—yelled.

A metal projectile arched across the valley toward the elves. A grenade? Jev hoped so. That might be effective.

He winced when an arrow sailed out, striking the grenade and knocking it from its trajectory. But it exploded close enough to the elves' trees that branches flew. The roar echoed up and down the valley.

Jev leaned out again, hoping he could catch one of the elves scurrying for cover farther up the slope. He spotted someone, a hand gripping a bow all that was visible.

Fearing it would be the best target he would get, Jev fired. This time, his aim was true, and his bullet pierced flesh. The elf swore and dropped his bow as he jerked his hand back behind cover.

Before Jev could feel any satisfaction, Vornzylar leaned out and pierced him with his icy eyes. The elf pointed his glowing silver sword at Jev, as if promising his death.

At first, Jev didn't worry, since they were almost a hundred yards apart. Then an invisible blast of energy slammed into him.

He flew a dozen feet into the air before landing on his back, all the air blasting from his lungs. He was out in the open, and he knew he had to scramble for cover again, but his body was too stunned to obey his mind. Another elf took aim at him from across the valley.

Jev rolled to the side, his lungs refusing to draw in the air he needed to cry for help. A hand gripped him as a hook slid under his armpit. He was yanked toward a boulder as an arrow slammed into the earth where his head had been.

"Common sense says it's a bad idea to irk elves," Cutter observed, releasing him.

Jev finally managed to gasp in a breath. "What about when elves irk humans?"

"That's rarely as deadly."

Another grenade exploded near the elves. Trees blew up, branches and leaves flying everywhere, and Jev grimaced at the destruction to his family's property. But he kept the image of the dead soldiers in his mind and knew this was a necessity. Unfortunately, the grenades seemed to be destroying trees without hurting any of their enemies.

"Lornysh," Jev called to the boulder where his friend crouched, returning fire with his own bow. "Can you communicate with Zenia or her dragon tear at all? Find out if they can send help? I'd settle for my father with some more men with grenades."

He assumed from the way they were being thrown one at a time that the soldiers hadn't brought that many.

"Do you keep those in your family's armory?" Cutter asked.

"Of course, don't you?"

"The people in your castle are busy with their own problem," Lornysh called back. Then he switched to hand gestures that wouldn't be visible from the far side of the valley. They seemed to translate to, "Cover me, and I'll try to sneak around to deal with Vornzylar."

Jev shook his head. Lornysh couldn't be the one to deal with Vornzylar. Even if he hadn't been injured, he'd already proven he couldn't kill his fellow elf.

Jev issued his own hand gestures as arrows continued to fly and rifle fire rang out. He tried to tell Lornysh to cover him and that *he* would sneak around. He would have no problem shooting that elf.

Lornysh shook his head vehemently, then leaned out to fire as one of the wardens briefly appeared to loose more arrows. Surely, the elves would run out of ammunition soon. Maybe Jev should simply wait. When their quivers were empty would be the time to charge. His team would still have to deal with those wicked magical swords, but maybe they would have a chance against the elves then. Jev's people *did* have the numbers advantage.

"Let's try to circle around and sneak up behind them," Jev whispered to Cutter.

"I don't know if you've seen me try to sneak, Jev, but Lornysh says it sounds like an elephant walking across roasted acorns."

"With all the noise from the soldiers, they won't hear us coming." Jev hoped. He pointed higher up the valley wall behind them. He and Cutter could climb up there, race back the way they had come, then across the valley and to the far side. It would take time, but they were at a stalemate now, and they might be able to surprise the elves from behind. "Do you have any magic you can use against them?"

"You want me to carve them a nice gem?" Cutter asked.

An arrow sped past, skipping off the side of the boulder inches from Jev's head. He ducked lower and shifted more fully behind their cover. Unfortunately, the boulder wasn't that large, and two of them hunkered behind it.

"We have to do something." Jev worried about what was going on at the castle—what if this was simply a diversion?

As he was about to climb up the slope to enact his plan, a rumble came from somewhere up the valley.

"That's magic," Cutter said. "I may not be able to hurl power at enemies, but I can sense it."

"What is it?" Jev asked as the rumble grew louder, turning into a roar.

"Water. The creek isn't going to be dry much longer."

"Take to high ground," Jev yelled to the soldiers.

A wall of water came into sight, roaring down the valley, tearing ancient trees from their roots as it rushed toward them. Jev feared it was too late to escape.

Zenia made it through the ancient dusty dungeon to the back wall before she faltered. The vision hadn't showed her how to open that secret door, and she eyed old shackles and torture implements uneasily, aware that Heber and more than a dozen of his men were chasing after her.

"What now?" Rhi blurted from her side.

The ground gave a final shake and grew still. Zenia wished that was a good sign, but she doubted it was. More likely, whatever had been happening under the castle had been completed. She envisioned a magical monster rising up, tearing away the earth and the castle itself as it grabbed people and ate them.

Shaking her head, Zenia reached for her dragon tear, hoping it could open the door. It glowed blue before she touched it. A groan emanated from the old stone wall, followed by a scraping sound. A door swung slowly open.

"What the—" a man asked from the stairs leading into the dungeon.

"Just get them," Heber barked, cutting him off.

The senior Dharrow had acquired a pistol and a mace along the way, and he charged forward, looking like he meant to use both weapons on Zenia. Often.

Rhi spun toward the horde of guards racing at them and fearlessly hefted her bo.

The dragon tear pulsed, and a wall of shimmering blue energy appeared across the dungeon. Heber and the guard running at his shoulder smacked face-first into it. They stumbled back where other men caught them. Judging by the livid expression that contorted Heber's face, Zenia had given him another reason to loathe her.

The hidden door finished opening, and she ran through it. After they'd stopped whatever trouble was coming, she could apologize to Heber and try to explain everything.

Cobwebs clung to her face as she ran into the dark, the glow of the dragon tear the only thing lighting the way. Rhi raced after her, and shouts trailed them down the ancient passage. One of Heber's men asked if there was a way around. Someone else said he had no idea where they were going. Neither did Zenia.

She kept her arms out, batting in front of her face and trying to knock away the dusty curtains of cobwebs. They were so thick that she almost missed seeing the rockfall blocking the passage ahead. She halted abruptly, and Rhi bumped into her.

The rocks and dirt completely filled the passage from floor to ceiling. Zenia couldn't tell how deep it went.

"How long will your stone keep that wall up back there so they can't follow?" Rhi asked.

"I'm not sure." Probably until Zenia needed the dragon tear to apply its magic elsewhere.

"Because those people seem really pissed. Like they think we were the ones making that earthquake."

Zenia shook her head and silently asked the dragon tear to make a hole through the rocks.

"Are you still going to want to marry Jev if his father horribly maims you?" Rhi asked.

Zenia sensed the dragon tear shifting its focus from the barrier in the dungeon to the rock pile ahead.

"It's down!" someone shouted back there.

She grimaced and was relieved when rocks shifted, tumbling free. But it was too slow. They needed—

Red light flashed, and heat blasted Zenia's face. She stumbled back, bumping into Rhi, and raised her arm, as if that would block the heat. Tremendous light and energy flooded the passage, and the rocks all around them groaned.

"That doesn't sound good." Rhi pulled Zenia farther back from the rocks, even though the angry shouts of Heber's men were growing closer again.

"Marriage may be the least of my problems today," Zenia muttered, squinting against the light.

It halted as abruptly as it had started, vanishing and leaving them in near darkness. The dragon tear still glowed softly on Zenia's chest. Its blue light revealed that the passage ahead lay clear now. Inches of a fine dust covered the floor where the rocks had been. They'd been pulverized.

"Thank you," Zenia whispered to the gem and jogged forward.

Dust flew up as they passed, and she sneezed repeatedly. Rhi coughed and batted at the stuff floating in the air like ash.

Zenia smelled water and mildew, the scent growing stronger as they continued on.

"I hear them!" someone blurted from behind them. "Right up there. Hurry!"

"Where could they possibly be going?" Heber snarled.

Zenia didn't know what to think about the fact that he didn't know about this place.

A glow came from around a bend ahead, and nerves knotted in her stomach.

An alarm rang in her mind. The dragon tear warning her of a threat. As if she didn't know.

Rhi must have also sensed the light was more than illumination, for she raced past Zenia, leading the way around the corner with her bo raised. Zenia rushed right behind her, not wanting her friend to be crushed by some magical monster before she had time to react.

The passageway opened up into a large underground chamber with a sunken pool of water in the center, a natural reservoir. Zenia barely noticed it. She was too busy staring at the large glowing oval apparatus mounted on a walkway to one side of the pool. The shadows of humanoid figures moved about behind a shimmering opaque field framed by the oval.

People? Elves? Since Zenia had expected a golem or other monster, she was confused. Until one of the figures sprang out of the field.

A blonde female elf in green and brown warden's clothing, a bow in one hand and a flaming sword in the other.

"Reinforcements," Zenia blurted, realizing this wasn't the seed of a monster germinating. It was some kind of portal. Oddly, it appeared to be a permanent structure—some old artifact?—not some fully magical creation.

Rhi rushed forward to challenge the elf. More shadowy figures moved behind the oval field. More elves preparing to come through.

"Can we destroy it?" she whispered, gripping her dragon tear and envisioning the portal exploding.

The dubious feeling that emanated from the gem was not reassuring.

"Try," she urged it.

Before Rhi reached their new adversary, the elf flicked her sword, and some invisible force hurled Rhi backward. She landed on the edge of the walkway, almost tumbling over the side and into the pool. Her bo flew from her fingers and clattered onto the stones.

Zenia growled, willing the elf to fly backward, back into the portal. Her dragon tear attempted to obey her wishes and hurled power at the intruder. The elf staggered back a step but quickly braced herself, eyes narrowing in concentration.

Rhi scrambled to her feet, snatched up her bo, and ran forward. While the elf was distracted, she swung the long weapon. Zenia thought it would connect, but the elf whipped her sword down in a block. Not only did it halt the bo's progress; it cleaved the weapon in half.

"Founders' assholes," Rhi blurted, scrambling back as the elf lunged in for a follow-up blow.

Rhi no longer had a way to block.

Zenia urged the dragon tear to send another attack, hoping their enemy was focused on Rhi now. Another wave of power struck the elf. This time, she wasn't prepared. She was hurled into the air and splashed into the pool.

Before Zenia could feel any relief, Heber and the guards ran up behind her. She jumped to the side, putting her back to the wall and hoping they would focus on this new threat instead of her.

As the elf used some magic to levitate herself out of the water, her long blonde hair plastered to her head and a fearsome snarl curling her delicate lips, two more figures sprang through the portal. Two male elves. They landed in fighting crouches, magical swords in their hands, one glowing green and one blue.

Heber stopped in the mouth of the passageway, his guards crowding behind him. He swore, his gaze landing on the intruders.

"Elves!" he yelled, saying the word like a curse.

Heber and the guards rushed forward, maybe not knowing what they were getting into—had they ever fought elf wardens?

"Their swords are magic," Zenia yelled in warning. "And so are they."

Men fired at the elves, but invisible barriers appeared, deflecting the bullets. They ricocheted around the stone chamber, and Rhi swore as one bounced off the walkway near her. She scrambled out of the way of the men and looked at Zenia, half a bo in each hand, an uncertain expression on her face.

Zenia shook her head, not sure what encouragement she could offer.

She envisioned the barriers dropping, hoping her dragon tear had the power to force that to happen. Just as it looked like the charging humans would bounce off the elven defenses, the same way the bullets had, the shields dropped.

Heber swung his rifle like a club at one elf while two of his guards launched themselves at the other male. The female had found footing on the walkway again, and she waved her sword in the air. Ten men flew off the stone walkway and into the pool, leaving Heber and the two guards at the front by themselves.

Rhi ran in to help, raising the halves of her bo like clubs.

More shadows stirred in the light of the portal.

"We can't let any more through or we're all dead," Zenia whispered, and once again envisioned her dragon tear somehow making the portal explode.

She sensed it trying, but the magic, similar to those bullets, simply bounced off.

Heber's attempt to club one of the intruders didn't work any better than Rhi's had. Though he was fast for an older man, he wasn't nearly fast enough to get through an elf's defenses. A magical blade cut his rifle in half. Heber tried to skitter back, his eyes bulging as he got the gist of what he was dealing with. The elf pointed his sword at Heber's chest. Heber dropped to his knees.

"You have great hatred in your mind for our people," the elf said, his voice ringing out over the shouts of men and clashes of swords meeting rifles. "Yet you are the undeserving vermin infesting this continent—this world."

Heber appeared to be held in a trance. Zenia wanted to help him, but she worried that more elves would leap through the portal any second.

What if you funneled energy continuously into it? she thought to her dragon tear, envisioning a stream of energy pouring into the thin rim of the portal. It looked so fragile. Was it possible that adding more and more magic might overload it somehow?

Her dragon tear seemed contemplative. She resisted the urge to yell at it in her mind, to urge it to hurry.

Heber made choking sounds, grasping his throat even though the elf wasn't touching him. To the side, the other elf battled more traditionally with the two guards that had gotten through, blocking their sword attacks or knocking rifles aside before they could be fired. Farther up the walkway, the female elf lunged toward Rhi. In the water, Heber's men swam toward the walkway, trying to find a place where they could reach the edge to pull themselves up.

A wave of weakness ran through Zenia, and she sensed her dragon tear attempting what she had requested. She also sensed that it would take time, if it worked at all, and that the gem was drawing upon her energy to help.

Heber's face was turning red. The elf sneered, holding the old man with his gaze as the magic of his sword did all the work, silently holding Heber prisoner.

Nobody was paying attention to Zenia at the moment. She crept closer to the battle. Her dragon tear needed to focus on the portal, but maybe *she* could help.

A pistol lay on the ground. Loaded?

Zenia picked it up and fired at Heber's assailant.

She expected the elf to anticipate the attack and create a magical barrier, but the bullet slammed into his shoulder. He stumbled back and fell into the portal, the rim now glowing cherry red, like an ingot dropped into a furnace. The top half of his body disappeared, but his legs and boots stuck out. Zenia hoped the artifact was scorching and burned him.

Heber pitched to his side, released from the sword's magical grip and gasping for air. Zenia rushed over to help him or at least pull him out of the way of the skirmish raging beside him.

But the elf she'd shot lurched back out of the portal, his golden eyes burning with rage. He still had his sword, and he thrust the point toward Zenia. She dodged, but power crashed against her and hurled her into the wall. She struck hard enough to see stars, and pain axed her neck and spine.

A twinge of uncertainty came from her dragon tear, and it seemed to offer to switch focus, to help. But Zenia sensed that if it stopped pouring magical energy into the portal, all that had gone in so far would evaporate without having done any damage. If it kept going, there might eventually be enough energy in that compact frame that it had to burst out, and the portal would be destroyed in the process.

Keep going, she thought to the dragon tear.

The elf ignored Heber and stomped toward Zenia, one hand gripping his wounded shoulder, but magic crackling in the air around him as he walked. Zenia saw her death in his eyes. She tried to push away her pain and scramble to her feet, but some force was pressing down upon her. An invisible hand wrapped around her throat. The elf sneered.

Everyone else was down or busy battling the other elves. As the vise tightened, cutting off her air, she knew she couldn't escape.

CHAPTER 17

T HE MASSIVE WALL OF WATER crashed through the valley, tearing up trees and dislodging boulders that had rested on that land forever.

As Jev clambered to the top of the slope, water splashed him in the back and doused his hair. He slowed his sprint to make sure Cutter stayed close to him. His friend had shorter legs and didn't run as quickly.

While they raced to high ground together, Jev kept glancing back down the slope in search of Lornysh, but his friend had disappeared. The boulder he'd crouched behind was now submerged.

A soldier caught in the flow sailed downriver, yelling and flailing ineffectively. Jev cursed himself for bringing Krox's people out here. Why had he believed that mundane soldiers would have a chance against elven mages? All he'd been thinking about was keeping his family safe.

"There's Lornysh." Cutter pointed.

Their friend crouched high in the branches of a tree, not on their side of the valley but on the far side.

How had he gotten over there? And *why*? Had he hoped to reach the elves during the distraction caused by the water? Jev didn't think that would work since the wardens had *created* that water.

"That tree's shaking and doesn't look stable," Cutter added.

No, it did not. It had a wide trunk, but who knew if its roots would hold under the torrential flow?

Worse, Jev spotted an elf high up on the opposite bank with his bow drawn. He only looked to have a couple of arrows left in his quiver, but he was nocking one and staring straight at Lornysh.

Cutter drew his hammer.

"That's not going to help." Jev yanked out his pistol and fired. No, he *tried* to fire. But the powder in the bullet had gotten wet.

"You sure? It's waterproof." Cutter pulled back his arm and hurled his hammer, the tool imbued with magic by Master Grindmor.

Jev couldn't believe his friend would risk losing it for such a crazy throw. He looked for the nearest soldier with a rifle.

"Shoot that elf," he barked, though he feared it was too late.

The elf loosed his arrow toward Lornysh as Cutter's hammer spun through the air across the flooded valley.

But Lornysh had seen the shot or sensed it coming. He hung from the tree branch with one hand and whipped his sword up with the other. He swatted the arrow out of the air with a faint clang that traveled across the roaring water.

The elf who'd loosed the arrow shouted angrily at Lornysh and waved his bow. He didn't see the hammer coming.

It slammed into his forehead with impossible accuracy, and Jev gaped. The elf pitched backward, his bow falling from his hands. He didn't get up again.

Cutter dusted off his hands. "That's how you do it."

"I wish you had more of those," Jev said.

"I'll have to retrieve that one. Good thing the water's going down."

Lornysh sprang from his perch. He didn't quite make it to dry ground, but he swam with powerful strokes and reached the far side. Two elves appeared on the top of the valley wall and looked down at him. Vornzylar and the elf with the green-glowing sword that sprouted vines.

"They'll kill him," Jev breathed.

A soldier ran up to Jev. "The lieutenant is missing, sir," he blurted. "What do we do?"

Jev snatched the rifle from the man's hands and shot at Vornzylar.

This time, the bullets weren't wet, and the weapon fired with a satisfying crack. His aim was as perfect as Cutter's had been, but the bullet bounced off some magical shield before reaching the elf.

Jev groaned. The elves didn't even glance in his direction. They strode resolutely to the spot where Lornysh was climbing out of the water, his sword in hand.

ELVEN FURY

Lornysh hadn't been able to defeat Vornzylar alone. He would be mincemeat in the face of two foes of that caliber.

"My hammer would break that barrier they've got up," Cutter said. "It's just as magical as they are."

"Then we're getting it." Jev thrust the rifle back at the soldier, spotted an axe on his belt, and grabbed it. "I'll bring this back to you later. Keep firing at any elves you see over there if you get a chance."

"You swimming?" Cutter asked.

Jev ran down the muddy slope with the axe in hand and launched himself into the water.

As Cutter had observed, the flow had lessened, and the water would disappear altogether soon, but a strong current still threatened to carry him down the newly flooded valley and out to sea. He jammed the axe through his belt so he could use both arms, and he kicked and paddled harder than he'd ever swum in his life. Meanwhile, he prayed to the Air Dragon that none of the elves were paying attention to him. In the water, he would be an easy target.

But maybe the elves were out of arrows. He made it to the far side without being shot at. He scrambled up the slope, glancing around to get his bearings. He'd traveled farther downriver than he wanted, and he had to sprint around torn-up brush and over downed logs, hoping the elves were still in the same spot. Hoping Lornysh was still alive.

Jev glimpsed Cutter and a couple of the soldiers also risking the swim, but he couldn't stop to wait for them. The roar of the water had died down, and he heard the clashing of swords up ahead. The elves had moved from the crest of the valley wall and disappeared into a thick stand of shrubs. Jev let the sound of the fight lead him to them.

From the rapid-fire clangs, it seemed that a dozen men must be battling, but Jev knew it couldn't be more than three, Lornysh and those two elves. The third elf was unconscious from Cutter's hammer strike, and Jev had shot the fourth in the hand earlier. He hoped that would make it impossible for him to swing a sword or draw a bow.

As Jev crept toward the stand, the leaves shuddered and shook. He spotted the hammer on the ground near the unconscious elf and snatched it up, remembering Cutter's promise that it would thwart a magical barrier.

With the axe in one hand and the hammer in the other, Jev slipped into the bushes. He spotted Vornzylar and Lornysh as Lornysh darted back from a barrage of thrusts and slashes, almost tripping over a root in his haste to get out of the way. He blocked Vornzylar's attacks, but he winced as their blades met again and again, as if his old injury—or some new one—was hampering him.

Jev circled, hoping to get to Vornzylar's back, but movement stirred at the corner of his eye. Instinctively, he ducked.

An arrow buzzed over his head and embedded itself in a tree trunk. Jev jumped up, spinning as the second elf, the one with the thorny sword, sprang over the brush toward him.

The glowing green blade slashed toward his face, grasping vines writhing like tiny snakes. Jev whipped Cutter's hammer up, praying for accuracy with the unfamiliar weapon, a weapon that wasn't as long as he was accustomed to for fighting.

The elven blade clanged against the hammer's handle. A jolt ran up Jev's arm, jarring his elbow painfully, but the hammer deflected the sword without breaking. The elf's eyebrows flew up. He must have expected the tool to break.

Hoping to take advantage of his opponent's brief surprise, Jev leapt in, swinging the axe at his chest.

His enemy sprang back, leaping a head-high bush as if it were a flower, but he landed awkwardly. Jev lunged around the bush and swung both weapons at the same time, aiming for different targets. The elf gyrated and twisted, evading the swipes and launching a thrust of his own, but the attack wasn't as fast as Jev expected, and he had no trouble blocking it.

Blood smeared the side of the elf's head—he looked to have been gouged by a bullet. Despite his mighty leaps, he also seemed to be favoring one ankle. Normally, Jev wouldn't find it honorable to battle a wounded opponent, but the elf was attacking *him* on *his* land. And all those injuries would do was even the odds.

"We're coming, Jev," came a bellow from downstream. Cutter.

The elf glanced in that direction and barked, "Reinforcements," in elven to his comrade as he parried another attack from Jev.

"Finish him!" Vornzylar snarled back, not glancing over. He battered Lornysh with blows like storm clouds pouring down boulder-sized pieces of hail.

Lornysh parried each blow, but his leg buckled, and he went down to one knee.

ELVEN FURY

Jev roared and lunged at his own foe, knowing he had to get him out of the way before he could help Lornysh. Knowing, too, that the elf had been ordered to kill him.

He attacked faster than he ever had, chopping with the axe and smashing with the hammer. The elf had only one blade, and though it whipped about so quickly it blurred, he struggled against Jev's angry onslaught. He backed away as he parried, and his shoulder clipped a trunk. The elf came down on his injured ankle, and it twisted, giving way.

Jev sprang, using the hammer to knock the elven blade out of his foe's hand. The sword's glow and magical vines disappeared as it flew through the bushes. The elf tried to roll away, but he was hemmed in by trees and brush too stout to push aside.

Jev lunged, pressing the axe against the side of his foe's throat. "Yield," he ordered, though he was tempted to simply crack the elf over the head, caring little if he lived or died, not when Lornysh was still battling his nemesis ten feet away.

The elf curled his lip. "To a human?" he asked in his own tongue. "Never! You are a plague upon the earth, and I will not let you sully my death by bowing to you."

Before Jev could reply, the elf whipped a dagger out of a belt sheath.

Jev stepped back, readying his weapons to block an attack. But the elf sneered defiantly and swept the blade across his own throat from ear to ear.

Stunned, Jev gawked as his enemy slumped to the ground, his life's blood spurting from his arteries.

The clash of blades drew him from his shock. He sprinted through the brush to find Lornysh and Vornzylar facing each other in a tiny clearing. Drawing upon some deep reserve, Lornysh had found his feet again and kept parrying, but his movements were slower than Jev had ever seen. Blood streamed from a cut lip, and he barely got his blade up to deflect a swing that would have cleaved his skull in half.

Jev advanced from behind, choosing the hammer for his weapon. He raised it, his eyes locking on the back of Vornzylar's head.

The elf must have heard or sensed him, for he started to turn, but Lornysh sprang at him, thrusting with his blade. Vornzylar was forced to whip back around to parry the fiery sword. Jev leaped in and slammed the hammer at the elf's head.

Vornzylar almost jerked away in time to avoid it, but the hammer struck the side of his head hard enough to stun him for an instant. Jev swung again, cracking him like the gong in the Air Order Temple. The hammer flared with silver light as it crunched through the elf's skull. That surprised Jev, and he jerked the weapon away, grimacing as the hammer's head caught on bone. He'd swung hard, but he hadn't thought a blow with a blunt weapon would penetrate the elf's skull.

Vornzylar's sword dropped from his limp hand, and his knees buckled. As he fell, he continued to glare at Lornysh, not even glancing back at Jev.

"You die dishonored," he snarled. "Traitor."

He reached up to touch his head, seemed surprised when his hand came back bloody, then crumpled to the ground.

"It is you who die, old friend," Lornysh said, his shoulders slumped.

Vornzylar's eyes closed, and he did not answer.

Feeling queasy, Jev looked down at the bloody hammer. He hadn't meant to kill the elf, but maybe it was for the best. Lornysh hadn't been able to do it, and if they'd let Vornzylar live, he might not have left Lornysh alone until he'd managed to kill him.

"I've always wanted to believe elves were wiser than humans," Lornysh said, kneeling as he caught his breath, "but I fear that's not true, that longevity and time don't impart as much wisdom as one would hope."

"It's disappointing that wisdom is in such short supply among all the intelligent races in the world," Jev said.

Foliage rattled as Cutter pushed his way into the clearing. He frowned at the dead elves and then at the weapons in Jev's hands.

"If you wanted to use my hammer, you should have asked."

"Sorry." Jev wiped off the blood and offered it to him. "I found it lying on the ground and assumed you didn't need it anymore."

"Well, I don't since it looks like you finished off all the elves." He glared grumpily at them as he accepted the tool—the *weapon*—and thrust it through his belt.

"One remains living somewhere. The one who was shot earlier. He may flee now that Vornzylar is dead." Lornysh stood and stepped forward, gripping his side, then bent to pick up Vornzylar's fallen blade. As with the other magical sword, its glow had disappeared once it fell from its owner's hand.

"Is it dangerous if someone finds one of those swords and picks it up?" Jev imagined children from the villages coming up here to treasure hunt after the flood receded, leaving debris from wherever in the mountains the elves had sourced that water. "Someone who's not an elf?"

"Not now that the owner is dead, no," Lornysh said. "By elven custom, the blades belong to whoever killed the wielders, though their magic will remain buried in the sword and inaccessible to someone who isn't elven. Still, they are fine weapons." He flipped it to hold the blade and offer the hilt to Jev. "Do you want it?"

Jev shook his head. "You're the one who battled him. I just snuck up and cracked him in the head."

"I already have a *kisyula* sword." Lornysh shifted his hand, offering it to Cutter.

"Don't look at me. That thing's taller than I am."

Twigs snapped as the soldiers approached.

"I can ship it back to his family." Lornysh lowered the blade.

Jev walked into the brush to retrieve the other sword, the vine-spurting one. He touched it, half-expecting some magical power to zap him. But its owner was definitely dead, and the blade lay quiescent. He picked it up and rejoined his friends.

After facing off against that elf—and that sword—twice, Jev wouldn't mind claiming it for himself. Less as a war trophy and more as a useful tool. He'd found a surprising number of reasons lately to set his pistol and rifle aside and use a blade.

Cutter looked at the sword. "Maybe Master Grindmor can make the magic inside it activate to your touch."

Lornysh appeared skeptical, and Jev decided not to pin his hopes on that.

"Would I have to prove my adequacy to her before she would try?" Jev asked.

"Likely."

Lornysh's eyebrows twitched. "Wouldn't Zenia object to that?"

"She—" Fear slammed Jev in the gut as he remembered the unknown trouble at the castle. "We have to check on her. On my family. Everyone."

Not waiting for a response, he sprinted for home.

Zenia couldn't breathe. She grasped at the air around her throat, as if there were hands she could physically pull free, but there was nothing she could grab. On her knees in front of the elf warden crushing her with his magic, she couldn't do a thing.

Heber's men threw themselves at the other two elves, but nobody disturbed her assailant. Nearby, Rhi was knocked against the wall and dropped to the walkway. Unconscious? Dead?

Her dragon tear offered to help again, offered to knock away her attacker. Zenia was tempted, just for a moment, so she could draw in a single breath of air. But she implored the gem to keep funneling all its energy into the glowing structure.

Another elf leaped through the portal, and she feared many more were on the way. If she did nothing else, she had to blow it up.

Energy rolled through the air like heat waves, flowing from her dragon tear to the portal. The rim glowed such a fierce red that it had to be close to exploding. Unfortunately, Zenia's head felt like it would explode too. Her lungs spasmed, trying to suck in air, but her throat was entirely constricted.

The female elf cried something in her own tongue. Zenia's attacker glanced aside, and for a heartbeat, the power constricting her throat lessened. She managed to get in a half gasp of air, but he turned immediately back to her. His gaze locked onto her dragon tear, and she realized the elves had figured out what she was doing. What *it* was doing.

Behind them, the portal quaked. The earth trembled under their feet. Zenia knew her dragon tear was close to destroying the thing, but the elf lunged for her, fingers reaching not for her neck but for the gem. She could see in his eyes that he meant to tear it off and hurl it into the pool.

A shot rang out.

Her attacker stiffened, his head jerking up. His hand never reached her chest. For long seconds, he stood frozen, eyes full of shock. Then he pitched over backward, collapsing in front of Zenia.

Heber knelt behind the elf, a thin trail of smoke wafting from his pistol.

"The heart, woman," he growled at her. "If you're going to shoot an elf, you shoot him in the *heart*."

"I'll try to remember," Zenia rasped, her throat raw.

Her entire body ached. She didn't know if it was from the elf's attack or from the energy the dragon tear was sapping from her. As she looked around the chamber, she sagged, feeling defeated even though her life wasn't in immediate danger. Rhi was down. Only two of the castle guards remained up, battling a male elf in front of the portal. The rest of the defenders were crumpled and unconscious—or dead—on the walkway. Some floated in the water.

The female elf stared over at Zenia and Heber, and her eyes locked on the dragon tear. She lifted her sword and sprang toward it.

As Zenia started to roll away, knowing she couldn't possibly escape, a final burst of energy poured forth from the dragon tear.

Light flashed and a thunderous boom echoed from the walls. Shards of something—metal—flew in a hundred directions, pelting the stone ceiling and walls. A piece gouged into Zenia's cheek.

A blast of energy came from the portal, knocking her against the wall again. Splashes sounded as others were thrown into the water.

All light vanished from the underground chamber. Even Zenia's dragon tear grew dark. Still. Dead?

For a few seconds, the only sounds were of people breathing, along with a few limp splashes from the pool. Then the earth shook again, and rocks started falling.

Zenia envisioned the ceiling tumbling down.

A hand gripped her. In the dark, she had no idea whose it was, but she was hoisted into the air and draped over a hard shoulder.

"Rhi!" she shouted, fearing her friend would be left behind.

Rocks slammed down. One struck whoever held her, and the man staggered. He recovered and felt his way along the walkway and the wall.

"Get out of here," he yelled. "Everyone, now!"

It was Heber.

Someone else shouted in elven. Heber cursed and walked faster, Zenia bouncing on his shoulder.

Lights appeared somewhere ahead. Not magical glowing lights but simple lantern light. As soon as she started to feel relieved, swords clashed.

"Get her," Jev barked. "Don't let her—"

A pained grunt sounded as more rocks slammed down. One clipped Zenia in the head. She twisted out of Heber's grasp. He cursed but let her go. As men rushed into the room carrying lanterns, half clambering over fallen rubble, Zenia spotted Rhi. She was in the same spot she'd been crumpled in before and wasn't moving. By the founders, she couldn't be dead.

"Jev," Zenia yelled. "I need your help."

She tried to call upon her dragon tear, but it was as if she wore a lifeless rock around her throat. It had used all its power to destroy the portal. What if she'd permanently burned it out and had forever lost the soul linked to it?

"Coming," Jev called. "I see you. Father, two elves ran by. Go get them before they can hurt anyone."

Jev rushed into the chamber as Heber and his surviving men pushed their way out.

"It's Rhi." Zenia pulled a chunk of rock off her friend's unmoving back, not caring about the elves that had gotten away. If Rhi was dead because she'd leaped in front of Zenia multiple times to protect her...

She found Rhi's throat in the poor lighting, praying to the Blue Dragon that she would find a pulse.

"She's alive," she blurted.

"I'll get her." Jev touched Zenia's shoulder, then gathered the unconscious Rhi into his arms.

"Thank you." She patted him on the back, surprised that his clothing was soaking wet. "That's not blood, is it?" In the dim light, she couldn't tell.

"No, I took a swim. I'll explain everything later, but we did kill Vornzylar, and Lornysh is all right. Injured, but that's his new normative state."

Zenia grunted, her entire body aching from the battering she'd taken, her throat bruised and raw. "I can empathize. Maybe later, we can—"

Shouts and a bang drifted down from somewhere above them, muted by the layers of rock.

"Never mind," Zenia said, trailing Jev toward the exit.

"Hold that thought. We'll find some time for recuperation later."

Zenia, worried for his family and the people who lived in the castle, didn't say anything. She was fairly certain only two elves had slipped out, but she knew firsthand how much trouble two of those wardens could cause.

"I had no idea this was down here," Jev said as they wound back through the dusty passageways. "I knew about the dungeon. Vastiun and I used to play down there when we were boys."

"A natural recreation area."

"We thought the old torture implements were particularly delightful."

"Boys are ghouls."

"Sometimes, yes."

More shouts drifted down from the courtyard, and Jev picked up his pace as they passed through the dungeon. Heber and his men must have already chased the elves out because Zenia didn't see anyone else in there.

A faint tingle emanated from her dragon tear.

She grasped it, relieved it had come back to life but worried it was warning her about something. Magic being used in the courtyard? Or was it simply letting her know it was there for her if she needed it?

She thought she sensed weariness in the gem, or the personality linked to it, and she tried to let it know it could rest, that she wouldn't need to draw upon it again. She hoped that was true.

The clang of steel rang out in the courtyard.

Jev sprinted up the last of the stairs, past the kitchen, and through the main hallway. He laid Rhi down in an out-of-the-way alcove behind an urn that had been knocked over, then drew a sword that Zenia didn't recognize and sprinted out. She followed, fearing they would have to battle those two elves again.

But as they burst into the sunlight, they spotted the elves right away, lying on their backs with swords pointing at their throats. The men holding the swords weren't Dharrow guards; they wore the king's blue, purple, and gold livery. Dozens of similar men on horseback blocked the open gate out of the castle, and several royal steam carriages were parked on the other side of the drawbridge.

Zenia spotted Targyon mounted on a horse in the back with the princess next to him, her eyes closed and a hand outstretched toward the elves on the cobblestones. She opened her eyes and glared at them, then spoke in elven.

Jev had stopped a few steps into the courtyard. Zenia looked to him for a translation.

"She's angry with their faction and calling them immature idiots for destroying her ship and her tower."

"Idiots? I didn't know elves had such simple insults."

"It has a lot of syllables in their language and rhymes with ship, so it sounds elegant."

"Ah." Zenia rubbed her face, relieved the situation was under control. She didn't think she could have asked for more from her dragon tear.

Heber Dharrow, his face bloody and his eyes livid, watched the goings on while the princess spoke—or maybe lectured. Zenia couldn't tell if Heber was angry at the two elven intruders who had barged into his basement or simply angry that elves of any kind were on his land.

Zyndari Bludnor was nowhere to be seen, but Zenia wouldn't presume that knocking out her dragon tear would change the situation between Jev and his father—and the arranged marriage. As far as Zenia knew, that was something Heber had wanted before the zyndari woman showed up.

"Let them rise," Princess Yesleva said in the kingdom tongue, her voice ringing throughout the courtyard, enhanced by some magic. "But take their weapons. I will send them back to my homeland where my father will decide what their punishment will be for intruding here and destroying elven property."

"And killing humans," Jev said. "We lost some of Krox's men out there." He pointed toward one of the castle walls.

"Where is Vornzylar?" Yesleva asked. "He will be held accountable for the actions of those he killed who were not *hyrishimo*."

Zenia looked at Jev again.

He sighed and quietly translated. "Traitors. She didn't state it, but I gather that killing Lornysh would have been acceptable." He glanced toward the fountain. Lornysh, looking tired and injured, sat on the edge closest to the wall.

Yesleva gazed in that direction, but Zenia didn't sense any animosity in her eyes. If anything, she appeared speculative.

"Vornzylar is dead," Lornysh said, then switched to elven to continue a conversation with her.

"He's explaining what happened out there," Jev told Zenia.

"What *did* happen? You say you didn't know you had a portal in your basement?"

He snorted. "No. That must have been from… I'm not even sure. From a time when Dharrows were friends with elves, and comings and goings were common."

"Your mother's time?"

"Before her, I think. If my father didn't know about that secret passage—" Jev shrugged, looking as tired as Lornysh. Zenia had the urge to hug him, maybe give him a rubdown and a bath, like one might do with a horse. A massage, she supposed it was called for humans. She'd never massaged a man, but she wouldn't mind trying. "I have a feeling it's been forgotten for a long, long time," Jev added. He explained how he and Lornysh and Cutter had been too late to stop the elves from using the communication stone but that they had run into Vornzylar and that Jev had ultimately been the one to kill him.

"What?" Lornysh blurted.

Jev looked back, his brows knitting, and Zenia felt bad for interrupting him and causing him to miss something. Maybe he would forgive her after that massage.

"You seem to be the logical choice," Targyon said dryly, speaking for the first time.

The two elven prisoners frowned darkly at Lornysh and also at the princess, but the guards were tying them, and Zenia sensed some magic keeping them still.

"You mean the *only* choice?" Lornysh asked.

"It is true that there are few of our people interested in coming to Kor right now," Yesleva said. "At least for peaceful purposes."

"Neither the king nor the elven diplomats in other nations would accept me."

"I am positive I can talk Father into accepting you, and there is no reason why you would have to interact with our ambassadors in other nations. You will send reports directly to Ormaleshon, and he will send his instructions directly to you. A simple chain-of-command."

"We'll rebuild your tower, of course, Lornysh." Targyon smiled.

"It's not *my* tower. I haven't said yes to this craziness."

Targyon's smile faded, his eyes growing serious. "*I* would be happy to see you there rather than some old elf I'm not familiar with and can't trust."

"You would ask me to act in your favor over that of my people?" Lornysh arched his eyebrows.

"I would ask you to help me maintain a diplomatic relationship with the Taziir, one I hope we can improve over time. To establish trade and invite elves back into the kingdom... I know it's early, but I hope this can be done."

"You're an optimist."

"What hope is there for a nation whose ruler isn't?"

Lornysh shook his head, his lips pressed into a thin line.

Zenia had no idea if he would accept the position.

Jev scratched his jaw and mumbled a, "Huh."

Maybe he had no idea either.

Someone cleared a throat behind them. Rhi.

Zenia spun, chagrinned she'd momentarily forgotten about her friend. Bruised, scraped, and with bumps starting to swell, Rhi leaned against the doorjamb and peered blearily at them.

"Usually," she said, wincing at the effort to speak or maybe the brightness of the sunlight, "injured people get deposited on beds with handsome male nurses there to sponge their grimy bodies and smear healing potions on their wounds. They're not dumped into alcoves next to a dusty urn with oddly long hairs zigzagging through the glaze."

"That's horsehair," Jev said, "and it was quite fashionable to include it in pottery a while back. My grandmother made a number of urns like that."

"It's gross."

"I always thought so too. Here, I'll carry you to a bed. I don't think we have any male nurses though." Jev looked around the courtyard, as if making sure nobody was going to start shooting in the next thirty seconds, and stepped toward her, holding out his arms.

Zenia thought her proud friend would object, but it *did* look like the doorjamb was the only thing keeping Rhi from falling back behind the urn.

"No male nurses with sponges? You're certain?" Rhi slumped into his arms when Jev came close.

He swept her up and headed into the castle. "I think Mildrey, our cook, has some sponges. One of her assistants is male."

"Aren't those sponges for washing dishes?"

"Likely so. Are you going to be fussy?"

"Is this assistant cook handsome?" Rhi asked. "Is he married?"

"No and yes. He has seven kids that live down in Red Hat Village."

"Maybe I'll see if Hydal is available to recite stories to me again."

"That does sound more promising than being sponged like a soup pot."

"You're a strange man, Dharrow. I'm not sure what Zenia sees in you."

Zenia smiled as she trailed after them, not wanting to risk being drawn into another conversation with Heber. She hoped the brief one they'd had earlier would suffice for Jev. He'd wanted her to remove the manipulation, and she had. Zenia doubted it was within her power to convince Heber that she was a well-mannered woman who would make a lovely daughter-in-law.

"Nor am I," Jev said, turning toward a wing of guest rooms. "It's a good thing her taste is questionable."

He spoke quietly to one of the staff he passed, eliciting a promise that the woman would find the healer to look in on Rhi as soon as possible, and then took her into a room. Zenia sat on a chair while he went to fetch water and some pain potions himself.

"He's a strange man but a good one," Rhi said, settling her head back on a pillow and closing her eyes. "You should have wild and passionate sex with him tonight and forget about what the gossiping ninnies in the castle say."

"I was thinking of offering him a massage."

"Do that. And then have sex with him. He'll thank you profusely."

Jev returned in time to hear her words, and his eyebrows rose. After the day she'd had, Zenia shouldn't have blushed at such silly talk, but she felt her cheeks grow hot.

"She's not wrong." Jev touched her shoulder on his way to Rhi's bed. "But we could start with dinner."

"I'd like that," Zenia said.

"After I have a long frank talk with my father. Did you, ah—" He waved to her dragon tear.

"Yes. I believe the link is broken, at least for now. It's possible the whole dragon tear is broken. If so, I may have to apologize, as destroying a priceless magical gem may go beyond my authority as an Agent of the Crown."

"Maybe so, but accidents happen." Jev sat next to Rhi and measured a dose of Grodonol's Pain-No-More.

"Jev," Zenia protested at his cavalier attitude.

He twitched a shoulder. "She was using it to further personal gain at the risk of ruining others' lives. She deserves to lose it. The Orders would agree."

Two dour-faced guards from Alderoth Castle walked in, and Zenia stood uncertainly. After talking about her dragon tear's deed, she half-expected them to tell her she was to be arrested.

"Captain Cham?" a feminine voice came from the hall outside. Princess Yesleva.

"I'm in here." Zenia faced the door as the guards stepped aside politely for the princess to enter. She didn't see Targyon in the hall. Maybe he was monitoring the situation in the courtyard. Zenia supposed it was too much to hope that Targyon was talking to Heber and informing him that arranged marriages were soon to be outlawed.

"I meant to speak with you earlier about your dragon tear," Yesleva said.

Zenia swallowed, nerves springing to life in her gut. Had someone finally figured out she was too ignorant and unworthy to wield such powerful magic? Had the elves lost it long ago and come to reclaim it?

The idea of losing the dragon tear—and the quirky personality it had shared with her—distressed her, and she had to resist the urge to wrap her fingers around it and sprint away before the princess could deliver any ultimatums.

"Oh?" she asked carefully.

"It is not my place to judge, but the soul linked to your dragon tear is in pain. Do you know this? It is unfair of you to use her so when she is not free."

Zenia swayed, the backs of her knees bumping her chair. "You know about him? Er, *her*?"

"I can sense her through your dragon tear, and I sense her pain." Yesleva frowned sternly.

Zenia almost blurted that it wasn't her fault, but she had a resource here who knew more than she did. She had to question Yesleva for all her knowledge while she had a chance.

"Where is she? Do you know? What do you mean she's not free? Why not?" Zenia thought of all the nightmares she'd had, of herself—or what had seemed like herself—chained in a cave with an orc sword-wielder approaching. "Is she truly a dragon?"

"Yes, she's a dragon. I'm not sure how her soul came to be linked to that dragon tear, as she seems quite young."

Zenia nodded vigorously in agreement. She'd always sensed a youthful enthusiasm and even playfulness from the dragon tear.

"It's possible that after she was imprisoned, she used her magic to siphon a portion of her soul into the gem in the hope that someone would find her and help her." Yesleva stepped forward and lifted a hand toward Zenia's chest. "May I?"

Zenia held the dragon tear out on its chain so the princess could touch it. It glowed a faint blue and emanated a sense of uncertainty tinged with wonder. Could Yesleva feel that?

Yesleva wrapped her fingers around the gem and closed her eyes. "Her physical body is far from here. Perhaps where she is, she could find nobody willing to help her, to defy those who hold her captive. And she thought a human could help her." Yesleva opened her eyes and tilted her head, as if puzzled by the idea. "I would like to think an elf would have helped, though I suppose our people rarely travel to Izstara. They are loathed by the orcs, trolls, and ogres that live there, ever since the Race Wars. It's also possible she has never seen an elf. But humans are more likely to be tolerated there if they offer some value. There are traders that travel the world and venture into those jungles."

"Izstara?" Zenia whispered.

Yesleva lowered her hand. "You should go there and free her. It is unfair of you to use her magic while she is in pain and a prisoner."

"Where on the continent is she?" Jev asked, speaking for the first time in several minutes.

"The northern end, I believe."

"That narrows it down to a couple thousand square miles," Jev said.

Yesleva spread her hands. "A dragon tear is not a homing beacon. If I were to go along, perhaps I could help, but I have much to do. A new ambassador to train and prisoners to take back to my father for punishment."

"Lornysh hasn't said yes, has he?" Jev asked.

"He will." Yesleva smiled cryptically and walked out the door.

Zenia grasped her dragon tear, distressed anew to learn that the soul linked to it truly was in pain in a cave somewhere deep in the Izstara jungles. She felt like a dunce for not having realized earlier, for not having grasped that those dreams had been an attempt to communicate.

"You don't look surprised," Jev said quietly, stepping over and wrapping an arm around her shoulders.

"I should have understood earlier. I have to find a way to free her." Zenia quailed inside at the idea of traveling to some distant and dangerous continent when she'd never been more than fifty miles away from Korvann. But the dragon tear—the *dragon*—had done so much to help her. She doubted she would even be alive if not for its assistance. Jev might not be either. All those dwarves she'd pulled off that ship before it exploded wouldn't have made it... "I have to free her," she repeated, lifting her chin.

Jev smiled and rested his forehead against her temple. "I know."

EPILOGUE

A S THE SUN DIPPED TOWARD the horizon, Jev walked out to the valley where he'd battled the elves that morning. His aunt had said Father was out there, and even though Jev was eager to return to Alderoth Castle and pack and recruit help for a journey to Izstara, he knew he needed to talk to the old man. Jev hoped the destruction of Zyndari Bludnor's dragon tear—she'd been ranting earlier that it had burned out somehow—meant her clutches had loosened on his father, but he couldn't be certain anything would truly change. In the old man's eyes, Fremia was the perfect daughter-in-law, zyndari, young, a descendant of great warriors… all the things he valued.

Jev spotted his father standing atop the valley wall where Cutter had stood to hurl his hammer. His arms were folded, and he gazed downward, toward the trickle of water that was all that remained of the flood the elves had conjured up. Somewhere in the mountains upstream, a lake had probably been emptied. Jev shuddered at the memory of that power.

He'd given the sword he'd claimed to Cutter, who was already on his way back to the capital, having promised to speak with Master Grindmor about attuning the magic to a human. To *Jev*.

Since he fully planned to go with Zenia to rescue her dragon, he wouldn't object to gaining ownership of a magical sword, but he wouldn't be surprised if Cutter was asking his mentor for the impossible. Jev couldn't remember hearing of any humans wielding elven blades in the legends. Even if it was possible—Grindmor was legendary among the dwarves, after all—it would likely take more than a day. Jev suspected Zenia wanted to set sail as soon as possible, as soon as Targyon gave them permission to take a leave of absence. And likely even if he didn't. She owed that dragon tear a lot. So did Jev.

Several men walked into view, striding out of the log-littered valley with bodies on stretchers. Jev grimaced, recognizing soldiers he had lost to the flood or the elven arrows. Lieutenant Cark was among the seven dead. Captain Krox would have words, maybe accusations, for Jev for losing the officer. And he wouldn't be able to shrug them off, for this had happened on his land in a battle to save his friend. In all, how many had been lost so Lornysh could live?

Not that Lornysh had asked for help. No, he hadn't wanted this. Jev had made the choice to assist his friend.

He hoped Lornysh took the job of ambassador and was able to act as a good liaison between Kor and Taziira. After so many deaths, it seemed he needed to ensure his life was for more than assassinating people.

"Burn that one," Father called down to the men at the end of the grim caravan.

They carried the body of one of the elves. The one Cutter had hit with his hammer, Jev thought. He hadn't believed the elf had been killed at the time, but maybe Cark's men had finished him off before coming to the castle.

Jev didn't see the bodies of Vornzylar or the elf who had committed suicide, so they were probably still up in the brush. He supposed he should direct some of the men that way so the dead could be collected and wouldn't be torn to pieces by wild animals, though elves wouldn't likely mind. They did burial cairns for those they loved and respected, but they always considered it proper that bodies eventually go back to nature in one way or another.

Father turned as Jev approached.

Jev had heard from Zenia and Rhi, before they had headed back to the city with Targyon and his entourage, that his father had been at the forefront, battling the elves that came through the portal. Jev wasn't surprised, though the old man was lucky to come out of that alive. He wore a gash across one cheek that would leave a scar, one that would only add to his naturally surly mien, and his clothes were ripped, hinting of injuries underneath. Jev wasn't that surprised that he hadn't waited for someone to tend his wounds before coming out to see what had happened to his land.

"They flooded this?" Father waved at the trickle of water below, the uprooted trees and bushes scattered everywhere, and mud slathered halfway up the valley walls.

"With magic, yes."

"Magic." Father spat. "I can't believe that *thing* was under our castle for the founders know how long. You weren't aware of it, were you?"

"I had no idea."

"I remember you boys playing down in the dungeon."

"What boy doesn't enjoy dangling from shackles that were once used to imprison people?" Jev smiled, though he didn't know why he bothered making jokes with his father. The man had the sense of humor of a dyspeptic badger.

Father grunted and frowned up and down the valley. "I'll have to get a team out here. Might as well gather those logs and mill them."

Jev almost volunteered to handle that job, mostly because he didn't want his father to stumble across the communication stone and decide to blow it up. Maybe that wouldn't be the worst idea, since it had proven a disadvantage that day, but Jev liked to think that with Targyon on the throne, a more peaceful time would return. One day, elves might once again be welcome on Dharrow land.

He clamped down on his offer to help with the logs. He had a quest to plan with Zenia. One day, Dharrow Castle and Dharrow land would have to be his priority, but that day had not yet come, despite his father's willingness to suicidally fling himself into battle.

"I need to return to the city tonight." Jev thought about mentioning the dragon tear and Zenia's quest, since it would take him overseas, but his father might accuse him of fleeing in order to avoid the marriage. He would have to let them know he wasn't going to be in the kingdom on the arranged date, but maybe he would do it in a letter. Or leave a note with Wyleria.

No, that was cowardly. He needed to tell his father his travel plans and that he wouldn't marry Fremia. Not this summer. Not ever.

He took a deep breath to explain the best he could, but his father spoke first.

"I figured. Do you know if Zyndari Bludnor left our castle?"

Jev hesitated, not wanting to speak of her at all. "The last I heard, she was lamenting the loss of her dragon tear. But I think you know more about that than I do."

He looked at the old man, curious about what had happened. Zenia had only said she'd spoken to him and that her dragon tear had broken the other one. She hadn't mentioned what his father's reaction had been, if any. It had sounded like chaos broke out right after that.

His father grunted. "I guess she was using it on me. I should have realized that. It wasn't like me to— I wouldn't usually." He glanced warily at Jev. "She's married."

Jev couldn't remember ever seeing his father embarrassed or uncomfortable. He was so busy being surprised by the broken sentences that it took him a moment to recover and speak.

"Those with mind-manipulation dragon tears should always be regarded warily," he said. "Most of them work for the watch or the king or the temples, but that doesn't mean they can't be tempted to use the power at their fingertips for their own gain." He groped for a way to suggest Zyndari Bludnor had only set up the marriage for her own gain.

"I hate magic. Any chance that Cham woman is doing the same thing to you?" The old man squinted at him.

Jev resisted the urge to take offense and get hot. So far, this was more civil than most conversations he'd had with his father.

"No. She had to turn in her inquisitor dragon tear to the temple when she left and switched to working for Targyon. The dragon tear she has now is for battling evil in the king's name." Technically, it could manipulate people's minds, too, but Jev had seen Zenia use it far more often to battle enemies, so he didn't feel that dishonest for emphasizing that ability.

His father grunted again. "Like elves. I saw it blow up that magic *thing*."

"The portal?"

"Whatever it was, it's in a thousand pieces now." The old man crossed his arms. He looked as pleased as he ever did, which was to say, he looked moderately un-surly.

"That's good," Jev said. "It's bad enough the shrews and cockroaches have free access to the castle. We don't need elves showing up in the middle of the night."

"You got that right."

They fell silent. A seagull flew overhead, cawing on its way down to the coast to hunt.

Jev took a deep breath. "About the marriage, Father—"

"You don't have to go through with it. I'll tell Zyndari Bludnor it's canceled. I wasn't in my right mind when I agreed." He grimaced. "Obviously."

Hope strolled into Jev's chest and bounced up and down.

"I wouldn't want *that* woman around the castle. The girl's pretty enough, but I reckon they both were just interested in getting their hands on Dharrow assets."

"I got that impression when Fremia asked about our mines and equipment," Jev said, careful not to sound too elated. Dare he bring up Zenia again? Was it possible that the old man had changed his mind? He'd apparently seen Zenia blow up the portal, and they'd fought in battle together…

"I want you to choose someone soon," Father said, "since I'm not getting any younger, but you can pick who you want to marry."

Jev opened his mouth, his bouncing hopes on the verge of soaring up his throat and out into the sky to fly with the gulls.

"But not Cham." His father frowned sternly at him.

Jev's shoulders slumped. "Oh."

"Not a common woman. You find a nice zyndari girl. There are plenty out there."

"After what you saw today, you don't think Zenia is worthy of becoming a Dharrow?"

Father scowled. "She's common. I don't care what she's done. That doesn't change that her blood is inferior."

Jev closed his eyes, struggling not to let his disappointment in his father and in the situation show.

"Just find a nice Zyndari woman. Let me have peace in my golden years and enjoy grandchildren without having my boy gossiped about all over the city." Father's frown grew even sterner. "Good night, Jev. Serve the king well." He turned and headed toward the castle.

Jev stared at the long shadows falling over the land, trying not to let his frustration out. He intended to marry Zenia, one way or another, but giving his father that ultimatum could wait. She wouldn't be interested in planning a wedding until after she freed her dragon. Jev didn't know how long that would take, but maybe it would give his father time to change his mind. At the least, Jev shouldn't have to worry about another arranged marriage being thrust at him any time soon. That would have to be enough for now.

As Zenia laid out clothes to pack, she decided with great reluctance that she needed to go shopping before she left. She'd thought she might raid the king's kitchen and armory for rations, ammunitions, and travel gear, but her small wardrobe consisted mostly of dresses. She thought of her trek through the mangrove marsh and assumed such ladylike clothing would be a significant impediment in a wild orc-filled jungle. She needed boots and sturdy trousers and shirts. Something oiled to repel rain? Yes, that too. Definitely a shopping trip.

"Tomorrow," she muttered, glancing out the dark window in her room.

Now that she knew her dragon-tear-linked dragon was in pain, she hated to delay, but she still had to arrange passage on a ship, so it was unrealistic to think she could leave tomorrow. She didn't even know if she could find a ship that sailed directly from Kor to Izstara. The journey might require passage on multiple ships and take weeks. Months?

She needed to ask Targyon for permission to go. She intended to go, regardless, but she would prefer to have his blessing, especially if this took as long as she feared it might.

Would he save her job until she returned? Or would he give it to another? Targyon would need someone to fill that position in her absence, especially if Jev came with her. She hadn't asked him to, and she knew she shouldn't assume he could leave, especially if that marriage was still looming, but she had a hard time imagining doing this without him. He, at least, had traveled out of the kingdom. Zyndar Garlok could likely step up to fill the captaincy position while they were gone, but would he be willing to give it back when they returned? For that matter, hadn't Jev said something about punching him and firing him that morning?

A knock sounded at her door.

"Come in," she called, hoping it was Jev. Or Rhi.

Zenia wanted to ask Rhi to come with her. If anyone would enjoy thumping the enemy orcs that held the dragon prisoner, it would be her bo-wielding friend. Zenia wondered how orcs had even managed to capture a dragon. All the stories said they were incredibly powerful creatures. Had magic been involved? An injury? Was her dragon simply so young that she hadn't come into her powers yet?

The door opened, and Jev strolled in. He had changed clothes, shaved, and his hair was still damp from a bath. She remembered that she'd wanted to give him a massage and lamented that the idea had fled from her mind at the princess's revelations.

"I thought I might find you packing." He smiled and spread a hand toward the clothing stacked on the bed.

"I'm mostly realizing that few of the clothes I own are suitable for a jungle trek. I'm going to need to go shopping tomorrow. I better not spend much money though. I'm not sure how much passage to Izstara costs, but I imagine it's not cheap. And I may need to hire a guide." She tugged at her braid, daunted because the princess had only been able to narrow down the dragon's location to the northern half of the continent. Zenia hoped the gem would be able to guide her once she was on Izstara soil.

"I can pay for some of that." Jev untied a heavy-looking purse on his belt, an item that wasn't usually there. "I went to the bank and got some gold and silver coins. I doubt Korvese kron bills will impress orcs, but these will be valuable anywhere in the world." He jangled the purse.

Zenia frowned, wishing she'd thought of that. She had simply intended to take regular money. "I can't ask you to pay for any of this, Jev. Thank you, but this is my quest."

"I don't think that's true. I owe your dragon tear my life a few times over now. And besides, Targyon gave it to you. If anything, it's *his* quest."

"He doesn't know about it."

"If he doesn't yet, he will shortly. I stopped by his office as soon as I got back to the castle. He wasn't there—he's probably still trying to woo the princess—but I left him a note."

"Ah." Zenia didn't know if she appreciated Jev taking the initiative or not. It seemed they should make a formal request to take off for another country, not simply leave Targyon a letter stating that they intended to do so.

"I also talked to my father before leaving." Jev took her hand and drew her toward the edge of the bed, a spot without any clothing on it.

"Oh?" She sat down next to him. "Has he decided I'm a delightful woman to fight elves with and that we should marry immediately?"

"Not... exactly. I do think he appreciated that you blew up that portal."

"I was just holding the dragon tear that did that." She rubbed the back of his hand with her thumb, enjoying the warmth of his gentle grip.

"No need to explain that to him. Unfortunately, he's still determined that I marry a zyndari woman, but he admitted—now that he's not being mind-controlled by Bludnor—that he was manipulated into agreeing to Fremia and agreed to call off the wedding and let me choose."

"A suitable zyndari woman?"

"That's almost exactly how he put it. At least he's giving me time. We'll figure out—I mean, I haven't asked you, so I guess I shouldn't assume." His brow creased as he gazed at her. "I know you don't want to be a mistress, and I don't *want* a mistress, but are you ready for—would you want—Zenia, do you want to marry me?"

"Was that a proposal?" She smiled, touched by him stumbling over his words.

"Uhm, not exactly. I would need to get a jade ring and an archmage to bless the union first. And there should be wine, good food, healed ribs." He grimaced, touching his side and straightening his spine. "But it would be nice to know you would accept if I offered."

Zenia slid her arm around his back and rested a hand on his chest, wishing she knew how to thoroughly heal all his injuries. Her body ached too. Maybe they should both find qualified people to massage them.

She shifted closer and kissed him gently. He returned it more eagerly than gently and wrapped his arms around her. Her thoughts drifted toward the memory of him half-naked and sparring in the gymnasium, and then of things they might do during the nights in a little tent together as they journeyed through the jungle... If they were engaged, even informally, then maybe it wouldn't be such a bad thing to enjoy blanket activities together.

Another knock sounded at the door.

Jev slowly broke the kiss. Zenia wasn't sure she would have broken it if it had been up to her. Surely, Rhi could come back in the morning...

"Was that a yes?" he wondered.

"I would love to marry you, Jev Dharrow."

"Good. We'll make it work then. One way or another." He smiled, but his eyes seemed a little grim underneath the determination.

She tried not to think about him walking away from his position as heir for her sake. But if he did, it would be his choice. She couldn't imagine giving him up if he was offering himself to her.

"Good," she whispered and touched his cheek.

A loud throat-clearing accompanied the second knock.

"Kings are busy," came a dry voice through the door, "and can't stand in hallways waiting overlong for doors to be opened."

Jev snorted and strode to the door.

Cheeks heating, Zenia smoothed her dress and tucked a few stray strands of hair behind her ears.

"Good evening, Sire," Jev said, opening the door. "Nice of you to join us. Did you see my note? Or has the princess sailed off to Taziira and left you lonely and bereft, thus forcing you to seek us out for company?"

The two bodyguards standing in the hall with Targyon were remarkable in their ability not to react to such comments.

"Actually, she's waiting for me in my dining hall where we're going to have a last meal together before she sails back north." Targyon smiled sadly and looked out the window. He held an envelope down by his side. Poetry for the princess?

"Oh?" Jev asked. "So soon? I thought she would wait to make sure a new embassy is successfully built."

"That's Lornysh's duty now, much to my bemusement."

"He's agreed to the position, then?"

"He has. He told Yesleva it was only until she and her father could find someone more fitting for the position. I certainly don't mind having an ally as the elven ambassador, but I think the idea of being committed to staying here where the Zsayon faction could easily find him again makes Lornysh nervous."

"Understandable. Let's hope Vornzylar was the leader of those set against him and that few others are interested in going after him."

Targyon nodded. "We'll see." He looked from Jev to Zenia. "You two have my permission, of course, to go find this dragon. Though I imagine you would have gone, regardless." He smiled.

Zenia kept her mouth shut, not willing to confirm that.

"I read your note, Jev," Targyon said, "and spoke to Yesleva, but I'm confused about how a young imprisoned dragon came to be linked to an old dragon tear that had been in the royal vault for generations, if not centuries." He cocked his head, regarding Zenia curiously.

She spread her hands. "I don't know anything more than the princess told me, Sire. I regret that I didn't figure out earlier that she— the dragon—is in trouble."

"Maybe she'll tell us how the link came to be," Jev said. "When we find her. Can dragons speak?"

"Some can speak telepathically, the stories tell us. Though they rarely deign to interact with the lesser races. In recent centuries, they've found the world too populated and rarely come out of their hermitages."

"Hermitages?" Jev asked. "I thought dragons lived in caves."

"Yes, in a hermitly manner." Targyon touched his forehead in a vague army salute and started to leave, but he looked down at the envelope and turned back. "I almost forgot. This came for you, Zenia."

As he held it up, a feeling of dread hollowed her stomach. Now that she could see the front, she recognized the stationery and the ink and handwriting. *Captain Zenia Cham.*

"Another warning?" she murmured.

Targyon's eyebrows arched. Zenia hadn't told him about her unseen and unheard ally of a sort, and Jev must not have either.

"How did *you* get it, Sire?" Jev asked as Zenia accepted the envelope.

"I was out with Lornysh, the princess, and my bodyguards, examining the ruins and arranging for the area to be cleared so construction could begin. When we were on our way back, an old blind woman stepped into the path of the entourage. My guards tried to shoo her away, but she had the look of one of those religious seers." He shrugged. "I don't like to irk the Orders or anyone who receives visions, real or imagined. It was a simple enough matter to go and talk to her, but all she requested was that I deliver this to my Crown Agent captain."

"Asking the king to be your messenger boy is audacious," Jev said.

Targyon spread his hands. "The religious Orders all think they're above us secular types."

"Did blind seers deliver the other messages?" Jev asked as Zenia opened the envelope.

"No. This is the first time anyone has seen who delivered one." That feeling of dread returned as Zenia unfolded the single page inside. She wasn't sure why. Before, the messages had all been helpful warnings. Maybe it was that they also always heralded trouble.

Death awaits in Izstara.

Zenia swallowed. That was all it said. Wordlessly, she showed it to the men.

"Uh, *whose* death?" Jev asked.

Targyon, not familiar with the earlier notes, merely appeared curious, or maybe slightly confused.

"And how did he or she know where we're going?" Jev added.

"How did they know Vornzylar was coming? Or that Lunis Drem had betrayed us?" Zenia shook her head, believing that her sensation of dread had been entirely warranted.

"Well," Jev said. "It doesn't change anything, right? We're still going?"

Zenia touched her dragon tear, and a feeling of uncertainty mingled with hope emanated from it.

"Yes," Zenia said firmly. "We're going."

THE END

Made in United States
Troutdale, OR
12/22/2023

16350702R00148